PENGUIN BOOK

FAREWELL TO MY CONCUBINE

Lilian Lee is the pen name of writer Li Pik-Wah, author of more than twenty books, including *The Last Princess of Manchuria* (1992), and screenwriter for fifteen feature films. In her native Hong Kong, several of Lee's bestselling novels have sold more than 100,000 copies each.

Andrea Lingenfelter, who also translated *The Last Princess of Manchuria*, is a doctoral candidate at the University of Washington in Seattle.

LILIAN LEE

———

FAREWELL TO MY CONCUBINE

TRANSLATED FROM THE CHINESE
BY ANDREA LINGENFELTER

PENGUIN BOOKS

PENGUIN BOOKS

Published by the Penguin Group
Penguin Books Ltd, 27 Wrights Lane, London W8 5TZ, England
Penguin Books USA Inc., 375 Hudson Street, New York, New York 10014, USA
Penguin Books Australia Ltd, Ringwood, Victoria, Australia
Penguin Books Canada Ltd, 10 Alcorn Avenue, Toronto, Ontario, Canada M4V 3B2
Penguin Books (NZ) Ltd, 182–190 Wairau Road, Auckland 10, New Zealand

Penguin Books Ltd, Registered Offices: Harmondsworth, Middlesex, England

First published in Chinese by Cosmos Books Ltd
This English translation first published in the USA by William Morrow and Co. Inc. 1993
First published in Great Britain in Penguin Books 1993
1 3 5 7 9 10 8 6 4 2

Penguin Film and TV Tie-in edition first published 1993

Printed in England by Clays Ltd, St Ives plc

Translator's dedication:

For my parents.
A.D.L.

Translator's Note

Farewell to My Concubine is set in the world of Peking opera, China's preeminent form of regional opera. Like the Kabuki theater of Japan, Peking opera was traditionally performed by an all-male cast, although female performers became increasingly common after the Revolution of 1911. This trend accelerated over the next half century, so that today Peking opera is more or less integrated. Nonetheless, during the period in which this novel is set, all-male companies were the norm, and the most famous performers of the 1930s and 1940s were men. Many of these actors trained for years in special opera schools. After roughly five years of general instruction in acrobatics, Chinese martial arts, and singing, a student was either given further training or relegated to working backstage. Those who continued training were chosen to play specialized role types (*dan,* "female lead"; *sheng,* "male lead"; *jing,* "older supporting male role"; or *chou,* "clown"), which they would play exclusively. The role of *dan* became the focal point of Peking opera during the

1930s and 1940s, with actors such as Mei Lanfang rising to international stardom. The two protagonists of this novel, Xiao Douzi and Xiao Shitou, enter opera school as young children and grow up to become a *dan* and a *sheng* respectively. The blurring between their onstage roles as lovers and their private lives backstage provides much of the dramatic tension of the story.

The reader may wonder why "Xiao" is the first word in all of the names of the children in Master Guan's opera school. Xiao simply means "small" and is common in Chinese nicknames. When the two protagonists, Xiao Douzi (Little Bean) and Xiao Shitou (Little Rock), begin their performing careers, they assume stage names, Cheng Dieyi and Duan Xiaolou, which are typical Chinese names, consisting of a family name followed by a personal name.

Pinyin romanization is used throughout the text to transliterate Chinese names and terms. I have made an exception in the case of China's capital, which I refer to as Peking, rather than as Beijing, the pinyin form. Using the more anglicized name allows me to sidestep the possibly confusing name changes the capital has undergone in this century.

FAREWELL
to my
CONCUBINE

Prostitutes have no heart;
actors have no morals. So
people say. A prostitute has to make her living by putting on
a show of feeling in bed; an actor may be the embodiment of
virtue and integrity as he struts upon the stage. He may be an
emperor, a statesman, or a great general. The stage is populated by brilliant young scholars and beautiful ladies whose
exalted passions are more vivid than the drab colors of our
workaday existence. Compared to their stories, everyday life
is like the plain and pale face of an actor stripped of his
makeup.

Without a stage to prop him up, the actor is just an

ordinary man, with an unmemorable face and unfulfilled expectations. His strength and power come from artifice—he relies on them to live, just as an embryo draws nourishment from the body of the mother, and the growing child holds fast to her hand. In the same way, women have long depended on men to sustain them. In exchange they reveal a part of the elusive secret that is their charm. But how much of that is just stagecraft?

After all, life is just a play. Or an opera. It would be easier for all of us if we could watch only the highlights. Instead, we must endure convoluted plot twists and excruciating moments of suspense. We sit in the dark, threatened by vague menaces. Of course, those of us in the audience can always walk out; but the players have no choice. Once the curtain goes up they have to perform the play from beginning to end. They have nowhere to hide.

But we are still in the theater, watching the opera being performed for us onstage. Both of the actors are in full makeup, and we see two brightly colored faces. One belongs to the actor playing the beautiful concubine Yu Ji. Opposite him is the actor who plays General Xiang Yu, Yu Ji's lover. Yu Ji's entire existence depends on Xiang Yu. And he has lost his kingdom to a rival.

Yu Ji is singing an aria to him:

"My lord is doomed,
I have nowhere to turn."

His life is over, and she will choose not to go on living.

But this is only an opera. The actors feign death, and the curtain falls. In the end they both stand up and walk away.

Actually, one actor really is in love with the other. Still, their story is not that simple. When one man loves another, it can't be simple; and it's hard to know how to begin. We might as well start at the beginning.

The theater is dark. As the houselights come up, the musicians enter and start to tune their instruments. The percussionist holds one hand ready to strike a leather drum while the other holds up clappers. He seems to be ready. The other musicians are still busy tuning. Everyone is filled with nervous excitement. Tonight they have a chance to participate in a moving drama. They will be part of someone else's story.

The lights dim again until there is nothing but a lone spotlight shining center stage. A faint creak, and the curtain parts.

It is their first meeting.

Winter, 1929. The eighteenth year of the Republic of China.

Strong, icy winds blew out of the North. It was the darkest and coldest time of the year, when a feeble sun wavered in the sky. Some days it peeked out; but on this day it was hidden behind the clouds. People looked up at the sky, wondering if it might snow, although it was still early in the season.

It was market day at Tianqiao, the Bridge of Heaven, and the clamor of voices filled the air. The Bridge of Heaven lay between Zhengyang Gate and Yongding Gate, just to the west of the Temple of Heaven. During the Ming and Qing dynasties the emperor made yearly offerings at the temple, and he always crossed this bridge on the way. The temple lay on the south side of the bridge, and people imagined the emperor's crossing from the north side to the south symbolized a passage from the earthly realm to heaven. Because the emperor, or Son of Heaven, used this bridge to cross to heaven, it was called the Bridge of Heaven. But after the fall of the Qing dynasty, in 1911, the bridge became part of the common world. Never again would it be used solely by the Son of Heaven.

A small but bustling marketplace grew up on the north side of this bridge. Lining the north-south street were teahouses, small restaurants, and secondhand clothing stalls. To the west ran a bird market, facing a row of stands that sold snacks of every kind. In the midst of all this, street performers plied their trades among the shoppers.

Little urchins wove through the crowds where they were thickest. One of them spotted a cigarette butt on the ground and quickly bent down to grab it. When he had gathered up enough discarded butts, he would take them all apart and salvage the tobacco. Then he would roll new cigarettes to sell on the street.

He had to be alert and snatch up the butts before somebody stepped on them. This last butt had narrowly missed being crushed by two pairs of feet, a woman's and a child's.

The woman had almost tread on the urchin's fingers with her worn cloth shoes. Once crimson, those shoes had faded to the brown of an old bloodstain. The woman herself had the sallow complexion of an opium addict, and her lips were tinged with a bit of lipstick. A red hairline mark, running like a scar between her eyebrows, suggested that she suffered from frequent headaches and had been pinching her forehead to cure them. Any careful observer would have known that she was an unlicensed prostitute.

The child at her side was about eight or nine, and his clothes were brightly colored and looked brand-new, in contrast to his mother's. The muffler wound around his neck and face covered everything but his eyes, which were beautifully shaped but wore a puzzled expression. He had never been to such a noisy marketplace before, and he clung shyly to his mother, clutching the corner of her coat with his left hand. He kept his right hand carefully hidden in his coat pocket, where he seemed to be fingering some mysterious object.

A newspaper boy was calling out, "Northeastern Army surrounded—Japs about to attack! Buy a copy, sir?"

A man who had just finished a breakfast of soybean milk and salted vegetables happened along, a half-eaten cruller still in his hand. He raised his other arm to strike the paper boy, who was blocking his way.

"Out of my way! We've got problems enough here at home—we can't even fill our own bellies. If the Japs want to go to war, let them!"

The man spotted the woman. He knew her.

"You're Yanhong, aren't you?" he leered. "I've been thinking about you!"

The child shrank from him, pressing closer to his mother and wrinkling his nose in disgust. Yanhong spat at the man and pulled her son after her. They hurried past stands selling an endless variety of snacks: wonton, roasted sausages, lamb stew with sesame paste and Chinese parsley, sautéed liver, sweet millet porridge, steamed breads, sticky rice balls with fillings of sweetened chestnuts or red bean paste, steamed buns, and more.

A loud bang made them jump. Up ahead, a tout with gold teeth was clanging gongs and cymbals to lure customers to his peep show. Men flocked to him, feeling an itch they couldn't scratch, hoping for a glimpse of something titillating through the little glass window in the case.

"Take a look, boys! See the lovely lady taking a bath!"

The farther the mother and son walked, the more boisterous the crowd became. Soon they found themselves surrounded by storytellers, conjurers, jugglers, wrestlers, martial artists, tumblers, vaudeville performers, sellers of tonics, and even sidewalk dentists.

Yanhong was looking for one of the entertainers. His name was Master Guan. At last she spotted him, a husky fellow in his forties, with a heavy black beard and hair growing out of his ears, which made him look very forbidding. But fiercest of all were his eyes, which burned like those of the intimidating door guardians posted inside Buddhist temples.

Yanhong walked up to Master Guan. Indicating the boy at her side, she waited expectantly. The man glanced at the child and nodded. Then he struck his gong as the audience crowded close to watch the upcoming performance.

"Look," the mother whispered to her son as a group of little boys assembled on the stage. Their shaved heads were smooth and shiny like watermelons. These were Master Guan's apprentices, and today they were performing an opera about the mischievous Monkey King, Sun Wukong. Each boy's face was painted with red, yellow, black, and white greasepaint, and each boy wore a crude monkey costume. They filed on stage and formed a circle.

The boy blinked his long-lashed eyes and rubbed at his forehead with his left hand. His right hand stayed buried in his pocket.

The biggest of Master Guan's apprentices was a twelve-year-old named Xiao Shitou, or Little Rock. He made a dramatic entrance by somersaulting across the stage and landing right in the center of the circle of smaller boys. He was the Monkey King, and he was furious at not being invited to the banquet given by the Queen of Heaven. She had invited a host of immortals to dine on the magical heavenly peaches she grew in her special orchard. But before any of the guests could arrive, the insulted Monkey King sneaked into the palace and stuffed his mouth with peaches. His belly full, the Monkey King ambled off across the stage, his arms swinging easily. Suddenly, he clutched at his neck and scratched at a louse, bringing down a torrent of laughter from the audience.

Now he was draining pantomime goblets of wine, and lustily gobbling down as many more peaches as he could. Not forgetting his brethren monkeys, he stole a sackful of peaches before somersaulting back home to his cave behind a waterfall.

Master Guan stood to one side, motioning each child in turn to somersault into a circle around the Monkey King. They capered about, each vying to impress their king and be rewarded with heavenly peaches. The audience cheered in approval.

Encouraged by these cheers, Xiao Shitou spun around, jumped into the air, and performed several twists. Suddenly, he cried out in dismay and the cheering stopped—the Monkey King had slipped and landed on top of the other little monkeys. The crowd burst into laughter and began taunting him.

"Clumsy! He's broken his nose!"

Xiao Shitou tried to execute another somersault, but he failed again, distracted by the catcalls.

"What a charlatan! And he has the audacity to come to the Bridge of Heaven and pass himself off as a real entertainer!"

The commotion attracted a handful of hoodlums, who also started to heap abuse on the boy.

"Why don't you go away for a few years—and don't come back until you know what you're doing!"

The little monkeys scattered, but they had nowhere to hide. Jeering men, women, and children surrounded them on all sides. Some of these onlookers had come to watch the performance, but others had only come to enjoy the even livelier spectacle of the actors' humiliation.

The frightened child performers squatted down on the stage and wrapped their arms around their heads to hide their shame. Master Guan had completely lost face, but he tried to laugh off this disaster.

"Be easy on them, people—they're only children!"

Master Guan knew better than to look rattled in front of an unruly crowd like this one, so he simply laughed along with them. Still, it would take more than that to restore his dignity.

The gong the troupe used for collecting money lay off to one side, and a hooligan gave a kick and sent it flying. One of the apprentices, Xiao Laizi, a boy with flaky patches on his scalp, took advantage of the ensuing confusion and dashed away in an attempt to escape.

"Hey!" Master Guan yelled after him. "Somebody catch that boy and bring him back!"

The crowd was starting to break up when Xiao Shitou stood up and called out in a clear voice, "Gentlemen! Ladies!

Don't go yet! Watch this! I'm not called Little Rock for nothing. See how hard my head is!"

He held up a brick for everyone to see and then struck himself on the forehead. The brick split in two with a loud crack, but there wasn't even a trace of blood.

"He really is a little rock!" somebody said.

Won over again, the audience showered Xiao Shitou with copper coins while he puffed out his chest like a hero.

Yanhong's little boy pulled on her hand. He had never seen anything like this before, nor had he ever seen a boy as brave as Xiao Shitou.

Fine snow had started to fall. Nobody had expected it, for it was early in the season.

Two rows of shallow footsteps led through the snow to the gate of the courtyard that housed Master Guan's opera school. There they ended abruptly, although the smaller set retreated a few steps before finally vanishing at the threshold.

"Come along, Xiao Douzi," said Yanhong, tugging on her son's hand as they crossed the courtyard. She was also carrying two packages of cakes, one large and one small. The cakes were wrapped in yellow paper that bore the faint red tracery of some auspicious symbol. The sound of shouting echoed in the courtyard.

"What the hell did you think you were doing back there? Do you call that Peking opera? Damn you all!" roared Master Guan. His eyes blazed, and the sinews on his thick neck were bulging.

His students stood in neat rows alongside the dining tables. Their arms hung limply at their sides, and their heads were bowed so low it seemed they were trying to bury their faces in the pits of their stomachs. They were all very hungry.

Xiao Laizi, the little mangy-headed boy who had tried to escape at the Bridge of Heaven, had been brought back. He now stood in the back, covered in filth from head to toe.

"You're all worthless, dammit! You can't sing and you're lousy acrobats! How do you expect to make any money?" Master Guan snorted derisively.

Nobody made a sound.

"You don't even make convincing monkeys! How can you expect to become men?"

With this he picked up a bamboo stick and began beating Xiao Laizi, cursing him roundly.

"This'll teach you better than to run away, you little ingrate!"

Xiao Laizi stifled his sobs, resigned to this punishment.

After Master Guan finished beating Xiao Laizi, he beat each of the boys in turn. Those who were caught whimpering had to endure several more strokes of the rod.

"You!" Master Guan hollered at Xiao Shitou. "First thing tomorrow morning I want you out in the courtyard practicing. I want you to do one hundred aerial somersaults!"

"Yes, sir," the boy answered respectfully.

"Speak up!"

"Yes, sir!"

The Master swept his eyes over his pupils and soon found another victim.

"You, there—Xiao Sanzi. When you make your entrance and strike your first pose, how do you widen your eyes? Show me right now."

Xiao Sanzi hesitated.

"Open those eyes wide!" Master Guan bellowed.

The boy obeyed.

"You call those wide eyes? Those are dead sheep's eyes! You look as dull-eyed as an opium addict who needs a fix. Get a mirror tomorrow and practice one hundred times!"

The session of beating and scolding dragged on. All the while, the children glanced furtively at the stacks of cornbread laid out on the table. Next to the bread was a large kettle of soup with a few greens floating on top. The boys' stomachs were rumbling, and they were getting light-headed. They felt as insubstantial as the limp greens drifting in the soup.

Finally Master Guan concluded his lecture.

"If you want to amount to anything, you're going to have to work hard and pay your dues! Now eat! And remember," he continued, "if you don't have any talent, you can't expect to dine on white rice and sautéed shrimp every night! Don't expect special treatment in the afterlife, either. If you don't work hard now, you'll get nothing but a few lumps of stale bread. Right?"

"Right!" the children answered in unison. Then they descended on the food, stuffing their mouths with coarse bread. Their hunger made this poor fare taste like the finest and rarest of delicacies. While the others ate, Xiao Shitou was drizzling oil into the soup. He took a copper coin, dipped it in an oil pot, and then held it over the kettle of soup, letting it dribble in one drop at a time.

Yanhong and her son slipped into the room.

"Master Guan," she said tentatively.

The master glanced briefly at the two outsiders before giving his students final instructions.

"When you're through eating, go over there and practice more drills," he said. Then he put down his rice bowl and turned to the visitors. "What's your name?"

"The gentleman is speaking to you," Yanhong urged her son.

"Xiao Douzi—Little Bean," he replied hesitantly.

"What's that? Speak up!"

Yanhong nervously unwound Xiao Douzi's muffler, revealing his face. His features were surprisingly delicate. He was almost pretty.

"Xiao Douzi," the child repeated. Master Guan had started to look him over carefully. First he felt the boy's head, then pinched his cheek and examined his teeth. He noted the boy's well-shaped chin. So far he was satisfied. Next, he turned Xiao Douzi around and checked his waist, back, and legs; but when he went to pull the boy's right hand from his pocket, Xiao Douzi resisted.

"What have you got in there?" the Master asked, yanking the hand from its hiding place. He stepped back in shock. Xiao Douzi had an extra digit that stuck out like a little twig beside his right thumb.

"He has six fingers!" the Master exclaimed. Despite the boy's numerous good qualities, it would be out of the question to accept him as a student.

"This child isn't fit for the Peking opera. Take him on home!"

"Master, please," the mother pleaded. "Can't you take him in? He's healthy and quite clever. He's very obedient—he'll do whatever you say, I promise. He was a mistake—an accident. If he'd been a girl, I could have kept him at the brothel, but . . ." She trailed off. "It's not that I can't afford to take care of him. It's just that I thought he might be able to make something out of himself if he studied with you."

She tilted the child's small face upward so that he was looking straight at Master Guan.

"See how pretty he is? He has a clear, sweet voice, too. Sing something—"

Master Guan peremptorily raised a hand, cutting her short.

"Look at his hand. He was born that way, and there's nothing you can do about it. It's no good."

"Is that the only reason, then?"

Yanhong turned and fled with Xiao Douzi. They quickly made their way into the kitchen—and found next to the stove the object for which they were searching.

It was already growing dark. Snow as fine as powdered jade danced aimlessly, without wanting to, without choice, buffeted by invisible currents as it fell to the dirty stone courtyard. Everything was quiet.

A piercing cry tore into the peaceful night. It had come from the direction of the kitchen. The students, interrupted at their drills, started at the chilling sound. Xiao Shitou felt the hairs on the back of his neck rise.

Drops of blood in the snow traced Xiao Douzi's path. He now crouched in a lonely corner of the compound, whimpering like a maimed animal. He had been a freak of nature. Even the simple good fortune of normalcy had been denied him. The cleaver had cut through flesh and bone, replacing his deformity with an open wound. But he had survived the shock. He was going to live.

* * *

Master Guan rolled out the bright red contract and cleared his throat. His modulated tones concealed his emotions as he read out the terms.

"I, the undersigned, Xiao Douzi . . ."

The other boys peeked around the corner of the door-frame like skittish ghosts; incense smoke coiled around the altar dedicated to the patron saints of Peking opera. Perhaps there was some deity, somewhere, looking out for Xiao Douzi. His right palm was wrapped in a rag that the blood had stained deep carmine.

He rubbed at his reddened eyes. His face was still wet with tears, and the pain of his open wound was almost unbearable. He bit his lip so hard that he drew blood.

"Come on, child. Come kneel here in front of your new Master. Your mother has chosen well."

Xiao Douzi obeyed and listened to Master Guan intone the terms of his apprenticeship.

"I, Xiao Douzi, aged nine years, seek to train under the esteemed Master, Guan Jinfa, as an apprentice for the term of ten years. This contract stipulates that for the next ten years my teacher, Master Guan, shall have complete authority to act on my behalf in addition to receiving any revenues earned through my performances during that period of time. In the event of any mishap or accident, be it natural or man-made, traffic accident, disease, death, or suicide, it shall be considered the will of heaven. Should I, the undersigned, neglect to practice, fail to attend class, or be disobedient in any way, I shall be summarily beaten to death—"

Xiao Douzi's mother tightened her already clenched fists. The Master read on: "When the term of ten years has been fulfilled, I shall bid farewell to my teacher and make my own way in the world, trusting in the benevolence of heaven. Verbal agreements being nonbinding, I hereby give my agreement in writing."

With this, Master Guan grabbed Xiao Douzi's right index finger—only the tip protruded from the makeshift bandage—and stuck it in a pot of pasty, red seal ink. When he took the inked finger and pressed a scarlet crescent onto the paper of the contract, a drop of blood oozed from the bandage and dripped onto the paper like a second fingerprint. Once signed, the contract could not be broken.

Under the stern gaze of the portraits of the Thirteen Great Opera Stars of the late Qing, Yanhong picked up a writing brush and traced a shaky X. She looked up and let her eyes linger on her son. This would be the last time they saw each other. She gave Master Guan the large package of cakes and slipped the smaller one to her son.

"Don't eat them all up at once," she admonished him quietly. "Break off little pieces one at a time so you can eat some every day. If another boy wants any, you must give him some. Remember, do as you're told. You'll have to learn to get along. Mama promises to come back to visit you soon!"

Having run out of words, she looked helplessly at the cakes. She was afraid of displeasing Master Guan. If she encouraged her son to eat well and dress warmly, Master Guan might think she didn't trust him to keep the children well fed and dressed. He might be offended. She said nothing.

It was time for her to leave. Wanting to appear resolute, she hurried out and nearly slipped in the new snow. Regaining her footing, she quickened her steps. If she wavered and went back for him, all of her efforts would be wasted, and the two of them would be back in the same hopeless situation where they'd started.

Yanhong's life had never been easy, and she'd been reduced to doing odd jobs, like rolling wax-coated pills in the back of some pharmacy during the influenza season, or washing other people's filthy clothes and fetid socks.

During the wintertime, mother and son slept on a makeshift bed made out of a wooden board set up in the loft of a down-at-the-heel courtyard. The thin blanket they used felt like a frozen sheet of iron, and their feet were often stiff with cold. The best Yanhong could do was to fill an old soy sauce bottle with hot water to warm her son's feet.

If she'd had an alternative, she would not have become a prostitute; but it was the only way she could make enough money to support her child. At times, it hardly seemed worth it. Once, when she was working, she had seen him staring coldly at her and her customer through the door curtains. The expression on his face as he watched the man mount her had been murderous.

Over the past three days, she had tried to teach her nine-year-old son everything he would need to know to take care of himself. She worried that her lessons might not have sunk in.

All he knew was that she had abandoned him, had sold him to a stranger, supposedly for his own good. After she left, he ran over to the windowsill, peeled back the paper set between the panes, and looked out. She hadn't gone far. His eyes followed her solitary figure as it retreated slowly and vanished into the first snow of the winter.

His lips formed the soundless syllables: "Mother!"

"It's late," Master Guan was saying to him. "One of the

older boys will show you where to sleep."

Xiao Shitou came up and patted him on the shoulder. Fearing he was being attacked, Xiao Douzi broke away.

"The bell in the Bell Tower is striking," the older boy said. "The Bell Goddess is calling for her shoe. Can you hear it? *'Shoe! . . . Shoe! . . . Shoe!'* It's bedtime."

"Who is this Bell Goddess?" Xiao Douzi asked skeptically.

"She's—a ghost!" Xiao Shitou said menacingly. Then he burst out laughing and ran away, leaving Xiao Douzi to hurry after him. When he caught up with him, he found Xiao Shitou waiting in the doorway to a grubby room.

Xiao Shitou motioned him in. The room was almost entirely taken up by a large kang, one of the heated clay sleeping platforms commonly used in North China. As big as the kang was, it wasn't big enough for all of the boys to squeeze onto, and they brought in the benches they used during practice and set them up around the edges of the kang. Only then was there room enough for everyone to sleep.

Ragged children occupied every square inch of this communal bed. The boys who had looked so carefree earlier in the day as they capered about dressed as little monkeys were now sleeping on their hard-won patches of bedding. But Xiao Douzi was a newcomer. Would they make room for him? He saw an empty spot and timidly crawled up, but Xiao Sanzi, the company bully, quickly put him in his place.

"Get off my spot. Find a place near the middle and stay there!"

The other boys started pushing and shoving, and nobody would make room for Xiao Douzi. He had stumbled into hostile territory and stood up on the kang, holding the package of sweets high over his head as though it were some precious inheritance.

Just then Xiao Shitou ambled in from the toilet. He was tying on his trousers, but as soon as he saw what was happening, he came to Xiao Douzi's aid like a knight-errant saving a traveler from bandits.

"What's going on here? Why are you picking on him?" Xiao Shitou demanded as he leapt onto the kang. With a grand flourish he tore Xiao Sanzi's and Xiao Meitou's bedding completely out from underneath them.

"Stop picking on him!" He motioned to Xiao Douzi. "Here. You can sleep over here." Turning back to the others, he continued sternly, "I'll take on anybody who doesn't obey."

He picked up a broken brick, and everyone else quickly lost interest in fighting and lay down docilely. But Xiao Sanzi was still muttering under his breath.

"Who does he think he is, anyway? I don't have to put up with—"

"What's that?"

There was no answer, and finally they all settled down to sleep. Xiao Douzi took Xiao Shitou to be a kind of leader at the school, but he also decided that he was mostly full of bluster and wasn't worth getting to know very well.

Xiao Douzi lay down on the kang and burrowed under a big cotton quilt, crowding in close like the others, desperate to escape the cold. There was so little space that if one boy had rolled over, everyone else would have had to turn over as well. But they were all too exhausted to move. Soon everybody was sleeping soundly. Everybody except Xiao Douzi. Staring into the menacingly unfamiliar darkness, and without any other distractions, he felt the pain in his hand growing more intense by the minute. His finger had been replaced by sharp pain. He bit down on his lip.

An eerie moaning broke the quiet. It sounded like the weeping of a ghost.

"Mother," Xiao Laizi was whimpering. "I can't stand it anymore. . . . I want to die. . . . Just make it stop. . . ."

Xiao Douzi felt sympathetic tears rolling down his cheeks.

"Why aren't you asleep, yet?" hissed Xiao Shitou, awakened by his sobbing. "You're driving me crazy! Go to sleep!"

"I want my mother!"

Xiao Shitou gave an exasperated sigh, but he spoke gently.

"Don't worry. She'll come to see you at New Year's. Now get some rest."

Xiao Douzi was eyeing him skeptically.

"How about your father?"

"He ran away. How about yours? Are your parents together?"

Xiao Shitou snorted derisively.

"I've never laid eyes on either of those two good-for-nothings. I just hatched from a rock one day! Listen, I'm sleepy. Good night."

Xiao Douzi felt somewhat comforted, but Xiao Shitou fell sound asleep almost instantly. Xiao Douzi felt painfully alone once again.

The next morning Master Guan shaved Xiao Douzi's head. His first pass with the straight razor released a clump of soft black hair that fell to the floor. He worked methodically, shaving one section at a time. With each sweep of the razor Xiao Douzi grew more dejected.

"Don't move!" Master Guan said as he held the boy's head steady with a forceful hand. "I said, don't move!"

When at last the job was done, fine dark hair covered the floor like drifts of ink-stained snow. Part of Xiao Douzi's past had been shorn away.

"Somebody bring me a uniform!" Master Guan turned toward the door and called out. "Xiao Zongzi—you go get some coal. And while you're at it see whether or not the water's boiling yet."

"Yes, sir!" the boys responded in unison.

Soon Xiao Shitou came in with a uniform.

"This ought to fit you," he said, as he handed it to Xiao Douzi.

"Thank you, Older Brother," Xiao Douzi replied deferentially.

With his shaved head and worn uniform, Xiao Douzi looked just like the other little boys at the opera school. They were all but identical, like rows of bean plants in a field. When he shook his head back and forth, it felt cool and light. It was a strange new sensation.

Soon he fell into the school routine. Every morning the children woke up in the dark, bleary-eyed, and washed their faces in a big soup kettle. Their faces were never entirely clean, and their bellies were never completely full as they set out every morning behind Master Guan. They marched behind him obediently, shoulders hunched against the cold, hands tucked inside their sleeves. They were going to Taoranting Park, at the southwestern edge of the city. It was there, in the outdoors, that they practiced their scales.

At the center of the park was a hill, topped by a temple with a view of the surrounding landscape. The temple itself was small but elaborate, with chambers full of intricately carved pillars, lacquered beams, and polished balustrades, all linked by winding corridors and marble steps.

The children walked past this impressive structure. Their teacher was leading them to the bank of a weed-choked pond that was encircled by burial mounds. This no-man's-land of wild grasses was the children's practice hall. They fanned out, each one looking for a choice spot. And then they began.

In the ghostly gray predawn twilight, they were like stranded spirits, waiting for the sun to banish them back to the underworld. Their plaintive cries filled the air, reaching the ears of another group of children who were on their way to school. Book bags slung over their backs, they ran down the lane, with a house servant in hot pursuit. His efforts to call them back were fruitless, and they raced away.

By the time Master Guan brought his students back to their school, the sun had come up and was shining down brightly. The breakfast stands lining the street had just opened for business, their stoves freshly lit; the people who lived in the neighborhood were getting ready to start another day.

Inside the compound walls, the opera students lined up and stood at attention. With legs spread wide and hands behind their backs, they listened to Master Guan's lecture. They wouldn't be permitted to eat their breakfast of coarse steamed bread until he had finished speaking, and their energy was faltering.

"Do you want to become actors?" he demanded.

"We do!" they shouted in unison. They were like the assembled courtiers who used to kowtow to the emperor in the Forbidden City.

"To whom are you grateful for your livelihood in the theater?"

"To the founders of the Peking opera!"

"That's right! Two hundred years ago, in the time of the emperor Qianlong, Peking opera was first performed here by the Four Greats of Anhui. Since then, the opera has grown and flourished. It becomes more popular every year. You have the good fortune to be entering the opera at a time of great opportunities." He swept his eyes over the children. "Nonetheless, while you need a teacher to teach you technique, you can only find the spirit of the opera inside yourselves. The founders have bequeathed to each of you a rice bowl—but whether or not it gets filled depends on what?"

"Hard work! As long as we're not afraid of hard work we'll succeed!"

Master Guan smiled with satisfaction.

The first lesson taught them to circle the stage taking small quick steps. This was the basic work of the supporting characters. Master Guan rapped a stick on the stage while the children pivoted their shoulders in time as they walked.

"Follow the beat. Faster, faster!" the Master shouted. "Keep your arms at your sides, and don't bend your knees! Take bigger strides!"

Practicing like this day after day, sometimes they had the feeling they were walking in endless circles and not going anywhere.

Without warning, the rapping ceased. This was a signal for the students to freeze and strike poses. Any carelessness was rewarded with a blow of the cane, and some of the children were seized with muscle cramps that left them unable to move at all. When at last they were permitted to rest, they found their legs were trembling with fatigue.

Next, the students stretched their hamstrings. With one leg resting on a bar, they leaned forward until their bodies lay flat against the raised leg. If a boy did not keep his supporting leg perfectly straight, he felt the sting of the Master's cane. Everyone kept a furtive watch on the stick of incense that was burning nearby. When it had burned down, it would be time to change legs.

Xiao Laizi was crying again.

"What's wrong with you?" the Master demanded angrily. "Can't you make your leg straight?" Pointing randomly at another boy, he ordered, "You—straighten out his leg for him. I want it completely straight!"

This exercise was difficult enough, but the one Xiao Douzi feared most was Chinese splits. They did these by pressing their backs against the wall, straddling their legs, and lowering themselves gradually. Each boy had a partner, who helped by adding bricks, one at a time, as the boy's legs rested on the floor.

While the pupils were doing Chinese splits, an old gentleman in wire-rimmed glasses came to visit. He worked for the owners of the Spring Blossom Teahouse, and he had come to inspect the apprentice performers. The Master had an ongoing arrangement with the Spring Blossom Teahouse, whereby his students gave occasional performances.

"Good morning, Master Shi," Master Guan said deferentially. He summoned his students. "Come over here. Mind your manners. And smile for the gentleman." He grinned obsequiously at Master Shi. "I've trained these children hard. They're quite disciplined. I think you'll agree that they pass muster. Take a look."

Prodded along by the Master's cane, the boys had achieved a wide range of acrobatic skills. They could execute backflips, pikes, black dragon rolls, cartwheels, double high kicks, somersaults, and backbends, all competently. The old man took a shine to Xiao Shitou right away and kept asking to have him repeat certain exercises. Finally, he had the boy perform a jump split, where he leapt up with his legs in an arabesque and landed in a split.

"There's a new arrival I'd like you see as well," Master Guan broke in. "He's very agile—and clever, too. Xiao Douzi, show us a turn in the air."

Xiao Douzi leapt up and seemed to hang suspended in the air, as though he were flying. Inside he was terrified of landing badly and losing his balance, but outside he appeared confident. Concentrating hard, he circled his extended legs around through the air before landing safely. The Master watched silently, but he was impressed. This boy had even stronger technique than Xiao Shitou. Xiao Douzi was blinking back tears of intermingled fear and relief, and the Master snapped at him.

"If you cry like a baby even when you haven't fallen, what's going to happen when you do fall?"

Xiao Douzi stopped crying, although he still felt unsettled.

"Show us a high kick. And this time don't make a fool of me!" Master Guan commanded.

Xiao Douzi raised his leg and extended it until his ankle nearly touched his forehead. His leg was shaking slightly.

"Higher! Higher, I said! And keep your leg straight!"

Xiao Douzi had started to wobble, and he suddenly lost his balance altogether and fell flat on his rump. The Master exploded. Everything was ruined. The earlier demonstration had been a complete waste of time.

"Damn you! Go practice Chinese splits until I tell you to stop!"

Xiao Douzi cast a worried look at the base of the wall. Xiao Laizi was still there, doing splits and crying with pain as though he were being tortured.

"It hurts! I want my mother! Mother! Maybe I'll see you if I die. I want to go home!" he whined.

Xiao Douzi blanched and did several leg swings to limber up. Xiao Sanzi was stacking bricks onto his legs. With each brick he added, Xiao Douzi's pain grew more intense, until he cried out. Unable to watch the younger boy suffer so, Xiao Shitou sneaked over to him while Master Guan was shamefacedly seeing off Master Shi. Glancing quickly to either side, he knelt down and massaged Xiao Douzi's legs. Then he casually kicked away the bricks, one by one, pretending that they were stones.

"Better?" he asked with a grin.

Xiao Douzi's face fell. Xiao Shitou turned around and found himself face to face with Master Guan.

"You haven't even learned your trade yet, and already you're trying to cheat me! I'm wasting my time with you!" he roared. "Everyone—line up behind me. Somebody bring me a bench. You all deserve a beating!"

One of the school rules was that if one child erred the

entire class would be punished for it. The children went up to the bench one by one, pulled down their trousers, and bent obediently over the bench. Sharp slaps echoed in the room with every fall of the switch on their bare skin. The other residents of the courtyard had long since grown accustomed to the sounds of beatings and tirades.

"You filthy, stinking little wretch! I'll show you what suffering is, you piece of shit. This whole place stinks because of you!"

Xiao Douzi awaited his turn. He was next. Xiao Shitou was being punished, and he spoke to the younger boy through clenched teeth.

"Tighten your butt. . . ." he said through clenched teeth. "It won't hurt as much. . . ."

Xiao Douzi's turn came. He tightened his buttocks as hard as he could, but the blows raining down on him still brought tears to his eyes.

"Should I beat your classmate again?" demanded Master Guan. "He got you into trouble, didn't he?"

Xiao Douzi didn't respond.

"Nothing to say? I'll teach you to be so stubborn!"

With that the Master unleashed a frenzy of blows on Xiao Douzi's frail body.

Spring arrived, and with it milder weather. Xiao Douzi had been at the opera school for three months. The snow that had heralded his arrival was beginning to thaw.

The shabby clothes provided by the school were made of old flour sacks, usually dyed black or some nondescript dark color. In wintertime, the boys stuffed these with cotton wadding, which they pulled out again when the weather turned warmer in spring. Come summer, they also removed the inner layer of these garments. When a child outgrew a piece of clothing, he handed it down to a smaller boy. When the clothes became too worn for anyone to wear, they were pasted together to make soles for cloth shoes.

The boys often performed at the Bridge of Heaven and did fairly well there; but street performers lose their luster if they stay in one spot too long. They couldn't spend their entire lives pretending to be monkeys at the Bridge of Heaven.

As they grew the boys learned the eighteen main types of martial arts: longbow, crossbow, spear, knife, sword, lance, shield, ax, battle ax, two-pronged lance, whip, baton, mace, bamboo pike, trident, lasso, cudgel, and hand-to-hand fighting. Of the four skills opera actors had to perfect—singing, acting, recitation, and fighting—it was fighting that formed the basis for the others. Once this foundation had been laid, Master Guan could start to instruct his students in singing and acting.

With the warmer weather, it came time to give the children baths, and so a big tub of water was heated. This was Xiao Douzi's first bath since entering the school and the first time any of the others had seen him completely naked. There were a dozen of them sharing the bath, and Xiao Douzi stepped in to join them amidst clouds of rising steam. As they washed themselves and took turns rinsing each other off with a wooden dipper, they lost track of the time. The tolling of the bell intruded on their play—*"Shoe! . . . Shoe! . . . Shoe! . . ."*—and Xiao Douzi couldn't help remembering the day he had come to the school. It was the last time he had seen his mother.

"Brother," he said to Xiao Shitou. "The sound of the bell scares me."

"There's nothing to be afraid of," Xiao Shitou replied, with the wisdom of a twelve-year-old. He was three years older than Xiao Douzi and much more experienced. "It's just the Bell Goddess, calling for her shoe. Listen—"

"I thought you told me she was a ghost." Xiao Douzi was quite certain. "Why does she want her shoes?"

Everybody started talking at once, wanting to show off by answering first.

"A long, long time ago, there was an emperor who collected every last copper coin in the city and forced every coppersmith he could find to try to cast for him the biggest, most gigantic bell the world had ever seen. One smith after another tried and failed—and failure was punishable by death. At last, there were only a few coppersmiths left. One of them was an old man who had a daughter. He had tried many times to cast the giant bell, and he told his daughter he was afraid the emperor would behead him soon.

"When she heard this, the daughter walked purposefully over to the giant crucible, full of molten metal, and leaped right in."

"Just like this!" put in one of the boys, who, still naked from the bath, demonstrated an acrobatic turn in the air. When he came down he slipped on the wet floor and landed flat on his behind. Everybody burst out laughing, and as the laughter died down, Xiao Shitou went on with the story.

"The old man tried frantically to save his daughter, but

it was already too late, and all he was able to rescue from the cauldron was one of her shoes. This time, though, the bell casting was a success, and it's the same bell that hangs in the back of the Drum Tower. Nowadays, when the bell tolls the watches at night, you can always hear her calling for her lost shoe."

Xiao Douzi looked fearful.

"Haven't you ever heard this story before? Didn't your mother tell you?"

"Maybe his mother didn't know, either!" Xiao Sanzi sneered.

"That's not true! She does know about it. She told me, only I forgot."

"She doesn't know!" taunted another.

"Your mother never told you!"

Xiao Douzi despised Xiao Sanzi and was about to lash out, but Xiao Shitou intervened.

"Stop bickering! Now forget it, all of you," he said. "None of us heard that story from our mothers. Uncle Ding, the old violin player, told it to us."

"Oh, no!" Xiao Douzi was in a panic. "Uncle Ding! We have to sing for him tomorrow."

He started reciting the lyrics of an aria:

"I am just a handsome lad,
Not a tender maiden—"

Xiao Shitou poured a dipperful of water over Xiao Douzi's head.

"That's not how it goes. It's: 'I am just a tender maiden, Not a handsome lad.'"

Several boys came into the room, dragging Xiao Laizi,

whom they unceremoniously dumped into the bath. He fell in with a heavy splash, like a sack of potatoes.

"Why don't you leave me alone?" he muttered. "I'm going to be dead soon, anyway. Ouch! Who stepped on me?"

Everyone was wrestling and splashing, except for Xiao Douzi. He was nervously trying to memorize the lyrics of the song he was to sing the next day.

"Try again," Xiao Shitou encouraged him. "Only this time pretend that you're a girl."

"Right," he said earnestly. "I, Xiao Douzi, am a girl. 'I am just a tender maiden, Not a handsome lad.'"

He sat in his corner, reciting lyrics, while the others played. They were all too busy laughing and tussling and comparing their penises to pay any attention to Xiao Douzi.

"How come yours is crooked?" one asked another.

Another boy innocently held his penis next to a friend's and asked, "Why is yours smaller than mine?"

Growing up close together, most of the boys had long ago lost their sense of modesty. But Xiao Douzi turned shyly away, reciting to himself, "I am just a tender maiden . . ."

The wound where his extra finger had been had completely healed, leaving nothing but a tiny scar. It was as though it had never been there at all.

The time had come for Master Guan to assign his young apprentices to the traditional role types of the Peking opera. The roles he would play determined how a young actor was to train. But first, they had to be divided into bit players and leads.

That morning they put on their uniforms and tied their sashes with care before diligently warming up their voices and stretching their limbs. It was an important day.

All the students had assembled in the main hall, lining up before Master Guan, Master Shi, and Uncle Ding, the old crooked-nosed violin player. Once they were settled, the adults began to evaluate the apprentices. It was a lot like buying pork in the market—one chose lean or marbled meat depending on one's own taste. The only essential was that a boy be good-looking.

Xiao Shitou was the first to be called upon.

"Come over here," Master Guan addressed him gruffly. "Show us your martial stance."

The boy did as he was told and sang a few lines of a martial air:

"Even my stallion knows that our defeat is nigh.
When I mount him at the stable,
He roars like the thunder!"

The next boy gave an unspirited but refined performance, competently singing a few pieces written for the role of *xiaosheng*, or young man.

Master Shi dismissed the next child as ugly.

"You can't really tell when he has on makeup," Master Guan said defensively. "What about this next one?"

"His fingers are too stubby. And the one next to him is as skinny as a rail. He's no good, either."

One by one, the most attractive children were singled out, leaving only the fat, the dull-witted, and the homely to stand to one side. They were the rejects, and they felt like complete failures, although they were only children. Perhaps, as children, they understood this system better than anyone. Brutal as a children's game, it was like paper, scissors, stone, where the winner takes all, and the loser is crushed.

"Somebody still has to play the supporting parts," Master Guan said huskily, in an effort to cheer them up. They were still in his care. "Without you, the opera couldn't go on. Someone has to turn somersaults and fight staged battles. You're just as necessary as the leads."

"Who is your star pupil?" Master Shi was asking.

Uncle Ding struck up his two-stringed violin as Master Guan summoned Xiao Douzi to sing an aria. The Master had started teaching him the most demanding pieces soon after he'd entered the school.

One day he and Master Guan had been listening to an old widow who lived in another part of the courtyard as she hawked her tea. In addition to the opera school, the courtyard housed two families who were very poor and eked out their livings doing odd jobs, selling bowls of tea on the street, or taking in mending. Some of the family members left early in the morning to find work as day laborers, shelling peanuts, hauling bricks, or cracking walnuts. Others, like the old widow, stayed in the neighborhood.

She sold tea for a living, and she was just setting out with her little wooden cart and big copper kettle.

"Come on over!" she yelled at the top of her voice. "Come drink a big bowl of tea. The water's boiling, and the tea is strong! It goes down easy and hits the spot!"

"Do you hear that, Xiao Douzi," the Master asked him. "Mama Wang is using her real voice. If you yell like that all the time, you'll get hoarse. Not only does it ruin your voice, it's also too much work. Don't forget—you have to use your diaphragm when you sing."

Xiao Douzi was keeping this lesson in mind as he prepared to perform an aria for Master Shi. He had practiced it over and over the night before and knew it by heart, but when he started to sing, his falsetto cracked on the high notes. With his voice stranded in the upper registers, he couldn't back down the scale gracefully, and he panicked and forgot the lyrics.

"I am just a . . . I am just a . . ." he fumbled. "I am just a handsome lad—"

"What's that?" the Master demanded, narrowing his eyes. He took a puff on his long-stemmed copper pipe, then rapped it hard on the table. The harsh clang it made caused Xiao Douzi to jump. Xiao Shitou looked on worriedly, and the other boys fell silent. They were like a flock of birds who have sensed an approaching tiger.

Without warning, Master Guan thrust the pipe bowl into Xiao Douzi's mouth and jerked it back and forth several times. Xiao Douzi's mouth started to fill with blood, and he stared blankly ahead.

"Have you forgotten the words? What's wrong with you? We'll just have to clean out that throat of yours!"

"Don't get carried away!" Master Shi tried to calm him.

"Sing it again!" Master Guan ordered.

Seeing that Xiao Douzi still couldn't remember the lyrics, Xiao Shitou stood where he could see him and silently mouthed the words for Xiao Douzi. This time he got it right.

"I am just a tender maiden,
Not a handsome lad.
Watching happy couples go by, I can only weep.
Two by two, in fine brocade and fancy silks.
Oh heaven, my heart is burning with longing."

His voice was superb, at once delicately ethereal and heartrending. Master Shi closed his eyes and tapped his fingers in time while Xiao Douzi's classmates looked on in awe. He had passed the test.

"You see!" Master Guan said smugly. "I only pushed you hard because I saw your potential!"

Xiao Douzi sighed with relief.

Just then, one of the other students burst in. It was Xiao Heizi.

"No! No!" he shrieked, jolting the adults and children out of their reverie. The violin stopped midnote.

"What's wrong?"

"No! It's terrible!" was all the terrified child could manage to say.

Very little light penetrated the recesses of the storage room. Swords, spears, and staves hung from a wooden storage frame, next to trunks full of primitive props and costumes.

The door opened with a creak, and the children peeked around Master Guan to get a look inside. Motes of dust danced in a thin beam of sunlight. Everything appeared to be normal.

Then they saw Xiao Laizi. His body was dangling from a crude noose that had been secured to a crossbeam. He had tied several silk sashes together and had hanged himself. A small puddle of urine had formed on the floor beneath him.

Most of the boys had never seen a dead body before. Xiao Douzi opened his mouth wide in shock. He was still bleeding from Master Guan's attack, and he felt a little blood trickling from his mouth. He imagined for a moment that it was gushing out and pooling on the floor beneath him. . . . Xiao Laizi's presence weighed down on him, crushing his head, his shoulders, his back, his entire body. . . .

Suddenly he felt something pressing on his shoulder, and he jumped. It was Xiao Shitou, putting his arms around him to comfort him.

Master Guan banged the door shut.

Although the spring days were warm, the nights were still chilly. Tonight felt especially cold to Xiao Douzi. While the others slept, he shivered under his blankets. Eventually, his shaking awakened Xiao Shitou.

"What's wrong?"

"I'm scared," he faltered. "Is Xiao Laizi a ghost now?"

Xiao Shitou rolled out of bed and got up to inspect the bedding and mattress.

"I had a dream," he said, "that the Dragon King let loose a big flood—except that the water was warm instead of cold. Hey! Somebody peed in bed!"

"I—"

Xiao Shitou pulled off the damp underquilt and turned it over.

"Now get some sleep." He saw Xiao Douzi was still shivering and added, "Come over here and put your arms around me. You'll warm up in no time; then you'll be fine. Ghosts are afraid of people's breath."

Xiao Douzi crept closer to the older boy and buried his face in his broad chest.

"If it weren't for you, I'd be scared to death."

"Only cowards want to die. Now, get some rest. Tomorrow you're going to have to practice hard and sing well. You're an actor, now." He chuckled. "You're going to be a famous singer. Maybe even Xiao Laizi will come to hear you!"

At the mention of Xiao Laizi's name, Xiao Douzi cried out in fear. He hugged Xiao Shitou even more tightly.

"Who's that?" barked Master Guan from the other side of the door. "Who's still awake? Do you want to catch your death?"

Holding up a lantern to light his way and dressed in a padded jacket, Master Guan strode into the room.

"I—" Xiao Douzi faltered.

"What's all the commotion about? You're making enough noise to wake the dead, dammit!"

The day's events had left him rattled and even more irritable than usual. When he noticed the wet bedding, he exploded.

"Who wet the bed? Who's responsible?"

By now, all the children were awake. They huddled in silence as Master Guan's eyes swept over the room, searching for the culprit.

"I am," Xiao Shitou exclaimed.

"No, it was me," Xiao Douzi put in quickly.

"Get up! All of you, get up!" Master Guan was even more furious than before, and everybody knew he was going to beat the entire class. As the children started to crawl quietly out of bed, Master Guan was seized by cold terror when he thought of Xiao Laizi's suicide and all the beatings he had given him. He recalled as well the many beatings he had received as a child, innocent of any wrongdoing but still held accountable, judged guilty. His teachers had treated him and his classmates even more harshly than he treated his own students—it was to toughen them up for their demanding careers.

He stopped short.

"Lie back down, all of you!" he said in a resonant voice. "Now that you know what kinds of roles you'll be playing, you'll have to work even harder. If you don't you'll be in trouble!"

With that, he blew out the tiny flame of the oil lamp. Everything went dark.

Early the next morning, Master Guan and Master Shi had a long discussion at the compound gate. Then they went out. The students waited and wondered, but soon Master Shi returned with a quantity of flaky sesame-seed pancakes. Assigning each of the children a partner, he instructed one boy to concentrate on a pancake without taking his eyes from it while the other boy moved it around.

"This is an exercise for your eyes. They should move with the pancakes, rolling up, then down, left and right, fast and slow—"

Loud voices echoed in the courtyard. Without even thinking about it, everybody turned toward the doorway. Two coolies were pulling a flatbed wooden cart across the courtyard. Riding on the cart was a rolled-up straw mat, beneath which the outlines of a body were visible. Master Guan nodded and bowed politely to a policeman as he escorted him out the gate.

The children followed the cart with their eyes.

"Xiao Laizi finally managed to escape from here," Xiao Douzi whispered in Xiao Shitou's ear. It seemed that dying was the only way out of this place.

He felt something hard strike his head. It was the Master's copper pipe.

"What can't we live without?" he demanded. "Spirit! And where does the spirit show itself? In the eyes! So exercise those eyes of yours! Don't move your heads or your necks. Nothing should roll around except your eyeballs."

They practiced diligently, until their eyelids, eyeballs, and eyebrows all moved in concert. They all knew their roles, whether *sheng*, male lead, *dan*, female lead, *jing*, supporting male, or *chou*, clown. Later, when they played these parts on stage, there would be sections of the operas without singing or dialogue. Their eyes would be their only means of expression. They were learning to speak with their eyes.

Xiao Douzi and Xiao Shitou had been paired as *dan* and *sheng*, heroine and hero. They practiced together until their eyes were in harmony and they saw only each other.

2

A warm breeze blew out of the south. Summer had arrived.

As the sun rose amidst a rosy and golden brocade of clouds, the opera students walked to Taoranting Park to practice singing scales. They were like the new bamboo shoots that had sprouted after the rain, each vying with the others to stand out.

"The Master chose me to play the heroine, and you to play the hero. So we're a boy and a girl—"

"I suppose so. Most operas have a hero and a heroine, don't they?"

"But I'm a boy, too."

"Then why are you so pretty?"

The children who had been assigned walk-on roles gathered around Xiao Douzi.

"You think you're great, don't you? None of us was good enough to be a *dan*. Only you," said one enviously.

None of them understood the implications of being a *dan*. All they knew was that Xiao Douzi had the finest technique of any of them, and they were resigned to careers as bit players.

Now that Xiao Douzi's course in life was set, Master Guan began to devote careful attention to his training. Every gesture and pose had to be so graceful and fluid that he seemed to be floating on air.

His once deformed hand became the embodiment of feminine beauty as his wrists circled elegantly, the posed fingers of his "orchid hands" weaving through the air. He practiced the light steps of a *dan,* making endless circles around the well in the courtyard. Slowly and carefully, he placed first the heel, then the instep, and then the toes, one foot at a time, as though he were strolling in a garden. At last he stopped before imaginary flowers and let his hands flutter up toward those phantom peonies. With a cloudlike ripple of his long sleeves, he made great arcs through the air before folding his arms across his chest. Putting one hand under his chin in a pensive attitude, he gazed out, his eyes resting on some indistinct point neither near nor far. He was in another world.

Xiao Douzi also learned to play the coquette. Today Master Guan had him sing "Thinking of Worldly Pleasures":

"Only sixteen and I'm trapped in this convent,
My hair shorn away in the flower of my youth.
Outside our gate I saw an acolyte with his friends.
He looked at me,
And I looked at him.
Now both of us are wracked with longing."

As he rolled his eyes coyly, flirting with the acolyte, Xiao Douzi's gaze came to rest on Xiao Shitou. He was practicing martial arts while Master Guan kept time for him with a gong. The Master roared over its sonorous tones.

"Thrust with the rhythm. Don't just flail about blindly. You're striking hard, but you don't have any control."

Xiao Shitou struck an imposing attitude. He was handsome and powerful, an ideal *sheng*. After several beats, he went back to fighting a choreographed battle with his classmates. They came at him with every manner of weapon while he fought them off with his spear and intimidated them with his booming general's voice. Suddenly he noticed Xiao Douzi, who was smoothing the hair at his temples with delicately tapering fingers, then miming the actions of getting dressed as he straightened his collar and pulled on his shoes. Next, Douzi threaded an imaginary needle and began to embroider. Looking up, he met Xiao Shitou's eyes, and for a moment they held each other's gaze. Soon my friend and I will be performing together on stage, Xiao Douzi thought contentedly.

"What are you looking at?" Master Guan barked. Xiao Douzi jumped. "There's nothing for you to learn over there. You're a *dan,* not a *sheng* or a *jing*. Now practice walking in your wooden stage shoes. Mind your own business, and stick to what you need to know for your own roles!"

Xiao Douzi had to learn to walk on tiny platform shoes, and it took all of his concentration to do so as he focused his attention on his feet.

The Master was a very large man. On hot days he would unbutton his shirt, revealing a hairy chest. He even had hair growing from his navel. All the children gathered round, hoping to see this burly man tiptoeing around to demonstrate how one should walk in the wooden shoes. But they were disappointed when the Master instructed Xiao Douzi to give the demonstration.

"Pull in your stomach. Now, take a deep breath, hold yourself tall, and try it."

The child stood poised a moment before taking a few gracefully swaying steps. He teetered precariously, but he kept moving. If he stopped, the Master would think him lazy. Xiao Douzi faltered, nearly losing his balance, and Xiao Shitou rushed over to prop him up. The two of them looked at one another and smiled.

Customers filled the small tables inside the Spring Blossom Teahouse. Some sat cracking melon seeds between their teeth, and others nibbled on cakes and sweets, waiting for their pots of fine tea to finish steeping. They were watching the opera being performed by Master Guan's pupils. Some of the customers placed several rows of benches up front near the stage, where they could get a better view. Those seated in the back of the restaurant grew rowdier and rowdier as laughter and rude talk gave way to arguments and blows. But the show went on, and a serving boy made the rounds with his copper kettle, refilling the teapots with hot water. Young children handed out moist towels for the patrons, and vendors circulated among the tables selling candies and shelled peanuts. In the wintertime, there were also candied chestnuts. In addition to whatever they might earn, the snack sellers also got to see a free opera.

Next to the open space set aside as a stage was a banner announcing the day's program: "A GATHERING OF HEROES," a tale from the Three Kingdoms. The hero was one of Master Guan's prize pupils, whom Master Shi had recommended to the teahouse's proprietor. Master Guan had brought the boy over one day, along with a token box of sweets.

The owner and Master Shi had turned their attention from a little bird they were teasing to size up the young hopeful. He met with the proprietor's approval, and the bargaining began.

"You put on a few shows for me, some repertory, and I'll provide the space. But I have several requirements."

He started to state his demands but was interrupted by Master Guan.

"Whatever you like! I want the children to gain some experience in the real world, and I'd be grateful if you could give them that chance, even though they aren't full-fledged professionals yet. As for the money, just give them a few coins to spend on sweets. That will be more than enough."

With that, the students began their performing careers.

Doors on either side of the stage led backstage, where there was a flurry of activity. Master Guan was helping the children apply their stage makeup by painting half of each child's face and letting him finish the other half himself. They examined their harlequin faces intently in the mirror—one side richly and strikingly patterned, the other plain—before shakily filling in the empty side.

"Use the white paint," one advised another. Then he sighed, "You used too much. Now you look like a ghost!"

Eventually they all finished putting on their makeup. They had been transformed from little boys to timeless characters. This would be Xiao Douzi's first stage appearance as a beautiful lady. His eyes were rimmed in black and drawn to appear large and uptilted like the eyes of a phoenix. Rouge spread over the planes of his cheeks to his hairline and over his brow bones to his temples. Only a newborn baby could be so ruddy, so flushed, he thought to himself.

"Here, let me help you." Xiao Shitou ambled lightly over.

"You'd better look after yourself, first. Don't worry about the others," Master Guan chided him. "You may think you're helping him, but you're not. If you put on his makeup for him, he'll never learn how to do it himself. Are you going to spend the rest of your life taking care of him?"

Xiao Shitou slipped away, muttering under his breath, "Fine with me!"

Xiao Douzi tried to catch his friend's eye in the mirror and made a face, but Xiao Shitou didn't respond. Instead, he just put on his costume and huffed out.

The Master came over again to appraise Xiao Douzi's makeup. He wasn't satisfied and added a few more strokes of color.

"You should be grateful to the founders of the Opera," he grumbled. "Without them your rice bowl would be empty. Thanks to them, you have a teacher to look after you, and you may even be famous someday. But at the rate you're going, that's a long way off."

At last, the drums and gongs sounded. The play was about to start.

"Is everything ready?" asked Uncle Ding. "Onstage, everybody!"

They made their entrances. The hero of the play, a historical romance, was General Lu Bu, and the heroine was Diao Chan, his consort. A host of famous figures filled out the cast of characters: Prime Minister Dong Zhuo, General and Prime Minister Zhu-ge Liang, Duke Guan, and General Zhang Fei. They bravely faced their audience and sang. But the children were trembling inside as though the teahouse were a theater of war and the patrons an enemy army.

Once the supporting players were on stage, Xiao Shitou strode on as Lu Bu. Xiao Douzi stole a look at him from the wings. His palms were sweating.

At last, it was time for him to make his entrance, and he joined Xiao Shitou in the middle of the circle formed by the others. The two of them sang the romantic arias with all their hearts, although, because they were still children, they couldn't really understand the feelings they sang about.

That day at the Spring Blossom Teahouse they were Lu Bu, Diao Chan, and a group of "heroes." But outside the theater, they were "ninth-class" citizens. As performers, opera singers, and actors, they stood on one of the bottom rungs of the social ladder in the China of the 1920s and 1930s. The time they spent in the limelight, dressed in elaborate costumes, was a brief respite from otherwise hard lives. For a few hours they embodied the dreams of their people, and then they went back to being objects of contempt.

Directly after the show, the children lined up backstage, in a neat row, hands at their sides, still in their makeup, while Master Guan critiqued their performance. He was always stingy with praise, and today's criticisms were even harsher than usual.

"Zhu-ge Liang was pathetic! Did you learn your technique from a stray dog? And Dong Zhuo—you cowered behind your henchmen like a frightened rabbit. Couldn't you muster even an ounce of courage? And you—what a poor excuse for Duke Guan. You should sing with authority. Instead, it sounded like you had a mouthful of chestnuts. Zhang Fei, you ran around wasting your energy and overacting. And you, Lu Bu, you did nothing but posture. The minute you get nervous, you close your eyes. You'd be more convincing as a cur than as an ordinary man—to say nothing of a general.

"That leaves Diao Chan. You're supposed to be charming—instead you just slouched around. Nobody in his right mind could ever mistake you for one of the Four Great Beauties of old China. What are you gaping at? Look at me!"

Master Guan stood thinking to himself. Actually, they weren't half bad, his students. Not that he would let on to them. It didn't do to overpraise children—they might become complacent.

At first they sang only in teahouses, but later on they moved up to small theaters. They always had a big pot of food backstage so that the young players could keep up their strength. Usually it was something filling like cornmeal porridge, noodles, or cornbread, although on holidays they ate steamed wheat buns.

★　★　★

Summer reached its peak, with heat that incapacitated people and animals alike. Master Guan went out to do some errands, and his students sneaked out to the riverbank. They jumped into the water in a chorus of exuberant whooping. Water fights became free-for-alls that ended with all the boys in a squirming mountain of bodies. Some of them were making fun of Master Guan. They mimicked his gruff demeanor and habitual gestures, bulging their eyes, fingering imaginary beards, and ranting and fuming.

There was a boy they called the Wet Log because he perspired a lot. The Master always dressed him down for it.

"You haven't set foot onstage yet, but you're already soaking wet, like something dredged out of the river," he would say. "You'll never make a living in the opera if you just stand there dripping water all over the stage."

This Wet Log had never felt such contentment as he did now, immersed in the river. His sweat mingled with the water and was carried away, as if it had never been there at all. When he stood up he felt the pleasant sensation of being wet and having the water running off of his body, without having to endure his teacher's curses. Happy and carefree, he intoned in a deep voice, "The Honorable Judge Bao of Kaifeng, presiding—"

Just then, the irascible Xiao Meiqiu came running by and gave him a shove, and he landed in the water with a hard belly flop. Then Xiao Meiqiu lumbered forward with a leading man's bowlegged walk, imitating Xiao Shitou.

"Heaven has forsaken me!" he wailed.

At this, everybody jumped into the fray, with all the boys splashing and tussling. Nobody was spared, except Xiao

Douzi, who sat by himself on the bank, singing an aria softly to himself. The song was sung by the wronged heroine, Su San:

"People say the flowers in Loyang are like brocade,
I have been locked in this prison for so long,
I do not know the spring."

So far, the others had been content to leave Xiao Douzi alone. At last, Xiao Sanzi, by far the most mischievous boy in the group, couldn't resist teasing him.

"Don't you know about sex?" he asked. Then, imitating the way Xiao Douzi mimed the role of the shackled Su San, he said in an affectedly bashful voice, "Xiao Douzi! 'I am just a tender maid—' "

All the boys wiggled their hips like the willowy young heroine and formed a line and snaked their way with tiny effeminate steps until they stood before Xiao Douzi. When they started to splash him, he ran and hid behind Xiao Shitou.

"Leave him alone," Xiao Shitou said good-naturedly.

"Look out—here he comes again!" Xiao Douzi called out from behind his friend's back.

"Look out!" Xiao Sanzi and Xiao Meiqiu mocked him with whiny voices. "Here he comes again! What a sissy!"

"What did you say?" Xiao Douzi asked. The rims of his eyes had reddened.

Xiao Heizi leaned in closer, saying, "He isn't really a boy. That's why the Master always has him play girls. Let's see what's inside his pants. Come on over, everybody!"

The others surged forward noisily, and Xiao Douzi fled in a panic.

"Leave him alone!" Xiao Shitou shouted. He did his

best to protect his friend, but he was outnumbered. The gang of boys caught up with Xiao Douzi and crowded around him. But Xiao Shitou hadn't given up, and he rushed at the knot of boys, butting them with his head, and striking out left and right. Soon they were all fighting.

Suddenly a loud cry rang out above the shrieks and yells of the battle. Everybody fell silent when they saw that Xiao Shitou had been pushed onto a heap of sharp rocks. There was a red gash at his temple, and it was bleeding profusely.

Xiao Shitou covered the cut with his hand, saying nothing.

"What should we do?" somebody asked.

"Wrap something around it tight to stop the bleeding."

"We can't let Master Guan find out, no matter what!"

Each boy untied his sash, thinking it would make a good bandage; but everyone's sashes were dripping wet. Xiao Douzi pushed through the cluster of boys, tears streaming down his cheeks. His sash was still dry, and he quickly unfastened it and wound it tightly around Xiao Shitou's forehead.

"It's all my fault," he sobbed. "This wouldn't have happened to you if it hadn't been for me. I'm sorry." As he wrapped the long piece of cloth around his friend's head, his hands began to weave through the air in the stylized movements of the opera without his realizing it.

"Does it hurt?"

"Not really."

"I can't stand it anymore!" Xiao Douzi said disconsolately. "If my mother came to take me home right now, I'd go with her and never come back! Would you come, too?"

Xiao Shitou kept silent for a while before finally answering.

"Your mother won't come back."

"Why not?"

"She signed the contract, didn't she? She sold you to Master Guan." He went on, "Don't fool yourselves, any of you. I spent three New Year's Days waiting for my mother before I realized she wasn't ever going to come back."

Shadows had begun to gather, and the children stood mutely in the approaching dusk. Some bowed their heads sadly, and some clenched their fists, while a few others fell to their knees in frustration. The ruddy light of the setting sun lingered on their naked chests and backs.

One of them spoke abruptly.

"We'd better hurry back to the school. Otherwise, the Master will find out and beat us!"

They all hid their feelings away again and trudged back home—if they could really call it a home. Their earlier high spirits had been replaced by homesickness and longing for their mothers.

The instant the group of children crossed the threshold of the school, Master Guan started to berate them.

"I'd given you up for dead! Where the hell were you? Did it have to get dark out before you remembered to come home? The moment I turn my back on you wretched creatures, you all go sneaking off to have water fights." He turned on little Wet Log. "Look at you! You're disgusting!"

Then he caught sight of Xiao Shitou.

"What's this?" he demanded. "Where did that cut come from? Can't you even take care of your own face? Nobody will want to watch you perform if your face is covered with scars! Where's the disinfectant? You—and you—" he said, singling out two of the more responsible boys, "Bring me the disinfectant in the bottle from Tongren Pharmacy."

The remaining students crowded close for a better view as Master Guan carefully examined the wound on Xiao Shitou's forehead. The examination, while thorough, was accompanied by an endless stream of abuse.

"It's right where everyone in the audience can see it! It's going to be hard to conceal. Just above the brow bone! That's bad luck. You know that a cut there means brothers will become enemies."

Xiao Douzi's heart fell when he heard these words.

"You have no common sense!" the Master ranted. "We finally booked a public appearance, and you went and let this happen! You'll still have to perform at the old gentleman's house along with the others."

The disinfectant burned Xiao Shitou's open cut, and he winced. But the more he tensed his brows, the more painful it was. Xiao Douzi looked on silently, wishing that he could suffer in his friend's place.

It was the last night of summer. The mansion and its extensive gardens blazed with hundreds of big red lanterns, and festive music filled the air.

A broad stage had been erected in the courtyard, under a marquee. Behind the stage hung a brocade curtain with a giant character in multicolored embroidery. It was the character *shou*, "long life." The orchestra struck up an overture. The host was celebrating his birthday.

China's imperial system had long since been replaced by the new republic, and most of the trappings of the former dynasty had faded away. Yet some people still lived in that era, longing for their old positions of power and dreaming of their days at the Qing court. The evening's host was one such man.

As the young company of actors were applying the final strokes to their makeup, old Master Shi came backstage holding a copy of the program.

"It's Master Ni's birthday," he said to Master Guan, with a bemused expression. "Why are you performing something as sad as *Farewell to My Concubine?*"

"I don't understand it myself," the other replied, shaking his head. "It's not the usual birthday fare, is it? But it's what he asked for."

Nearby, Xiao Douzi had finished his own makeup, pale pink near the chin and gradually deepening to an intensely rosy flush beneath uptilted black brows. He was holding Xiao Shitou's face steady with one hand while daubing on the last of his makeup for him. The open cut at Xiao Shitou's temple stung every time the greasepaint touched it, but he hid his discomfort so as not to upset his friend. The painfully slow process was made all the slower because not only was Xiao Douzi afraid of making a mistake, he was also afraid of being caught by Master Guan. But tonight Master Guan pretended not to notice. It would be too great a loss of face to berate his students on such an important occasion.

Just then, the stage manager hurried up, urging everyone in the company to get ready. The play was about to begin. Gathered backstage, the young actors peeked at their audience through a gap in the curtain. The people they saw were all richly dressed in old-fashioned clothes. Young or old, man or woman, they were all still loyal to the vanquished Qing dynasty. Some were holdovers who longed for the good old days. Others were spiritual refugees who had no memory of those times but still wished for their return. None of them wore a braid, the old symbol of loyalty to the Qing, but there was an invisible queue winding around the bodies of the assembled guests like a filament of spider web. They were trapped in the past, with no desire to slip their bonds. They had nowhere else to go but here, nothing else left to do in life but sit cracking melon seeds, watching operas, and smoking opium.

A number of guests were clustered around Master Ni, a sixty-year-old with a wrinkled and florid face that looked like dried pork belly. He had salt-and-pepper hair, and his face was smooth and beardless, with eyes that drooped kindly at the corners. But his coldly grating and androgynous voice belied his benevolent appearance.

"Please, please," he said, deflecting his guests' well-wishes and compliments. "You needn't be so formal. Do sit down, please."

At last the retired eunuch sat down and comfortably awaited the beginning of the show. The opera started, and the stirring melodies and inspiring lyrics washed over him like the capable and knowing hands of a masseur. He half closed his eyes in pleasure.

Then Xiao Douzi made his entrance as Yu Ji, stepping so slowly and lightly that he seemed to float. He wore an elaborate headdress, a yellow shawl embroidered with flowers, a large golden locket, and a many-pleated silk skirt. The costume belonged to the opera company, and many people had worn it before him. It had never been washed and smelled of decades of stale sweat, but when people in the audience looked at Xiao Douzi, all they saw was a sweet and charming lady. Nobody noticed how heavy the costume was, or that it was a little large for him. He sang an adagio:

> "Since I first followed my lord on his campaigns, east and west, north and south,
> I have borne the wind and frost, and hardship year after year.
> But I regret nothing, save that a wicked emperor has plunged the people into misery.
> I am only angry that he has condemned them to lives of toil and pain."

"Bravo! Good boy!" the members of the audience called out as one.

The neighing of his black stallion, Wuzhui, heralded the entrance of General Xiang Yu. Xiao Shitou marched on stage, wearing a black robe embroidered with a serpent. Symbolic black banners on his shoulders identified him as a general. He sang with presence.

> "I went into the enemy camp and killed two of their generals with my sword.
> Many brave heroes have died in these battles—they lie buried all around.
> Give the orders—no man shall leave camp and those who are away shall return."

This was followed by more shouts of "Bravo!"

Master Guan listened backstage and heaved a sigh of relief. He had been even more nervous than if he had been singing himself. Although he didn't smile easily, he was smiling to himself now. The audience was pleased, and so was he.

After the show, Master Ni's steward came up to him and

thrust a pouch of silver coins into his hand.

"Compliments of Master Ni!"

"Thank you, thank you," Master Guan said distractedly. He had been watching Xiao Douzi and Xiao Shitou take off their makeup.

"It's just a token! It's nothing," the steward laughed. "This company of yours has some hidden talents!"

Master Guan was just about to make a few politely self-deprecating remarks when Xiao Shitou gave a little cry. Xiao Douzi had been wiping off his greasepaint and had rubbed the cut at his temple, causing it to break open. With great concern, Xiao Douzi cupped his friend's face between his hands and touched the open cut with his tongue. He sucked at it gently until it stopped hurting.

"Master Ni requests that your little Yu Ji go pay his respects and give his thanks."

"Xiao Douzi! Master Ni wants to see you. Hurry up!"

The boy looked up at the men with clear, guileless eyes. There was a trace of black greasepaint from Xiao Shitou's forehead on his crimson lips. Obediently, he followed the steward.

Old Master Ni leaned back on his opium bed. He wore a blissful expression, having just smoked two pipefuls of opium.

Xiao Douzi stepped into the bed chamber as the door was silently pulled closed behind him. He was immediately overwhelmed by the luxurious surroundings—he had never seen anything like this. Not knowing where else to look, he let his gaze rest on the dark rosewood bookshelves that lined the opposite wall. They were filled with rows and rows of books, their titles running down the backs of their hard bindings in bright green script. These were the *Twenty-four Histories*—official histories of China's twenty-four dynasties, stories reaching back millennia.

Old Master Ni blew a puff of smoke toward Xiao Douzi, who nearly gagged. Nonetheless, he minded his manners and bowed deeply.

"I have come to wish Master Ni long life on this his sixtieth birthday—" he said shyly.

The old man pointed a long bony finger at him, cutting him short.

"What year is it?"

"The nineteenth year of the republic—"

"Wrong," said Ni with a peremptory wave. "It is the twenty-second year of the reign of the Qing emperor Xuantong!"

Master Ni took out a fine white silk handkerchief and wiped the black mark from Xiao Douzi's lips. Without looking, he dropped the handkerchief, and it floated into a spittoon. The little pot was decorated with red peonies outlined in gold, and it stood on a dark sandalwood pedestal.

Master Ni beckoned Xiao Douzi to come closer and set him on his lap. Tenderly but playfully, he began stroking Xiao Douzi's face and pinching his buttocks in an almost maternal fashion.

"Who does Yu Ji die for?" he asked smoothly.

"She dies for the General."

Master Ni was pleased by this response. Relaxed by the opium, he was beginning to feel aroused.

"That's correct. Yu Ji is a woman, frail and weak, and yet she shines with integrity. She is so loyal that she dies for her lover, cutting her throat with a sword. All the officials and generals of the Qing dynasty combined weren't equal to this courageous woman!" As he grew more excited, his voice rose in pitch. "These are sad times! I chose that opera today just to humiliate them!"

Xiao Douzi began to feel unsteady as the old gentleman got more and more carried away.

"What's wrong, little one?"

"I have to go peepee," he answered timidly.

Master Ni gestured toward the fancy spittoon, and Xiao Douzi stood down. After a brief glance at Master Ni, he turned away modestly and dropped his trousers. But the old eunuch had glimpsed it—the child's penis, complete and undamaged, unlike his own. He fought to control his excitement, but it showed in his face.

"Slow down!" he said, his lower jaw trembling slightly.

Xiao Douzi gave a start.

The old man lifted up a white jade bowl from the night table. Translucent and glossy, it had been a gift from the emperor in some long-forgotten year. It was priceless.

He held the bowl in front of Xiao Douzi, saying gently, "Here. Please, use this."

The urge to urinate overcame Xiao Douzi's embarrassment, and he felt relieved as he let go. The old man was transfixed.

"You are so . . . perfect, so beautiful," he sighed. As he tenderly blotted the boy dry with a corner of his silk robe, he suddenly lost his senses and put the boy's penis in his mouth. He sucked and sucked. Xiao Douzi's eyes widened and his mouth was dry. . . .

★ ★ ★

By the time they emerged from the front gate of the mansion, it was in the morning of the next day. Master Guan was in high spirits and was humming a tune as he sauntered ahead of his pupils. Many of them still had traces of makeup left on their faces as they chattered excitedly about the previous night.

"I've never seen a door as tall as Master Ni's front door!"

"And the stage was ten times as big as the one at the teahouse!"

Xiao Shitou had hidden handfuls of pilfered shortbread and candies in his shirt. He was showing them to Xiao Douzi.

"Look what I got! This supply should last me a long time. It's the best candy I've ever had! Here, have some."

Xiao Douzi said nothing. He looked a little melancholy.

"What's the matter?" Xiao Shitou asked. "Aren't you feeling well?"

Again Xiao Douzi didn't respond. He felt bewildered and afraid.

"Cat got your tongue? Speak up!" After a moment, Xiao Shitou went on impatiently, "If you have something to say, then say it. If you keep things bottled up, you can't expect other people to know what's bothering you!"

They were passing a heap of garbage at the mouth of an alley when they heard a faint cry. Xiao Douzi turned back and walked over to take a closer look. The cry had come from a bundle of cloth. He pulled aside the cloth and was astonished to see a newborn baby, red all over and still streaked with blood. The infant was so new that its hair was still damp. An old rag was wrapped around the tiny belly.

Master Guan walked over to investigate.

"It's just a foundling. It's none of our business," he said, putting the bundle back where it had been. "Now, get going!"

"Master—" Xiao Douzi had tears in his eyes. "Can't we keep her? It's a girl."

"Don't be a fool! What do you want with a baby girl? Girls don't belong in our company—they don't sing Peking opera. It's that simple. She'd just be one more mouth to feed, and we can't afford that."

Xiao Douzi knew not to argue, but he couldn't help sobbing. Even Master Guan was moved by the sight of the child's small shoulders wracked by sobs.

"You have food to eat and clothes to wear," he said gruffly. "And you have the chance to grow up and become an actor. You're luckier than most children."

Xiao Shitou patted him on the back, encouraging him to move on. But he dragged his feet and started crying uncontrollably. He kept thinking of her—a rosy-faced little girl, just born and abandoned on a heap of garbage. She would cry herself to death, and nobody would come until it was too late, when she would be thrown into the river with the other refuse.

Xiao Douzi kept thinking of her soft, damp hair. She had cried herself hoarse. She must be hungry, he thought. Where was her mother? Had she felt no remorse at abandoning her child? He was filled with intense longing for his own mother.

Master Guan came over to Xiao Douzi and Xiao Shitou. Fumbling in his pockets, he took out two silver coins and gave one to each boy before pulling them after him, one on each hand. As he continued on down the street, he admonished them:

"Others are riding on horseback, but I ride an ass,
When I think of it, I say I'm not as good as they.
But when I turn around and view the road behind,
There are people bearing burdens and plodding all the
     way."

My mother will come back to see me, Xiao Douzi told himself. All I have to do is work hard, and I'll be a success. I'll have lots of money and never go hungry. He wiped away his tears.

"It's almost New Year's," Xiao Shitou was saying. "We can visit the temple fair. By then we'll have enough money to buy ten squares of steamed pudding—all dipped in sugar. I can already taste it!" He licked his lips in anticipation and went on to describe the other treats he was planning to buy. He grew more excited by the minute, unaware of Xiao Douzi's lack of enthusiasm.

It was New Year's Eve. Everybody was in high spirits and ran around the lanes and alleys near the school playing hide-and-seek and setting off strings of firecrackers. People were singing New Year's songs, and a festive mood pervaded the capital. The scents and sounds of holiday cooking were everywhere. Knives rapped sharply on wooden blocks as families minced meat and sliced vegetables for special dumplings. Some people had no money for this kind of celebration, but they took up their cooking knives anyway, chopping at empty cutting boards for the neighbors to hear. Otherwise people might laugh at them.

Xiao Douzi sat on the kang, cutting intricate designs in brightly colored paper to make window decorations. He was very adept and turned out lacy butterflies and flowers with great ease. As he cut, his fingers were poised delicately in the "orchid hands" of his stage performances.

The door opened with a creak. Xiao Shitou poked a sweat-soaked head around the corner and walked in. He had been outside playing with the others.

"Come on out, Xiao Douzi. What are you doing cooped up in here? We're setting off firecrackers—the loudest ones we could find. And Xiao Meiqiu is going to light some more fireworks—fountains of sparks and snakes, too."

"I'll be out in a bit."

"What are you making?"

Xiao Shitou casually picked up one of the cutouts, but he was a little rough and tore it accidentally. Xiao Douzi shot him a dirty look.

"What's this? A butterfly?"

"Butterflies are nice. Here, I'll give you one. I can paste it up for you."

"I don't want a butterfly," Xiao Shitou said, setting it down. "I'd rather have a five-clawed golden dragon, or a fierce tiger."

Xiao Douzi didn't respond. He didn't know how to make either of these designs.

"Never mind! I don't want one anyway." After a moment he said, "Why waste your time cutting them out yourself? I have enough money to buy you one—any design you like. What do you say? Let's go!"

Fireworks popped and cracked with the irrepressible spirit of the season. Cheerful shouts of "Happy New Year!" rang out all around.

New Year's was the only day of the year that the members of the opera troupe got to eat refined white rice. The rest of the year they had to make do with coarser kinds of grain, but on this day everybody ate to his heart's content. After their meal, they donned their costumes, getting ready to perform the lion dance. They would go from door to door bearing greetings and hoping to collect a few red envelopes containing money, in accordance with the New Year's tradition.

Xiao Shitou and Xiao Meiqiu had put on the lion costume and were ready to go. The vividly patterned red, orange, and yellow of the lion's body made the very air around it seem to pulsate with energy and a sense of hopeful expectation. No matter how troubled or difficult the times, people always looked forward to the New Year, with its promise of better fortune.

Xiao Douzi was fastening up the buttons of his coat. It was bright blue and embroidered with small, white flightless butterflies. The jacket sleeves were wrapped at the wrist, and his trouser legs bound at the ankles. His role today was to tease the lion with a ball of multicolored silk threads.

He wove from side to side, holding the ball right in front of the lion's eyes, then tossing it high in the air and jumping up to catch it. Try as it could, the lion couldn't catch the boy or the ball. It shimmied and swayed, following the boy down wide avenues and narrow lanes as onlookers pressed close for a better view. Even babies in little tiger-headed slippers and sequined caps delighted in the spectacle. The sound of applause was thunderous.

They danced their way to Longfu Temple and climbed the stone steps, from which one could see the front of its nearby companion shrine, Huguo Temple. The road that ran between the two temples had become a flower market, and a riot of purple and red blossoms, freshly cut and in full bloom, overflowed the stalls.

A steady stream of temple visitors lit offertory sticks of incense and prayed for good fortune. Master Guan first led his group of young players to worship the gods of Longfu Temple shrine before heading for Huguo Temple.

The inscription on the gate of Huguo Temple was a poem:

These two temples, east and west, are the busiest of all,
They don't collect fine jades or precious gems
From the high and mighty or the wealthy clans.
Here we love only the colors of spring brought by the
    faithful,
The scent of sweet incense wafting through the air
    makes it springtime all year round.

While New Year's made every child feel like a little tycoon, none of their mothers ever came to visit them. Xiao Douzi knew he couldn't have endured it without his "big brother."

Changdian was the liveliest place to be during the first month of the lunar year. If you set out from Heping Gate and crossed the railroad tracks, you would be met by painted canopies and tents stretching as far as the eye could see. There was a rushing sound like that of the ocean, which came from pinwheels. They spun round and round in dizzying but hypnotic swirls of dazzling color. Xiao Shitou and Xiao Douzi were among the onlookers who found themselves irresistibly drawn in, unwilling or unable to break the spell.

The kite sellers' stalls were festooned with fantastically bright and elaborate kites in every shape imaginable. There were centipedes several yards long, butterflies, dragonflies, goldfish, wind socks, and lucky three-tailed kites.

Xiao Shitou had already spent every last cent of his pocket money on sweets. He had sampled steamed puddings, conical corn biscuits, sticky fried rice-noodle bars, and pea cakes. He had amassed a big sackful of treats, plus two skewers of candied gourds. These were stuck on three-foot-long bamboo sticks and topped with brightly colored paper flags. He turned to hand one of these sticks of candy to Xiao Douzi, but he had disappeared.

Xiao Shitou found him standing in front of an embroidery shop, entranced by the embroidered figures displayed there. The finely detailed beauties and handsome knights-errant had captured his imagination. After some contemplation, he pulled out the silver dollar he had been saving for the past few years and bought a pair of handkerchiefs embroidered with butterflies and flowers. He held one out to Xiao Shitou, but his hands were full of sweets.

"You carry it," Xiao Shitou said, gesturing with his chin.

Xiao Douzi felt hurt.

"I bought it especially for you to dry yourself off with when you sweat."

Xiao Shitou sang a few lines from an aria:

"I have troubled my lady,
Today I return home in defeat.
Oh, my heart is uneasy indeed."

Xiao Douzi sang in reply:

"I beg of my lord, please grieve no more,
But take your ease and be merry."

Xiao Shitou laughed.

"You just spent your whole savings on a couple of hankies?"

"I have to start somewhere. Today, I'm buying handkerchiefs. Later I'll save up to buy the best costumes I can. And props and headdresses and jewelry, too. Everything I use will be all my own," he said wistfully. "What about you?"

"Just give me something good to eat, and I'll be happy!" he laughed.

Xiao Douzi gave him a conspiratorial look.

They were passing a small shop that sold antiques and curios. It was packed with fine and expensive bronzes, porcelains, jewelry, and clothing—once the property of rich families now down on their luck.

They both saw the sword at the same time. It was displayed on the wall—a double-edged sword, with a tasseled and carved scabbard that had a subtle patina. It was like a closed eye that barely hinted at the luster of the blade inside.

Xiao Shitou stopped in midstride.

"What a sword! Anybody who wears that is bound to become a general for sure! It's really something!"

"I'll get it for you, Brother," Xiao Douzi said without thinking.

"Don't be stupid!" he laughed. "It costs one hundred silver dollars. The two of us put together aren't even worth that much. Let's go."

He had already eaten all the snacks he'd bought earlier, and he headed for the door, one hand on Xiao Douzi's shoulder. Xiao Douzi's eyes remained fixed on the sword, as though he were trying to see into its heart.

"I promise. I'll get that sword for you someday."

"Hurry up!" Xiao Shitou said as he impatiently dragged him out. "We'll be in big trouble if we're late. It's important."

Master Guan knelt stiffly in front of the row of clean-shaven little boys who had assembled in the courtyard of the Temple of the Patron Saints of Opera. They waited quietly, each young face a copy of the Master's stern expression. None of them even cracked a smile, and they stood without moving for so long that they began to feel numb.

The photographer ducked his head under the voluminous black cloth covering his camera and checked his composition in the viewfinder. The sun shone down on the children's bare heads. At first it had felt warm, but after a while it started to itch and they began to fidget.

Some time passed, and still nothing happened. A kite drifted overhead, one of the ten-foot-long centipedes that had been on sale at the fair. Rippling in the breeze, free and independent, it seemed to be looking down on them from its height.

One of the boys saw it and twisted his head around to watch. Another boy caught sight of the kite and laughed out loud. One after the other, they looked up longingly, their hearts soaring with the paper centipede.

The photographer held up a flashbulb and called out, "All right, everybody. Get ready!"

The children turned back to face the camera and resumed their sober expressions. All stood respectfully behind

Master Guan. As the saying went, "Once a teacher, always a father." If he had ordered them to stand until they dropped dead, none of them would have disobeyed.

The flash went off with a great blinding pop, and the shutter clicked, fixing each of the subjects in his place within a rectangular frame.

Red curtains screened the altar table. Incense burners and candle holders had been placed before yellow tablets inscribed with black characters. Each tablet bore the name of a deity: Guanyin, Goddess of Mercy; Celestial Marshal Wuchang, Master of Stars; Yisu, the patron of opera singers; the Master of Drums; Bell Boy. There was also a plaque dedicated to the five venerable institutions of Heaven, Earth, Emperor, Parents, and Teachers.

Master Guan led his students up to the altar and kowtowed deeply.

"May all of my pupils shine brighter than any one star, brighter than all the stars in the sky, and brighter than the sun."

Ten years later, Xiao Shitou and Xiao Douzi stood before the same altar. Xiao Shitou was leading his colleagues in prayer.

"May our success be sweeter than sugar spun with honey," he recited. He raised his head, revealing a handsome and honest face. Beside him was a slim young man with delicately arched brows and gracefully uptilted eyes.

Xiao Shitou and Xiao Douzi had grown up.

3

Xiao Shitou and Xiao Douzi completed their training. After graduation, they joined an itinerant opera company and would soon take new names: Xiao Shitou would become Duan Xiaolou, while Xiao Douzi would become Cheng Dieyi. With trunks full of props and costumes, they crisscrossed the countryside, performing on makeshift stages in villages and hamlets.

The company's most popular piece was *Farewell to My Concubine*. The stars of this piece were both quite young. The *sheng*, or male lead, was only twenty-two, while the *dan*, or heroine, was all of nineteen. They had just emerged from the critical years when the voice matures from a child's to a man's, during which time the voice may crack unpredictably. Some of the young singers in Master Guan's training passed through the change only to find they no longer had good singing voices. Others, like Xiao Douzi and Xiao Shitou, were more fortunate. Xiao Douzi's voice had matured smoothly in a mere three months.

Xiao Shitou had a fine voice, a handsome face, and a good physique. Xiao Meiqiu had emulated his disciplined practice of martial arts; but there was more to Xiao Shitou's talent than that. He alone had both a solid foundation in the martial arts and a clear and powerful voice. When he sang the role of General Xiang Yu, he sounded like a man who could command great armies.

Xiao Douzi made his entrance, parting the beaded curtains and posing gracefully as the audience cheered. His voice was sweet and smooth, and his movements exquisite. With his slim body and delicate features in costume and makeup, he was utterly convincing as the beautiful Yu Ji. He also had a more elusive quality—he knew how to be seductive. A *dan* without this kind of charm had no future; and it was not something that could be learned. Xiao Douzi had been born with it.

The two old friends and classmates had become a *sheng* and a *dan*. They played the hero and his lady, the scholar and the maiden, and other romantic couples. They played whatever roles came their way—an actor couldn't afford to be too picky. They learned their roles quickly and well, memorizing the text of every opera they performed. Soon they would be making their formal debuts, and yet neither of them could read a word. It was time they learned to read and write their own names, at least.

The company manager held up strips of red paper, with the actors' names written on them neatly in black.

"Master Duan and Master Cheng, will you two please come over here and sign your names?"

Xiao Shitou took the piece of paper and read from it haltingly. "Duan. Xiao . . . lou. Little brother, the manager gave me a good-sounding name that looks good, too!"

"What about mine? Cheng . . . Die . . . yi." This was his new name—and his future. "Mine isn't so bad, either."

"Let's try writing them ourselves."

Brandishing a writing brush the way General Xiang Yu might brandish a sword, Xiaolou (formerly Xiao Shitou) gripped it determinedly and began to write his name, one painstaking stroke at a time. The character he wrote the best, *xiao*, was also the simplest. It consisted of three vertical strokes—one long one flanked by two short ones. The other two characters of his name were more complex, and he wrote them so badly he wadded up the practice sheet and threw it aside in shame. Dieyi (formerly Xiao Douzi) saw this and snatched the paper up from the floor. It was Xiaolou's first signature, and Dieyi meant to keep it.

"Try writing it again," Dieyi encouraged him.

"All right. Here, take a look at this. What do you think?"

Conferring and offering advice, they helped each other learn to write their names. Their naive writing seemed to have come from the hands of children, rather than grown men.

* * *

Incense sticks and candles burned brightly in the Temple of the Patron Saints. Those flames seemed never to burn out and were always at their peak. The temple was a world unto itself, timeless and filled with hope.

The company manager was pleased to have two very fine actors in his employ, and he treated them deferentially, making sure they received their full complement of silver coins. They had been performing repertory in nearby rural areas. Now it was time for them to travel farther afield, but Dieyi was somewhat concerned.

"Big brother," he said to Xiaolou. "Next month is Master Guan's fifty-sixth birthday, and we won't be able to make it back to Peking in time to congratulate him. Perhaps we should send him a little money."

Cheng Dieyi could never forget that he had also once been Xiao Douzi, and he was as dutiful toward his former teacher as a son to his father.

"That's a good idea," Xiaolou replied.

Although he was not as conscientious as his friend, he hadn't forgotten the Master's birthday, either. When he was away from Peking, Xiaolou often sent gifts, including packets of fine tobacco, to Master Guan.

The old courtyard hadn't changed.

Dusk was gathering, but the oil lamps in the compound hadn't been lit. Another crop of children was practicing swordplay in the fading light, whirling pairs of swords in the air. They were already quite proficient and danced with powerful grace.

Master Guan didn't notice the two men who had just

walked into the courtyard, and he kept shouting out instructions to his students.

"Immortals pointing the way," he directed, and they extended one arm before them while raising the other one overhead. "The White Snake flicks her tongue," he commanded, and they stabbed their swords forward. "Embrace the moon," he shouted, and they held their swords inside rounded arms. "Sweep lotus with the wind!" he instructed, and they kicked their legs. When he said, "Golden needle pointing south," they lay down, swords pointed at the sky. At "Jiang Taigong goes fishing," they went into arabesques that mimed the act of fishing. "Clever maiden threads the needle," he directed, and they wove their swords through the crooks of their arms. "Two dragons breathe water," "Wild horses part their manes." He called out combination after combination.

Swordplay and sword dancing were Dieyi's specialties, and *Farewell to My Concubine* was a showcase for this talent. The high point of his performance as Yu Ji came after the General had sung the melancholy arias that acknowledged his defeat. Then Dieyi would take up a pair of swords, and dance with them as he sang his final aria.

As he watched the group of young students, he couldn't help but feel that while their technique was strong, they somehow lacked feeling. Without feeling, the dance was lifeless. He was musing over this problem when suddenly a child cried out in fear.

"A rat!"

The boy was rattled and fell out of step.

Master Guan walked over and struck him several times on the head and face.

"When you practice swordplay," he bellowed, "you have to pay attention to what you're doing! If you let your mind wander even for an instant, you can get seriously hurt!"

The Master's beard, which had once been black, was now flecked with silver, and Dieyi thought back to the first time he had seen the Master. He hadn't even dared to look directly at that fierce face, with its beetling brows that made him look like the terrifying statue guardians at Buddhist temples.

"Haven't I told you that there are words we must never say?" Master Guan hectored. "Xiao Si, you've been here the longest. Can you tell everyone what we call those creatures?"

A large thirteen-year-old started to respond when Xiaolou broke in.

"We call them 'Great Sage Number Five'," he called out from the gateway. "Listen carefully, children. We call mice 'Eighth Grandfather Gray Ashes'; hedgehogs are 'Fifth White Grandpa'; we call long worms or snakes 'Seventh Grandpa Willow'; yellow weasels are 'Yellow Granddaddies'. If you ever break these taboos in the theater and call these things by their original names, the spirits of our founders will come back to punish you!"

The Master turned around.

"Why, it's Xiao Shitou!"

Dieyi smiled and also went over to the Master.

"Master, we've come to pay our respects, sir."

He glanced at these men whom he had raised from boyhood and addressed his students.

"Get back to work. This time pay attention and do it right."

Dieyi added, "Hasn't the Master taught you not to flail

around like madmen, or to fight like vicious, wild animals?"

"That's what the Master always criticized *me* for doing—not you. The way you're talking, everyone would think he'd criticized you for it, too. Don't you know the saying, 'Everyone wants to take the profit but no one ever wants to take the blame'?" Duan Xiaolou teased him.

"I had ulterior motives," Dieyi replied.

Master Guan coughed, and the two fell into a respectful silence. He graciously accepted the gifts of money they presented to him in lucky red envelopes.

"How was your tour?" he asked them.

"We've taken stage names: Duan Xiaolou and Cheng Dieyi," Xiaolou reported. "They're lucky names, with a nice ring to them. We've also been learning to write them in our spare time."

"You can write your names?"

"Not very well," Dieyi said diffidently.

Master Guan gazed at his former pupils.

"You two are actors in your own right, now."

"We owe it all to you. We haven't forgotten that it was you who taught us everything we know. If we sing well, it's because you beat it into us."

"You can't learn opera without a teacher, but a teacher can't do everything. A lot depends on you. What piece do you sing best?" Master Guan asked them.

"*Farewell to My Concubine,*" Xiaolou announced proudly.

"That's good. Just don't slack off. Unless you give it all you have, you're cheating the audience."

The Master had grown older, but he hadn't really

changed, Dieyi thought to himself. He looked around him and suddenly recalled that day, ten years before, when his mother had brought him to this place. They had been standing in this very spot when she signed the X that had changed his life.

Duan Xiaolou and Cheng Dieyi expected many years of touring ahead. They decided to take some publicity photos, both in costume and in street clothes, to use in promoting their performances. So one day they went to the Wansheng Photo Studio and sat for a few portraits. A tall plant stand holding an arrangement of dried flowers had been placed before the backdrop, a painted curtain depicting a pallid landscape of false mountains, false stones, and false vistas.

Both Xiaolou and Dieyi had put on a little makeup. They looked quite handsome in robes of dark green silk and satin, with white lining peeking out at the cuffs. Xiaolou held a dignified pose, a fan grasped firmly in his hand, while Dieyi straightened his collar for him.

Dieyi's hands fell into a graceful attitude, seemingly of their own accord. He felt somewhat embarrassed at being photographed, but as long as he reminded himself that it was just another performance, he would be able to carry it off. He simply had to remain in character.

"When will the photos be ready?" he asked the photographer.

"Quite soon. Four or five days."

"Please take special care with the tinting."

"Of course. You needn't worry about a thing," he said deferentially. "I understand that you two gentlemen will be touring quite a few cities in the South."

"Yes, that's right. We want to post these pictures in the theaters where we play."

"Have no fear—" began the photographer unctuously, when he was suddenly drowned out by a surge of angry voices. Moments later there was the sound of shattering glass, and Dieyi's and Xiaolou's haughty expressions turned to terror. The photographer's face fell.

"Dammit! It's probably those geisha pictures in my front window."

He rushed outside, leaving Xiaolou and Dieyi standing in front of the deserted camera. They didn't hesitate long and followed him into the street.

The wide boulevard was filled with people, chanting slogans.

"Down with Japanese imperialism!"

"Wake up, China! Stop the policy of nonresistance!"

"Boycott Japanese goods! Don't be enslaved!"

"Give us back our land! Give back Manchuria!"

A group of student protesters had broken the plate-glass windows of the photo studio and were now zealously tearing up pictures of geishas and scattering them in the air. Shredded paper rained down on the two elegant young men as they emerged from the studio.

Up ahead, another store that sold Japanese goods had been stampeded by an angry mob. Everything inside had been smashed and then set on fire. The owner, wearing Japanese wooden thongs, futilely tried to hold the protesters back with outspread arms.

In the midst of the confusion, one of the students recognized the pair of actors.

"What's this?" he challenged. "Actors?"

"One look at those two gives them away. They're just a couple of sellouts. Been posing for pinups again, have you?"

At a loss for words, Dieyi glanced at Xiaolou.

"Don't you people care what's going on around you? You theater types all live in an ivory tower, never thinking about your families or your homeland. Are you really Chinese, or not?"

Xiaolou had hailed a ricksha, and he hustled Dieyi aboard before hopping on himself. After directing the ricksha puller to head away from the demonstration, he turned to Dieyi.

"They still smell of their mothers' milk—all they can do is bawl," he said angrily. "If the city is surrounded by Japanese soldiers, they ought go and fight them. Instead, they stay in town and pick on other Chinese!"

Educated people had always looked down on theater people and their gypsy existence, while actors, filled with self-loathing, avenged themselves by disparaging educated people. Xiaolou felt disgust for the students. Who cared about family or country, indeed! If those little baby bookworms wanted to go save the nation, let them. Did they think they mattered? It was like adding a few sesame seeds to a whole bushel. It made little difference in the end. When has the nation ever cared about its citizens?

They had driven quite a way before Dieyi felt safe enough to relax.

"As long as I'm with you, nobody can hurt me," he said gratefully. "How can I ever repay you?"

Heaving a sigh, the ricksha puller slowed down. They were rolling through Liulichang, Peking's bustling antique market street. Dieyi looked down a side street.

"What a shame. That curio shop has been turned into a coffin builders'. I tried to find out, but nobody knew what had happened to that sword."

"What's that?" Xiaolou asked distractedly. An attractive young woman had caught his eye, and he had twisted around to get a better look at her.

"Oh!" He turned back around and let out a laugh. "You still want to make good on that promise you made when we were kids?"

Dieyi gave Xiaolou a searching look. Had his friend not heard him clearly, or did he simply not believe he was serious? He felt slightly insulted that Xiaolou seemed more interested in a bunch of strangers milling around in the road than in him.

They reached the theater, and the ricksha puller let them off in front of the door.

It was 1939, the twenty-eighth year of the Republic of China—the second year of the Japanese occupation. Evidence of this was everywhere, but people ignored it, preferring instead to look at the bright and gaudy lights of the capital's entertainment district.

Strings of lights blazed around two names on the theater's marquee: DUAN XIAOLOU and CHENG DIEYI.

"Look," said Xiaolou, pointing. "Those are our names!"

He went forward for a closer look at the playbill posted at the entrance. It listed the program as well as the actors. Xiaolou found the character for *xiao* at once, and he was just able to make out the other two characters of his name. He was very pleased.

"That's me!"

Dieyi spotted his name, too.

The highlight of that evening's program was to be *Farewell to My Concubine,* and Dieyi was secretly delighted to see that he had top billing.

"Why is my name on top of yours?" he asked, feigning displeasure.

"The operas you appear in always attract a big audience. That's why. But I don't mind. It's an honor just to appear on the same marquee with you!"

"It shouldn't matter who's on top and who's on the bottom. It's not right!"

"It's fine by me if you're on top," Xiaolou said with bafflement. "Why are you angry at me?"

He had always looked after his younger friend. What was Dieyi upset about, he wondered. They had been working hard together for years, and now that they were beginning to enjoy some success, what did it matter whose name came first and whose came second? They were just a *sheng* and a *dan*. If either of them was missing, the show couldn't go on.

Dieyi patted his arm.

"Never mind. I didn't mean it."

"I did," Xiaolou said, clapping the other man's bony shoulders. "I'd be angry if you didn't expect me to take a back seat."

The company manager had seen them and hurried up to greet them.

"The stalls are overflowing, and people are getting impatient." He drew near to Dieyi and whispered in his ear. "Master Yuan is here just to see you. Is that a coup or not? You'd better hurry up."

Xiaolou had already gone backstage, swaggering like a

general. He had played the role of Xiang Yu so many times that he had unconsciously taken on some of that character's qualities.

The master of ceremonies was pacing backstage, drenched in sweat, as Dieyi completed his transformation into the lady Yu Ji. Once his own makeup was finished, he put the last touches on the General's makeup. This had become their ritual.

Wildly clanging gongs and staccato drums came to a crescendo. The actor who played the General's groom waited in the wings, still as a statue, while the stage manager informed him, "There's been a delay."

Turning around he said, grinning obsequiously. "Master Duan, they've been playing this allegro for a quarter of an hour!"

"I'll sing a few notes to let them know I'm here. That should calm them down."

He matter-of-factly faced the curtain, took a slow, deep breath, and let out a long cry. When the audience heard this, they cheered excitedly.

"Bravo! Bravo!"

Xiaolou signaled he was ready. The stableboy burst onto the stage with a leap and a somersault. His was the first entrance. The opera had begun.

The stalls were a sea of bobbing heads. Shuttling back and forth among them were snack sellers, cigarette vendors, waiters handing out hot, moist towels, and servants carrying kettles of hot water for replenishing teapots—the gentlemen who sat in the front row customarily brought their own teacups and choice teas. Other waiters placed saucers full of melon seeds or candied fruit on the edge of the stage, within easy reach of the patrons.

The most prestigious seats were the boxes. Yuan Siye had reserved one for himself. He was a large-framed man in his forties, with a high-bridged nose and piercing eyes. He had a rather forbidding air and looked like a black tower in his long brocade robe.

A pair of attendants stood behind him. Another made him a pot of fine white peony tea, but he paid no attention— he had entered the world on the stage.

The General was facing defeat:

"My strength can uproot mountains, and my vast spirit reaches every corner of the land.
But the times are against me, even my horse cannot advance.
My horse cannot advance, what shall I do?"

"I am moved to tears by my Lord's spirited and heroic song," Dieyi's Yu Ji answered, gracefully wiping away her tears. "Would you permit your humble consort to dance for you to ease your sorrows?"

The General Xiang Yu politely accepted, and Yu Ji forced a cheerful smile. She withdrew slowly, and returned soon after. She had taken off her cape, revealing a suit of chain mail. With a sword in each hand, she began to dance and sing a slow tune.

"Pray my lord, take this cup and let me sing you a song.
I'll dance to ease your sorrows.
Evil Qin has ruined the empire,

Forcing brave men everywhere to take up arms.
Remember the saying, for it is true:
Victory and defeat, flourishing and dying, all pass within
the blink of an eye.
Pray rest here a while and drink your fill."

The audience watched in rapt attention, moved by the spirit of Yu Ji. Even as she faced death, she thought only of pleasing her lover as he faced his death.

Yuan Siye was keeping time with his fan.

"The young lady is delightful!" he exclaimed, pointing at the stage.

"This role is Master Cheng's specialty," one of his companions hastened to reply.

Yuan Siye gave a deceptively neutral nod and went back to watching the performance. From high up in his box, he commanded a view of the entire stage, so that all the actors seemed to rest in the palm of his hand. Yu Ji moved slowly at the center of the rapidly spinning swords that whirled so fast they looked like flowers.

Yuan Siye's gaze did not wander from the lady for the rest of the show.

☷☷☷
4

A performance is a brief encounter between actors and audience. Its sweetness lies in its brevity and in its melancholy aftermath. A performance lets the actor be someone important, while those in the audience have bought a piece of that extraordinary life. The actors bask in the admiration of hundreds of strangers, who are transported out of their small lives by the deep emotions enacted before them. But the encounter only lasts for several hours of an evening. By the next day, all of the participants have returned to their quotidian existences, strangers again.

After tonight's show, the wooden benches were awry,

and melon seeds lay scattered across the floor like so many stars. A few dirty and trampled hand towels were strewn on the ground.

Duan Xiaolou and Cheng Dieyi were taking off their makeup, with the pleasantly monotonous drone of the orchestra tuning their instruments in the background. Dieyi passed Xiaolou a handkerchief. Wiping the sweat from his face and neck, he casually set the handkerchief aside and leaned back in his chair, relaxing with his friend.

"The crowd was really enthusiastic tonight," Xiaolou said with satisfaction. "I think they were louder than we were."

Dieyi grinned.

"Do you want to know how I keep my voice from cracking on tough passages?" Xiaolou asked. "When I come to the break in my voice, I can get through it smoothly by bracing my arms against my waist. That way, I can get enough breath."

"Where do you press?"

"At my waist."

Dieyi walked over and stood behind him. He put a hand on either side of Xiaolou's waist and pressed lightly.

"Here?" he asked.

"No, a little lower—there, that's it. That's where I find enough breath to get the power and volume I need. It always impresses them." He suddenly became aware of Dieyi's probing fingers, and he felt a bit awkward.

"Speaking of being impressed," Dieyi said, "a very important patron has been coming to see us every night."

"Who's that?"

"His name is Yuan. Yuan Siye. The people working at the theater told me."

"He's probably up to no good. Watch your step."

"Don't worry." Dieyi was silent for a moment. "Did you realize, Xiaolou, that we've already played husband and wife two hundred and thirty-eight times?"

Xiaolou picked up a tiny teapot and took a sip from it. He wasn't listening.

"I've been putting chrysanthemums in my tea lately—they give it a very delicate flavor," he said.

"Tell me," Dieyi persisted. "How many times have we played husband and wife?"

"What's that?" Xiaolou said absently. "More than a couple hundred times, I suppose."

"Two hundred and thirty-eight exactly!"

"You keep that careful a count?"

"Of course I do. I take my work seriously." He paused. "I've set aside enough money to buy some of my own costumes. That way I won't have to rent them anymore."

"Why is it that ever since you were a little kid you've done nothing but talk about that kind of thing?" Xiaolou laughed. "What's the difference between buying and renting costumes? When the show's over you have to take them off and put them away. It's not as if you can take them to bed with you! Sometimes I think you're so impractical."

"You're wrong. Yu Ji and Yang Guifei are with me all the time. They *are* me."

"Fine. You just save your money like a good little boy, and get yourself some costumes and a great big iron trunk. You can lock up all of your precious belongings inside it—

costumes, hair ornaments, jewelry, rouge, eyeliner, the whole lot. You can use it as a bench during the day and a pillow at night. If you want to go out, just put four wheels on it and call it a car! I guess you're being practical, after all!"

Xiaolou mimed his descriptions exaggeratedly.

"You don't know anything about opera! All you know how to do is make trouble!" Dieyi burst out.

He picked up the little teapot and brought it to his mouth with a sweeping gesture. Suddenly, he noticed that it was not the one they normally used.

"A new teapot?"

Xiaolou grunted.

"It's very pretty. I see it has chrysanthemums painted on the sides."

"It—it was a gift."

Dieyi let his gaze drift from the pot to Xiaolou, doubts and suspicions crowding into his mind. Before either of them could speak, Xiao Si rushed in excitedly. He had first seen the two actors the day they came back to visit Master Guan's school, and he had been so impressed that he'd begged his parents and Master Guan for permission to become their errand boy. This job would be a way for him to broaden his horizons and gain some experience. Although Xiao Si was still an apprentice performer, Master Guan allowed him to come to the theater on nights when Xiaolou and Dieyi were performing. Xiao Si often concealed himself behind the curtains of their dressing room door, watching and listening in with fascination, and filled with a mixture of envy and admiration.

"Master Cheng, you have visitors," he reported.

The theater manager, the company manager, and several others came in behind him, escorting Yuan Siye.

Yuan politely paid his respects to the performers, bowing his head and raising clasped hands.

"You two gentlemen certainly live up to your reputations." He gave a casual wave, and a member of his entourage came in with a tray. The theater manager lifted up the piece of silk laid across its top and uncovered an array of crystal-encrusted hair ornaments and jewelry. The stones sparkled in the light. The ornaments were a gift for Dieyi.

"I couldn't possibly," he said.

"Next time, we'll be sure to inquire as to what would please you most," Yuan Siye said engagingly.

"Please, sit down," Xiaolou said with a bow. "And please, you don't need to give us any gifts. Your company is a great enough compliment to us. Your appreciation of the opera is well known, and I hear you're a talented amateur, too."

Yuan Siye was not a great general or leader. He had been born in the wrong age. But he wielded the power of a general in the imaginary world of the theater, holding sway within the narrow confines of a realm that had been frozen in time for almost two centuries.

He had read a great many books: the biographies of great men recorded in the histories of the Sui and Tang dynasties; the "Tale of Wang Baochai"; the *Romance of the Three Kingdoms;* and of course, his favorite opera, *Farewell to My Concubine*.

Times had changed, but the characters were still the same.

There were men who depended on the Japanese, or the government, for their power and prestige. They ruled like despots in their own spheres.

The strongmen of the stage took their strength from the loud crash and clang of drums and cymbals. Their singing, acting, recitation, and fighting all made the characters come to life. Without the proper background to throw them into relief, they were nothing. But with it, they were indomitable.

"This opera, *Farewell to My Concubine,* has quite a long history," he told Dieyi. "It's based on the old Kunqu opera *A Thousand Pieces of Gold.* Many great performers have tried to sing the role of Yu Ji, but only Master Cheng here has succeeded in doing it justice. His singing and acting are superb, and his impeccable swordsmanship is a delight to watch." He smiled at Dieyi. "You made me think that the spirit of Yu Ji might have been reincarnated!"

Dieyi felt his face flush. Yuan Siye's heart skipped a beat, but he turned to Xiaolou.

"Master Duan, you are an outstanding singer, truly first-rate. But I have some questions about your technique."

Yuan was surrounded by an attentive audience of nervously smiling faces, and he enjoyed this.

"For example," he said, grimacing slightly, "when the General returns to camp and goes to see Yu Ji, convention dictates that he take seven steps. But you take only five. He is the ruler of Chu—and yet he does things in a slapdash fashion. He should be a man of substance, don't you agree?"

Xiaolou smiled insincerely.

"How could one disagree with the opinions of someone as expert as yourself?"

Sensing Xiaolou's sarcasm, Dieyi hastily covered for him.

"Perhaps sometime when you are free, Master Yuan, you might talk to us about opera."

"That would be delightful! If you would be so kind as to come to my home, we could share a little wine and have a chat. Why not tonight?"

"I'm terribly sorry, Siye," Xiaolou said in mock dismay, "but I have a prior commitment. Please forgive me. Maybe some other time? I would very much appreciate your advice."

Dieyi forced himself to keep smiling, but his heart was sinking. His gaze lingered on Xiaolou's new teapot. Another engagement? With whom? he wondered. Why hadn't Xiaolou mentioned it before?

The House of Flowers was a theater of another kind. It, too, was a stage for glamorous illusion, from the hall where guests were received to the private rooms in back. A man was standing in the receiving hall and reading from a list of the girls' names.

"Rainbow Phoenix, Double Happiness, Water Sprite, Dainty Plum, Sweet Orchid . . ."

As he called out each name, a girl would descend the stairs and strike a pose in front of a semicircle of prospective customers. Whenever one saw a girl he liked, he summoned her with a wave, and she would walk over languidly in her high heels, hips swaying. The girls all wore long *qipaos*, traditional Chinese dresses with collars and side slits. These were usually made of crimson or pale yellow silk, embroidered with flowers or willows, symbolic of courtesans and passionate liaisons. The willows and flowers seemed to ripple in some unearthly breeze when the women walked, and the overall effect was as gaudy as a garden in spring.

Xiaolou arrived punctually. He was handsomely dressed from head to toe in dark purple.

"Can someone tell me where Miss Juxian's room is?" he called out loudly.

"She'll be right out," someone answered. "Please have a seat. She won't be a moment."

The madam came out to welcome him.

"General Xiang Yu is here!" she exclaimed. "We've been expecting you!"

"I came here tonight so that I could personally thank the young lady for her kind gift," he said, producing the little chrysanthemum-painted teapot.

"Do you really use it when you perform?" the madam laughed. "Don't try to deceive us girls!"

"When this pot is filled with spirits, I sing better than ever!"

As he was speaking, someone burst through the beaded curtains that led to the bedchambers and crashed into Xiaolou. It was a woman in a satin *qipao* with multicolored embroidery and a scallop-edged collar. She wore necklaces and earrings of pearls and jade, and there was a chrysanthemum in her hair. Her name was Juxian—Chrysanthemum. Although she was carefully dressed, her bangs were mussed, and her eyes revealed a mixture of haughtiness and fear.

"I won't drink it!"

Before she had a chance to notice who she had bumped into, a man with a jade-tipped cigarette holder dangling from his lips came running after her.

"What's wrong with you?" he leered. "I've paid for your services, and I expect to get my money's worth!"

The madam apologized profusely to the irate customer before turning her attention to the girl.

"Juxian," she said peevishly. "He's only asking you to drink a cupful."

"He wants me to drink it from his mouth. I won't do it!" Then she noticed Xiaolou. "Help me, please!"

"Don't worry about a thing!" he blustered.

"An opera singer?" somebody exclaimed.

"What's she to you?" asked the unsavory customer, whose name was Zhao Dexing.

"I am a man, and she is a woman. That's all that matters."

"You're no different from anybody else!" Zhao laughed crudely. "Every cock wants a hen. Just because you have a bigger voice than the rest of us doesn't mean you can take whatever you want. No one has the right to spoil another man's fun."

He plopped a sackful of silver coins down on the table in front of him.

"Come over here, cutie!" he smirked at Juxian.

She edged closer to Xiaolou, who stepped forward to protect her.

"I shall engage the services of every girl here in the House of Flowers and take them all to see you perform. You'd better sing well! Otherwise we'll all be disappointed. Right, Miss Juxian?"

"I'll look after Juxian!" Xiaolou said impulsively.

Juxian gave a start. Although she had met him recently, she already felt some tenderness for him. If she had been an ordinary woman, it would have been simple. Love at first sight and true love were things that existed for ordinary women, but not for women like her, not for prostitutes. As prostitutes, they spent their days and nights with playboys—love was just a game for most of them. If a girl allowed herself to be genuinely touched, she would only end up getting hurt. People said that whores had no feelings; but it was simply self-protection.

She gazed fixedly into Xiaolou's eyes.

"Do you want to marry me?" she asked evenly.

"If you're willing! Let's drink a cup to our engagement!"

Lifting up a cup of wine, he took a gulp and then held it out to Juxian. Before she could take it, he rotated it so that she would drink from the same spot that he had.

The onlookers were shocked. Zhao cackled.

"You must be joking! It sounds as if you're reciting dialogue from some badly written play. Anyway, hundreds of men have tasted those lips of hers, including me. Only a moment ago—"

Before Zhao could finish his sentence, Xiaolou hurled himself against him, knocking the wind out of him and pushing him backward onto the wine tray. The two started to grapple, Xiaolou pounding his opponent with strong fists— the martial arts he'd learned in opera school served him well. A handful of other guests joined the fray, and soon fists and feet were flying. Someone brought a wine pot crashing down on Xiaolou's head, and while the vessel shattered, Xiaolou fought on as though nothing had happened.

Watching the fray from a safe corner, Juxian began to form a plan. Perhaps it was time for her to change her life.

★ ★ ★

The next evening, Dieyi and Xiaolou were backstage at their makeup stations, readying themselves for their performance. Dieyi had applied his base and was now painting rosy contours over his cheeks and brows. In the mirror, he caught sight of Xiaolou, who was removing the fine hair from his forehead with string. Unable to avoid the cut on his brow, he winced in pain.

"I hear you made quite a splash last night in the red-light district," Dieyi called over to him.

The two men's makeup tables were on opposite walls. Each could look into his mirror and see himself and the other—their two faces side by side, multiplied infinitely.

"You were like Wu Song brawling in the Lion Wineshop—just like the opera!" Dieyi snickered.

Xiaolou didn't deny it.

"Are the girls there pretty?" Dieyi asked at length.

"They're so-so."

"Isn't there even one who's any good?"

"There's one who's not too bad. She has a heart—and integrity, too."

Dieyi momentarily lost his grip on the brush he was using to paint his eyebrows. He quickly wiped away the stray mark with his little finger.

"How did you happen to find a whore with heart and soul?"

Xiaolou turned and rose from his dresser and walked over to stand behind Dieyi.

"Why don't I take you there? We can spend some time relaxing together. What do you say?"

"I don't go to places like that," Dieyi said as evenly as he could.

"What's wrong?"

"I don't think you should go to places like that, either," he said sternly. "You can get all sorts of filthy diseases from prostitutes if you're not careful. Diseases that can ruin your voice—and we singers have to take care of our voices— they're our livelihood. Don't throw away your future on fleeting pleasures! You have the rest of your life to think of."

"What's left of it!" Xiaolou muttered. Dieyi sounded so vehement that there was no point in arguing. As far as Xiaolou was concerned, if you didn't have a little fun you were wasting your youth.

Dieyi's commitment to his art was all-consuming. When he spoke of a lifelong commitment, he meant every minute of every day. Any time taken away from the opera was time ill spent.

Neither of them spoke for some time, but Dieyi's curiosity got the better of him at last.

"What's her name?"

"Juxian."

Dieyi didn't respond, but went on painting his eyes, filling in the overdrawn lines around them. When he blinked, they resembled a pair of peach leaves quivering in the breeze.

"Oh," he said flatly. "She's your mistress, then—the one who gave you that little teapot? Doesn't it have chrysanthemums painted on it? Is she the one?" He paused. "By the way, did you win her hand?"

"You've been listening to too much gossip! That was just talk. I didn't mean anything by it, honestly."

Full makeup for the opera required that more than the face be painted. Neck, ears, and even the backs of the hands were covered in a water-based white foundation. Honey was added to it to make it long-lasting, and the pallor it imparted seemed all but indelible. If it had been intended to conceal a wan complexion, then it was a failure.

Ordinarily, Dieyi would have touched up Xiaolou's makeup for him. But tonight he turned his back on his friend and stared blankly at the shifting patterns on the gauze window covering, his lips trembling slightly.

The show went on. *Farewell to My Concubine* was reaching its climax.

"Wake up, my lord! Wake up!" Yu Ji frantically called out to her lover, General Xiang Yu.

She had been taking a walk outside the camp when she heard singing all around. The enemy had surrounded them, and the enemy's soldiers were singing songs from Xiang Yu's kingdom of Chu to let him and his followers know they had conquered it.

The General awakened and heaved a great sigh.

"My lady, I think of how you have stayed by my side all of these years, accompanying me on military campaigns. Your devotion has touched me deeply. In all this time, we have never once been parted. But now I realize that today we shall be forced to part, and for the last time."

There were two loud reports as gunshots rang out from a dark corner of the theater. A man who looked like a gangster slumped to the floor in a pool of blood, and the hall erupted in an uneasy babble. Such disturbances were becoming increasingly commonplace. This was the third such incident of the month.

Xiaolou leapt down from the stage in alarm while Dieyi stood and watched. Then he saw her. She was sitting in the first row, calmly cracking a melon seed between her teeth. Although she looked a little pale, any trace of apprehension left her face when she saw Xiaolou signal to her that the trouble was over. She must be the one, Dieyi thought to himself. Sprawled in her seat, she smiled coyly at Xiaolou, at once flirtatious and vulnerable. No wonder Xiaolou had fallen for her. Dieyi noted with perverse satisfaction that this delicate creature had littered the floor around her with melon husks.

Dieyi regained his composure. The show had to go on, and he forced himself to keep singing, concentrating hard so as not to lose the melody or the beat. Yu Ji was comforting her lover at the hour of his defeat.

"The high crags and tortuous ridges of Gaixia hem us in. Perhaps there is some way for us to break through enemy lines and seek help."

There were stirrings of motion in the audience, and a ripple passed through it like a gust of wind on a dark lake. The police had arrived, and they quietly carried off the dead man's body.

The performance continued uninterrupted. General Xiang Yu was speaking as a servant brought him a little wine.

"Here is some wine."

"Pray, my lord, drink this cup," Yu Ji said with false cheer.

As the music came to a crescendo, the two shared a cup of wine. But they could not ignore the enemy singing that surrounded them.

Juxian watched the heart-wrenching scene unperturbed. She had found a champion in Xiaolou. The curtain fell on Dieyi and Xiaolou's final scene.

★ ★ ★

Dieyi had some spare time and went to a letter writer's in the marketplace. The scribe was an old man in a gray scholar's robe. He sat in his stall all day, looking into people's hearts and composing letters that bridged the gaps of years or miles.

"Mother, I am doing fine here," Dieyi dictated. "Please don't worry about me. My classmate Xiaolou looks after me very well. We rehearse together day and night, and we also costar on the stage. We've known each other for more than ten years, now, and our mutual affection is very deep."

He paused to take a small white pouch from the bag he wore at his waist. Removing a bundle of bills, he handed them to the old man. Pressed between the bank notes was a hand-tinted photo of him and Xiaolou.

"I am enclosing a little money for you," he went on. "Please use it to buy yourself a nice meal."

He related a few more details of his life and finished the letter.

"I'll sign my own name," he said emphatically.

Picking up the old man's writing brush, he painstakingly wrote his signature: "Cheng Dieyi." Reconsidering, he added beneath it, "Xiao Douzi"—Little Bean, his childhood name.

A handful of schoolchildren had clustered behind him and were peering over his shoulders and watching him write. One of them, a little girl, read aloud from his letter.

"Mother, I am doing fine here. Please . . . don't— worry. . . . My classmate—" Here she craned her neck to see what came next. "Xiaolou looks—"

"What are you looking at?" Dieyi demanded.

"What are you looking at? What are you looking at?"

she chanted, mimicking his slightly effeminate tone of voice. With that, she and her classmates scattered.

The scribe had folded up the letter and put it into an envelope, which he sealed with a few grains of rice.

"What address is this letter being sent to?"

Without saying a word, Dieyi took the letter from him and walked away. When he was halfway home, he tore it up and threw it away.

Somewhat later he arrived at the theater and went backstage to prepare for the evening's performance.

The madam was astonished. She had experienced a great many things in her life and had associated with people of all kinds as proprietress of the House of Flowers. But Juxian had caught her off guard.

Watching the girl through narrowed eyes, she folded her arms across her chest. She started to pick her teeth with a toothpick that looked like a broom straw, and her thick, red lips were contorted in a lopsided grimace. She was well past forty and heavily made up, but her hair was still glossy and black. Manual labor and the work of serving her house's many patrons was something she left for others, like Juxian. Now Juxian wanted to buy her way out.

Between the two women was a table of Yunnan marble covered with a round embroidered cloth. On it lay a heap of silver coins, jewelry, and bank notes; but it would take more than this to satisfy the madam. She eyed the many fancy hairpins set with jade and pearls that still adorned Juxian's hair. The girl responded by taking them off. One by one she pulled them out and added them to the pile of valuables.

The madam looked on implacably. It was still not

enough. But Juxian was not going to give in. Smiling wanly, she slipped off her fine silk shoes and placed them on the table. Each one was embroidered with a phoenix looking back over her shoulder; but Juxian was not going to turn back.

Visibly moved, the madam hesitated a moment. She had prepared to lecture Juxian about the immorality of actors, but the girl anticipated this and spoke first.

"Thank you, Foster Mother, for taking such good care of me for all these years." Hands steepled in front of her chest, she gave a formal bow.

The madam watched her turn and walk out. The girl had nothing left but the clothes on her back; but she had bought her freedom. When she stepped into the street, her white-stockinged feet would sink into the mud. Life outside the indolent precincts of the house of pleasure was harsh and grimy. She had lived a soft life, relying on her gentle charms. Now she was taking a big gamble.

The older woman knew exactly what was at stake. She was losing the money tree she had cultivated with painstaking care over many years. Juxian's last earnings from selling her body lay heaped on the table, but they were little consolation. The madam was so angry she couldn't speak.

Never again would Juxian paint her face and sell her body. She had forsaken that life for one man, Duan Xiaolou.

5

Dieyi was backstage, still in the costume he wore on stage as the courtesan Yu Ji. He sat before the mirror, just another woman about to take off her makeup for Xiaolou. First he removed his elaborate headdress, and then his hair ornaments. One by one, he took off the rhinestone flowers he wore at his temples, the satin flowers, and the pearl-studded hairpins.

Xiaolou had already changed out of his costume and came over and gave Dieyi a friendly pat on the shoulder.

"Hey, what's wrong? Are you still angry at me about that fight I was in the other night at the House of Flowers?"

"I've forgotten all about it."

Xiaolou was about to reply when he caught sight of the beautiful woman reflected in the mirror.

"Ai! She's here!" he exclaimed as he spun around. "What are you doing here? Juxian, I want you to meet my classmate and costar, Cheng Dieyi."

Xiaolou led her over by the hand. Dieyi looked up.

"Miss Juxian," he said awkwardly.

"Make yourself at home!" Xiaolou was urging Juxian. Dieyi was silent.

"Xiaolou has told me so much about you," Juxian said warmly. "He's always talking about you. I feel as though I already know you."

Dieyi smiled stiffly.

"Please, do sit down, Miss Juxian," he said with excessive politeness. "I'm busy right at this moment." He noticed the easy and familiar way that Juxian linked arms with Xiaolou.

"Let's not wait around," Xiaolou said. "Let's go out for a midnight snack—"

"Don't go yet," Dieyi cut in. Then he remembered something else and quickly added: "Didn't we arrange to go out with Master Yuan this evening? He was going to take us to the opera."

"I'm afraid it has to be 'farewell to my concubine' in real life, my friend!"

"Xiaolou, is there something else you had planned to do tonight?" Juxian said tactfully.

"When his lady is nigh, where else has a gentleman to seek?" He laughed and made to exit with her on his arm.

Juxian's face froze.

"I can't—"

Only now did the moonstruck Duan Xiaolou take a thorough look at his beloved. He realized that she was in her stocking feet. It finally occurred to him that despite her outward calm, this might not be a casual visit.

"How did that happen?" he fumbled.

She looked at her feet. The dirt on her stockings looked like another pair of shoes.

"I bought my freedom!" she said with quiet intensity.

Xiaolou gaped at her, unable to move.

"The House of Flowers doesn't keep a girl around after she's drunk her engagement wine."

The full significance of her words was starting to sink in, and he was still speechless. He was like a wooden marionette waiting for the tug on his strings so he could speak.

"Right—" he said flatly.

Juxian didn't respond, but watched and waited for him to say more. She had forfeited everything she owned. Tears began to form in her eyes.

Nearby, the other members of the company were going about their own business, tidying up after the show. Only Cheng Dieyi was paying any attention to the pair of young lovers, although he pretended he wasn't. He had not yet removed his stage makeup, and it hid his expressions as he listened intently and cleaned his set of hair ornaments. Using a small brush dipped in tooth powder, he polished each piece until it shone, then wrapped it up in tissue paper. A semi-opaque gauze partition separated him from Xiaolou and Juxian, but he was able to keep an eye on them nonetheless. As he watched he saw Xiaolou's face suddenly freeze.

"All right! I always keep my word!"

Had he decided? Dieyi wondered to himself.

The members of the company were roaring their approval, and their exultant shouts came to Dieyi.

"Bravo! You have a good heart and a pure soul!"

"Congratulations, Master Duan!"

"This is even better than *Spring in the Jade Hall!* You know, the opera where the girl runs away from the brothel and her boyfriend saves her from jail. You've done her one better!"

"Well now, Master Duan," said the company manager, his jovial voice rising above the din. "That's just wonderful! If you can find someone who truly understands you, someone to share your troubles in this vale of tears, then you'll have nothing to regret in this life. When's the wedding?"

"Well, as you know, this is a once-in-a-lifetime sort of thing . . . ," he stammered. "Actually, I haven't bought the rings yet."

When she heard these words, Juxian felt her spirits lifted. She knew he would take care of her.

"First of all," he was saying, again looking at Juxian's muddy feet, "we need to buy the bride some shoes."

Before they could take a step, a pair of embroidered shoes landed at Juxian's feet. Nobody knew when Dieyi had slipped from his seat. Now he emerged from the crowd, swaying as he walked, ever in character.

"I'll give you these shoes, Miss Juxian." He paused and then asked, "So you've been practicing to be the heroine in *Spring in the Jade Hall?*"

"Me?" she responded, deflecting the insinuation. "What business does a person like me have learning to sing opera?"

"If you can't sing opera, then you shouldn't overact!"

He narrowed his eyes. He felt almost overcome with resentment, but he tried to keep his feelings hidden. He was an actor, and he had his pride. He refused to lower himself by arguing with a prostitute.

He turned dramatically and walked away.

Xiaolou, the only person in the room who missed the meaning of this exchange, sauntered over to Dieyi at his makeup mirror. For a moment the two men seemed at once surrounded by and separated by their reflected images.

"Brother, this is my big day. Let me pick out a hairpin for your future 'sister-in-law'!"

They were old friends, like brothers, and he felt it only natural for him to help himself. After brief consideration he selected a butterfly-shaped hairpin studded with rhinestones.

Whatever Dieyi felt was concealed by the thick layers of rouge and white greasepaint still covering his face.

Xiaolou was excitedly urging his friend. "Now remember, come to my house a little early. You're the best man!" Then he added, half to himself, "We've got to get some good wine!"

So this was how Xiaolou kept his word, Juxian thought to herself complacently as they stepped out.

Dieyi's gaze lingered awhile on their retreating figures before he collapsed despondently into his seat. Seized with anger, he began furiously to scrub off every last trace of makeup from his face, as though he wouldn't be satisfied until his skin had been rubbed raw.

Once stripped bare, his fine-featured face stared tiredly from the mirror. He felt dead inside, his heart as cold and gray as ashes. He knew how it felt to be an abandoned woman and remembered an old saying: A woman without a man is a vine with no stakes to support her.

Something quivered in the mirror behind Dieyi's head—a peacock feather attached to a costume warrior's cap and the tassel of multicolored silk that dangled from the root of the quill.

The reflection of Yuan Siye's face appeared over Dieyi's shoulder. Yuan gave the feather a sidelong glance.

"Feathers this fine are hard to come by," he said. "It's not a question of money—it's the peacock himself. This poor creature couldn't even protect his own tail! You can tell his tail feathers were plucked while he was still alive. Plumes taken from a dead bird are always too stiff; but a feather taken from a live bird will always have a nice spring to it." He looked back at Dieyi. "A very fine plume indeed. I'll be waiting for you, Master Cheng." There was a hint of menace in his voice.

Yuan Siye went home, leaving behind a few of his retainers, who would escort Dieyi to Yuan's later on. They waited quietly. Yuan was a powerful man, and Dieyi had no choice but to accept his invitation.

Somewhat apprehensively, Dieyi picked up a cloak and went out with Yuan's men. As he passed through the area backstage, he noticed a couple of eleven- or twelve-year-old bit players sleeping underneath a trunk stand. Another boy of about fifteen was embroidering flowers on a costume in the feeble lamplight. This was how junior members of the company earned the right to become real performers someday in the future. Dieyi had once been like them—he and Xiaolou both. Like these children, they had eaten, slept, and worked together. They had become brothers.

He frowned and threw the cloak over his shoulders.

Yuan Siye greeted Dieyi inside the main door of his mansion. He led him to a spacious hall that was hung with fine paintings and calligraphy and opulently furnished with rosewood tables and chairs, cabinets made of red sandalwood, and a marble-topped altar table. Yuan had placed some incense burners on top of the altar. The stage was set.

Dieyi's host had changed into lounging clothes—a long gown and a mandarin jacket. He seemed at ease as he took Dieyi's hand in one of his and covered it with the other. Shyly, Dieyi allowed himself to be drawn in as Yuan showed off his impressive collection of antiques and curios.

"Look at this ceremonial vessel of carved jade," Yuan said expansively. "It's priceless—and sturdier than it looks."

Moving on, he indicated a scroll. It was a portrait of Guanyin, the Goddess of Mercy.

"This image of Guanyin embodies the combined spiritual essences of both male and female. Guanyin is male and female in one body, transcending the crude materialism of this world. Can you see the way she seems to float up toward the heavens?"

"Do you pray to Guanyin, Siye?"

"Me? I'm still adrift on the seas of desire," he laughed. "I just hope Guanyin will forgive my sins!" He made a sweeping gesture. "Let's go to my bedchamber. We can sit and chat."

Siye's room was light and airy. A large cloisonné clock sat securely under a glass dome. Even time was kept imprisoned here, Dieyi thought to himself. The clock ticked uneasily, the sound muffled by the glass.

A maroon coverlet spread over Yuan's immense bed. It looked like some strange and boundless sea, the surface of which concealed untold dangers.

A servant placed a hot pot full of thinly sliced meat and vegetables on top of a marble-topped table in the center of the room. The charcoal fire beneath the pot sparked and flickered, filling the room with a dusky orange light that threw weirdly shaped shadows against the walls. Dieyi shivered.

Yuan Siye was still talking about his painting of Guanyin.

"The material world is filled with temptations—drink, sex, wealth, pride. And yet, I wouldn't want to become an immortal, either. I'd have to live up in heaven, and I wouldn't be able to hear you sing."

Siye had a neatly trimmed stiff black mustache. When he smiled, the two halves worked up and down like a pair of oars.

"As a man has character, so an opera has its moral content. This is why I cannot praise Duan Xiaolou. Please, have some wine," Siye said, offering a cup to Dieyi. "This wine was brewed during the reign of the emperor Guangxu and given to the court as tribute. Ordinary people could never hope to taste this wine."

He drained his glass and watched Dieyi drink his. Then he poured another round as Dieyi sat politely, waiting for him to continue his lecture.

"When one is performing the roles of Xiang Yu and his

lady, Yu Ji, every last gesture must be perfect. One must pay meticulous attention to every aspect of one's artistry. Only then can one hope for that sublime merging of players and play into one. There is a saying that if the actor is not himself deeply moved by his performance, then the audience won't be touched, either. Take Duan Xiaolou, for instance. His heart's clearly not in it—his mind is a thousand miles away. Watching the two of you is more like seeing *Farewell to My General* than *Farewell to My Concubine!*" said Yuan laughing.

Dieyi forced a smile.

"Xiaolou should have been here tonight," he said. "Perhaps you could remind him that we are forever indebted to patrons like you. As the saying goes, if you learn so much as one word from a man, then you should always look up to him as your teacher."

Yuan chuckled.

"Enough small talk! I have a surprise for you." He called to a servant: "Bring it in!"

Dieyi felt uneasy. The strong wine was making his vision blurry.

Suddenly he heard the beating of papery wings. A little bat flew at his face, all claws and jagged white teeth that looked like a forest of white. The wings seemed to grow and spread out into a huge umbrella. Dieyi froze.

"Excellent!" Siye exclaimed. "This bat was captured in a little town in the South. They had to travel day and night to bring it to me alive."

He put his arms around his frightened guest.

"Are you afraid?" he asked.

Yuan's servant snatched the bat out of the air. Taking out a small knife, he drew it across the creature's throat. At first the bat struggled, its mouth gaping desperately as the man held it over the simmering hot pot. He let its blood drip slowly into the broth, and the drops bloomed like flowers as they spread into the soup. Only when the blood had stopped flowing did the servant take the bat away.

Yuan Siye felt his blood quicken as he watched the bat die; but Dieyi's skin was crawling. The dying bat reminded him of Yu Ji, slitting her throat at the end of the opera. He pressed his lips tightly together.

Siye was cooking a thin slice of lamb in the hot pot, teasing it with his chopsticks. He plucked it out half-cooked and ladled out a bowl of soup.

"Drink up!" he said. Holding the bowl to Dieyi's lips, he tilted it toward him. "It's good for the blood."

Dieyi blanched and stood up. He tried to flee but realized he had retreated into a corner.

"Drink!"

Feeling the potent effects of the wine, Dieyi lurched. As he attempted to right himself, he noticed a sword hanging on the wall. Was it his imagination? Yuan came at him and poured some broth down his throat; Dieyi choked and spluttered. He looked back at the wall. The sword was still there.

"That sword—is it yours?" he asked unsteadily.

"Have you seen it before? I acquired it about ten years ago, at a little shop in Changdian. It cost me one hundred pieces of silver. Did you see it then, too? Maybe it's fate that has brought us together."

Dieyi took the sword down from the wall. It was the same one. The blade whispered as he slid it from its sheath.

"Do you like it? A sword is a suitable gift for an intimate, I think. Would you like to be my intimate, Master Cheng?"

What did he mean by the word *intimate?* Dieyi wondered. His knees wobbled, and the sword shook in his hand. Chills, alternating with feverish sweats, passed over his body. Overcome with drowsiness, he wanted just to lie down, to drift off. It must have been the wine.

"Shall we sing a duet?" Yuan was asking him. "Come, let's take this opportunity to do some playacting!"

He was a talented amateur, and once he had put on his makeup, wouldn't he also be General Xiang Yu? Dieyi allowed Yuan to rub on his rouge for him, and Yuan did it carefully and delicately, as though he were stroking a piece of fine jade.

Relaxed by the wine, Siye sang first:

"Our fields lie fallow—we must return,
We've followed the army these many leagues—
But for whom?"

Hand in hand, the two men sang their duet. Aided by the wine, they surrendered themselves to the opera.

"My lady," Siye recited. "I hear the enemy singing the songs of our land of Chu all around us. Does this mean that Liu Bang has occupied our kingdom? All is lost!"

Dieyi sang through his tears:

"Enemy troops surround us,
Singing the songs of Chu, they mock us.
My lord is doomed,
I have nowhere to turn."

He extended his arm languidly and flourished the sword. Siye snatched it away.

"This isn't a prop! It's real!" He looked into Dieyi's eyes probingly. "You don't believe me?"

Yuan made a tiny cut in Dieyi's collar. Dieyi shrank back with a fearful whimper, and Yuan cackled and made another false pass with the blade before flinging it aside. Grabbing Dieyi's limp body, Yuan pushed him down onto the table. He pressed his coarse face against Dieyi's rosy skin as though he were crushing the petals of a peach blossom. With their two painted and patterned faces, they were actors performing in some bizarre theater.

Dieyi realized that Yuan Siye wanted him, but it was too late to escape.

Dieyi had stumbled into a savage realm of purple, carmine, and black, where a bat darker than the depths of hell beat its wings and attacked. He fell forward as it spread itself on top of him, glaring with bloodshot eyes. Hundreds of tiny knives stabbed him as it raked at his flesh with its hands and teeth. He struggled to fight it off, knowing that it wouldn't be satisfied until it had torn him to pieces. Blood covered his body, and his breath came in short, painful gasps.

The clock, imprisoned in its glass case, groaned faintly. Far off, a somber bell tolled the first watch of the long night.

The Milky Way blazed in the heavens, and the morning star winked its tired eye. Soon it would be light.

Dieyi sat alone in a ricksha, hugging the sword tightly to his chest. Filled with shame, he wrapped his cloak around himself more securely.

He had lost or given away everything that he might have called his own. Only the sword belonged to him now. He had known what might happen when he set out for Yuan's house the previous night; but he had gone anyway. It could not be undone; but he had no regrets. He had got back at Xiaolou.

Very few people were about, and it was unusually quiet for the hour. Perhaps there was going to be a storm. But instead of rain, he heard the clatter of horses' hooves, which grew louder and louder. The horses belonged to a detachment of cavalry.

The ricksha puller stopped dead as the horses nearly crashed into them. The red suns on the riders' flags had rays that burned with the power of empire in the predawn twilight. Horses and riders alike had an air of invincibility. The Japanese cavalry had entered Peking.

Like a frightened rabbit, the ricksha puller ran around in circles, frantically looking for a way out. He turned sharply into an alley, but it proved to be a dead end. High walls blocked them on three sides, and the driver jolted to a halt, his head hanging in despair.

The Japanese had said they'd come, and here they were, Dieyi thought to himself ruefully. He wondered if he would ever have anything to smile about again.

When he looked up he saw a little boy in the cul-de-sac. The boy was about ten years old, and he was smiling and holding a newborn baby. The baby was still streaked with blood from the afterbirth, and her hair was damp. Someone had tied an old rag around her belly. Dieyi peered at the boy quizzically—it was Xiao Douzi. It was himself!

A contemptuous smile crept across Xiao Douzi's mouth, like the icy grin of an evil ghost come to torment Dieyi's dreams. They had been abandoned, all of them.

Perhaps he was already dead. Maybe his mother had killed him when he was ten, and the man he was today was only a ghost. Or maybe he was that abandoned baby girl. Suddenly, he didn't know who or where he was.

Dieyi looked through the curtains of the ricksha toward the mouth of the alley. An endless parade of Japanese soldiers streamed by.

Still hugging the sword to his chest, Dieyi entered the hall. He walked with dignity, the famous singer, the famous *dan*. Without hurry, he threaded his way among the tables littered with greasy plates and empty wine cups—the debris left over from a wedding feast. Not long before, the tables had been filled with heaping platters. Now the food was gone and the wine was running out, but the guests lingered on. Some were asleep on the floor, overcome by drunkenness. Others were still wide awake and were noisily playing drinking games.

Dieyi scowled. It was an even bigger mess than most weddings.

Xiaolou came up and confronted him.

"What kept you?"

"Brother, please have a seat!" someone said. It was Juxian. She looked especially beautiful in her scarlet wedding dress. Dieyi looked at it wistfully. That and the deep red silk flower she wore at her temple were reserved by custom for brides and brides alone.

Standing beside Xiaolou, she seemed intimately connected to him. Dieyi felt abandoned. They even seemed to breathe in unison, he thought to himself.

The ceremony was long over, and the musicians had all

gone home for the night. The only people left were revelers. There was nothing left to do but celebrate with the happy young couple.

"Last night, Xiaolou sent people out to find you. They spent the whole night looking. Xiaolou refused to start without you, so we kept delaying the ceremony."

Dieyi felt somewhat gratified but said nothing.

"We'll have to hold another banquet just for you so that we can toast you properly," she continued.

"Should we punish him or not?" Xiaolou asked jovially. "He was even late on his big brother's important day!"

"Here, have some wine," Juxian offered.

Ignoring her, Dieyi held the sword out to Xiaolou.

"This is the sword, Big Brother. It's definitely the same one."

Taking the sword from Dieyi, Xiaolou unsheathed it. It gleamed in the light as he turned it from side to side admiringly.

"You found it! It's great!"

The other guests clustered around to get a better look, and Xiaolou called to Juxian, "Hurry, come look at this. I've dreamed of this since I was a little boy."

Juxian leaned on his arm and looked at the sword.

"Take good care of it, my friend," Dieyi said brittlely. Then he walked over to the household altar to the patron saints and piously offered a stick of incense to the founders. He closed his eyes and bowed his head, the embers from the incense and the tiny flames of the red candles flickering on his mysteriously cloaked figure.

"This is certainly the finest wedding gift we've received," Xiaolou said to the others. "There is no way to thank someone enough for such a gift."

Dieyi turned to him.

"Now that you're married, I'll have to sing solo," he said blandly.

Only Juxian suspected what feeling lay behind those words.

Dieyi accepted the cup of wine Xiaolou held out to him and tilted his head back to drain it in one swallow. This was the second time this evening he was getting drunk, he thought ruefully. Things certainly couldn't get any worse.

A burst of shouting in the street outside silenced the wedding party. No one understood the words being shouted—they were Japanese. But before they could ponder long, someone yelled out a translation in Chinese.

"Put up a Japanese flag! Show your support for Japan and Greater East Asian Co-Prosperity!"

Someone staggered in the front door. It was Xiao Si, Dieyi's personal servant.

"They're all over town!" he said breathlessly. "Japanese soldiers are ordering every household to fly the rising sun."

The wedding party looked at him blankly.

In the lane outside, a few people were poking their heads out to see what the commotion was about. Some of them had not been to bed yet; others had been jolted awake by the noise. But they all did as they were told and silently raised the flags the invaders had given them. Somewhere a child started to cry, but the sound was quickly muffled.

Dieyi alone seemed unaffected by these events. He felt his personal loss so keenly that there was no room for anything else. He had spent many black nights backstage, a melancholy child without home or family. He had found a place for himself among the trunks full of costumes, pieces of scenery, and opulent brocades. He had found something in which to believe. The theater was a world of illusion, but it was the only world he knew. The rest of the world seemed to drift by him, no more substantial than a dream.

He was only twenty, but he was already widely acclaimed. His brilliant career had only begun. If loneliness was the price he had to pay, so be it. He didn't belong in the ordinary world, anyway. He looked around him. Everyone in the room was toasting his health and shouting his praises.

After that night, Dieyi became even more successful, aided by his immense talent and influential patrons like Yuan Siye. The war of resistance against Japan raged on, and many men went away to the front. But many people stayed behind, and ticket sales at the opera houses soared. The entertainment business flourished as people sought to escape from the grimness of life during wartime.

The company manager came into Dieyi's dressing room.

"Master Cheng," he said unctuously. "I've had a red banner made up for your new program. The lettering is gold, and there will be marquee lights running all around it. I'd also like to post a large portrait of you in costume. Which of these pictures do you prefer?"

Dieyi looked over the photographs the man spread out in front of him. They were all taken from famous scenes in operas. There was *Picking Up the Jade Bracelet, Sword of the Universe, Goddess of the Luo River, Yang Guifei Gets Tipsy,* and a few others. Xiaolou's marriage had forced Dieyi to change his program—these were all solo shows that featured a *dan.*

"This one will do," he said lazily.

"Very well, sir. And don't worry—your name will be the biggest of all. You're the star, Master Cheng."

Dieyi tried to forget about Xiaolou and enjoy his success. Yuan Siye constantly showered him with gifts. One day he sent an ornate box containing a set of hair ornaments and jewelry of jade and cut crystal. There were also silver hairpins, a phoenix medallion, long pearl earrings, and brightly colored silk flowers. A different fabric was used for each of the four seasons: satin, damask, gauze, and velvet, all intricately fashioned into blossoms. Yuan sent Dieyi trunks filled with costumes and props of every description. He had gold bars melted down and spun into thread that was used to embroider the costumes, and Dieyi's skirts and mandarin jackets seemed to flash like lightning.

"It's so heavy," Dieyi complained as he hefted one of these outfits. "This thing must weigh five or six pounds."

The ever-smiling company manager picked up one of the ornaments.

"Look at this hairpin! It's set with cat's-eye. That's very impressive."

While the company manager was delighted with Yuan's attention to Dieyi, other members of the troupe talked behind Dieyi's back, calling him a gigolo. But none of them dared snub him in public.

It was the first evening performance of *Picking Up the Jade Bracelet,* in which Dieyi appeared as the coquettish Sun Yujiao. She happens upon a jade bracelet lying on the ground and is sorely tempted to pick it up. Hesitating at first, she pretends accidentally to drop her handkerchief, which falls so that it covers the bracelet. She quickly gathers up the bundle and carries it away with her, stroking it fondly.

A *dan* has to be even more feminine than a woman. In real life, a woman's charms are enough, but something else is needed for the stage. It takes a man to understand what other men desire. A *dan* must have that elusive quality and the ability to merge into his character until the actor and the opera are one.

As Sun Yujiao, Dieyi had slyly taken the bracelet and put it on. Then the male lead made his entrance, seeking his lost bracelet. When he saw Yujiao, he was smitten and went to her side, and she made as if to return the jade.

Dieyi looked into the eyes of his costar. He wasn't Xiaolou. He was just a minor player, the boy who shared Dieyi's bed. On stage, Yujiao was making a great show of trying to return the bracelet.

"Please take it! I don't want it!"

In the end, he didn't take it back. The bracelet was like Xiaolou—no matter how hard he tried, he couldn't separate himself from him. Longing for Xiaolou informed Dieyi's performance, and the audience was captivated by the emotional intensity of his singing.

Two days later, Dieyi starred in another program, *Yang Guifei Gets Tipsy*. He chose it because there was no costar. He portrayed the emperor's consort, Guifei, as she admired the fish in a pond, smelled flowers in a garden, raised a cup of wine to her lips, and became intoxicated. Finally, at the end of the scene, she collapsed to thunderous applause.

In that brief instant he was Chang'e, the Goddess of the Moon. Even the golden carp in the water and the wild geese in the air came to pay tribute. For a moment he forgot Xiaolou.

Although her beloved emperor had forsaken her, Guifei was still devoted to him. She imagined she heard him approaching, but he had been detained. She sank into a reverie.

"I need no wine, I am intoxicated without it," Dieyi sang.

Just then, a handful of leaflets sifted down like snow from a corner of the balcony and scattered among the audience. Written on them were the words: "Resist Japanese Aggression, Save Our Nation, Be Patriots." A ripple of confusion passed through the hall. Some people picked up the sheets, while others ignored them. Dieyi was still singing, and when he swept his long, flowing sleeves through the air, the breeze stirred the leaflets that had landed on stage.

The house went dark. Blackouts like this were becoming increasingly common. Whenever the Japanese wanted to locate clandestine Nationalist or Communist radio transmitters, they would shut off the electricity, one district at a time. The first time this happened, Dieyi had been flustered, but now he was used to it. What happened outside the theater was no concern of his.

The theater was his life; he would finish his aria. In the darkness on stage, he became the indistinct figure of the lady Yang Guifei.

"It is not our desire that misleads us, but ourselves."

"Bravo!" came the satisfied shouts of the audience.

After the incident with the leaflets, the Japanese Military Police launched a search for the culprits. The theater was forced to suspend performances indefinitely, but the actors still spent their days there.

Today, they had all gathered backstage, including Xiaolou and Juxian. Dieyi noticed how calm she seemed to be when she was with Xiaolou. With her face washed clean of the paints and powders of her former trade, she had almost become a respectable woman.

Dieyi was cleaning and polishing his prized set of hair ornaments so that they would be ready to use when the theater reopened. He was watching Juxian and Xiaolou out of the corner of his eye. They sat nearby, and Juxian was wrapping a skein of yarn around Xiaolou's outstretched hands. When Xiaolou playfully grabbed her wrist, Dieyi saw her look up at her husband and smile as though at some private joke.

"I'm going to finish knitting this sweater soon and make you wear it. It will warm up your blood—and that will be good for me."

"Are you saying I'm lukewarm?"

"Men with hot blood father sons, that's all."

"You can't fool me! Eating ice chips is supposed to make you have sons, too."

Xiaolou shrugged and sent the ball of yarn tumbling to the floor. It rolled a few feet and got tangled up around Dieyi's ankles. Trying to appear calm, he worked furiously to extricate his feet and tried to kick the ball away, but he only managed to get all the more tangled up.

"Miss Juxian," Dieyi said with an insincere smile. "If you knit a sweater for my brother here, he'll never wear it. You can't teach an old dog new tricks. Don't waste your time."

"What do you mean I wouldn't wear it?" Xiaolou objected loudly. "I always sleep in a sweater."

"Since when do you wear anything to bed?" Juxian countered.

Xiaolou pulled the yarn and reeled Juxian in until she was close enough for him to whisper in her ear.

"You are a very naughty boy!"

"It's you who's tempting me!"

The more he listened to their banter, the worse Dieyi felt. He withdrew to a corner and furiously started to scrub a silver hairpin. He gripped it so tightly his fingernails dug into his palms.

Juxian slapped Xiaolou affectionately. This was more than Dieyi could take.

"The theater's been dark for three days already. We're going to get out of practice," he said peevishly.

"And all for a few lousy scraps of paper," Xiaolou interjected. "There are leaflets scattered all over town; but those good-for-nothing military police are just looking for excuses to make trouble for people." He paused. "What the hell. If they want to shut us down, let them. We won't sing anymore."

"Not sing? You can't be serious?" Dieyi was startled. "How would we eat?"

"We could always work as day laborers," Xiaolou said optimistically. "Don't worry! They can cart away all of our worldly goods. As long as I have so much as a grain of rice to my name, you'll never go hungry. We're family."

Dieyi smiled at Xiaolou, and Juxian walked over and placed a hand on Dieyi's shoulder.

"Don't be silly, Xiaolou! Dieyi can have a family of his own."

Dieyi scowled.

"I have a good friend," Juxian continued. "She's stunningly beautiful, and a very capable girl, as well. Xiaolou and I would be pleased to discuss a match with her—"

Dieyi stood up abruptly and made to leave.

"Another day wasted. I think I'll go home now."

He took a few steps and realized his feet were tangled in the ball of yarn again. Unable to free himself after a couple of kicks, he made sure no one was looking and then broke the thread with a violent jerk.

"The whole world's a mess these days—the economy is a mess, people's lives are a mess. Even our own theater is a pigsty."

Just as he turned to leave, there was a commotion outside. Xiao Si came running in along with a few of the company's other errand boys.

"Master Cheng," Xiao Si said anxiously. "Don't leave yet. The manager says you should wait awhile."

"What's happening out there? What's all the noise?"

"It's a girl student—"

They could all hear the voice of a girl pleading loudly outside the stage door.

"I'm not a fan. I'm the woman he's going to marry. Is there something wrong with a wife coming to see her husband?"

They heard the sound of someone being slapped.

"What's going on?" Dieyi asked again.

A policeman ordered everyone to disperse, and they all heard the sound of fleeing footsteps.

The theater manager came in to apologize, bowing deeply.

"A student named Miss Fang came here to see you,

Master Cheng. She said, 'One smile from Master Cheng is like a thousand springtimes, one tear like a thousand sorrows.' She's madly in love with you and was determined to get in to see you this time. She's already been here many times, and we've always turned her away, but today she tried harder than usual. She even slapped the gatekeeper on the face. She just wouldn't give up!"

Dieyi laughed helplessly. What else could he do? He had many fans like Miss Fang; but she was certainly one of the most dedicated. She might be arrested and need to be bailed out by her parents. In the long run that might be better for her, sparing her feelings and preventing her from making crazy promises she couldn't keep. With luck, her parents might marry her off to someone who lived far away. Otherwise she might never recover.

Dieyi's fervent admirers were deluded, however. It wasn't him they loved—it was the idea of him. Men loved him as a woman; women loved him as a man. Nobody knew who he really was.

Dieyi's room was a study in indolence. The walls were adorned with a group of portraits in ink and watercolor—the "Thirteen Greats" of the late Qing. There were *sheng* and *dan,* men who played men and men who played women. They were all dead now, but their images seemed to eye Dieyi covetously as he sprawled languidly on a chaise longue. For a long time he didn't move.

He'd let his hair grow a bit long, and he had it combed back so that the ends hung softly down his neck. His head lolled back against an embroidered pillow, and he looked drunk, but he wasn't. An unmistakably sweet scent hung in the air, while a silver-tipped opium pipe lay at Dieyi's side, his companion in sleep. The ancients had imbibed cinnabar potions, hoping for immortality. In Dieyi's time, the magical potion was opium.

His lids drooped and he dozed off, his troubles forgotten for the time being.

Mirrors decorated with portraits of the "Four Famous Beauties" of ancient China hung from the walls. When Dieyi looked into them, he always saw the face of some long-dead beauty staring back. Frames of all sizes and shapes held photos of Dieyi in costume or in street clothes. He also had a copy of the group portrait taken when he was still a boy in opera school, as well as the picture he and Xiaolou had taken together at the Wansheng Photo Studio. Time had been frozen inside those frames.

Dieyi's other companion was a cat, black with green eyes. The opium had made it sleepy, too. When Dieyi exhaled, he blew smoke into the cat's face, one puff at time, making it blink in ecstasy. It had become as dependent on the drug as its master.

Dieyi stroked his cat as though it were another person. His soft, pale hands had never done a day's labor—never tilled the soil, never fired a gun, never slid the beads of an abacus along their spools, never rolled pills of herbal medicine, never struck another man. It was as though they had been emasculated the day he cut off his extra finger.

Xiao Si walked in, a pair of new costumes draped over his arms. He had been serving Dieyi for several years now, and he was bright and obedient. He had also grown very handsome, and Dieyi imagined he had found the face of his own lost youth when he gazed upon Xiao Si's as yet unformed features.

"Master Cheng, when you went out this morning little Lucky became listless. He wouldn't even open his eyes. It wasn't until you blew a little smoke his way that he came back to life."

"He's a divine little creature, isn't he?" Dieyi commented affectionately.

"No more divine than his master."

"What would I do without you, Xiao Si? I don't think anyone else would put up with me!" He added, "You haven't disappointed me."

Xiao Si gently laid the costumes on the bed, smiling to himself. He was devoted to Dieyi.

"Master Zhu just came by," he suddenly remembered. "He wanted to know if Master Duan would be appearing with you in tonight's performance. A lot of fans have been sending inquiries to the theater lately. They're all begging you two to perform together. Even the military police sent someone by to ask."

"I suppose we're about due for a reunion," Dieyi sighed. "It's been a long time since we last sang *Farewell*. The next time we get together, it'll be *Farewell* again!"

"Sir—"

"What are you waiting for?"

"Master Zhu said he'd been looking for Master Duan but wasn't able to find him. Usually he goes out drinking and gambling. He likes cricket fights."

The year was 1943. China was under Japanese occupation, but life had to go on. Some worked hard just to get by, while others sought to escape into gambling and carousing.

A gang of partygoers and drinkers had gathered at the house of one Master Chen, an acquaintance of Xiaolou's. As usual, they were eating and drinking to excess. Each guest had also brought a delicate porcelain cup in which he displayed his prized crickets.

Xiaolou sat beside one of the gaming tables.

"This bronze-armored general of mine dined on ants' eggs last night—he'll be fierce!" he called out loudly. "If you don't believe me, come fight a round!" He turned around to Juxian and smiled confidently. "Juxian, collect my winnings for me!"

He had won again, and the cash was heaped up on the table in front of him. His companions clustered around to flatter him.

"You're as great a general as Xiang Yu. Even the crickets you lead into battle are mighty warriors!"

"If they weren't any good, they wouldn't dare appear in front of a real soldier like him."

Xiaolou laughed loudly and showed off his operatic voice.

"The wiiiine is heeeere!"

"Bravo!" everybody chorused.

Seeing that Xiaolou was in an expansive mood, one of his fellows asked, "Master Duan! Things are going well for you tonight. I was wondering if perhaps you could lend me a little cash."

"It's yours!" he said, handing the man a small handful of money.

After the man had gone, Juxian turned angrily to Xiaolou.

"No matter how much money you have, you can always spend it three times over!"

"Why don't you run along home now?" he said, ignoring her complaint. "Maybe you could make us some braised pork for dinner."

Juxian left angrily, and Xiaolou went back to the game with renewed enthusiasm.

"Let's have another round!" he shouted. "Women don't understand anything!"

Just then, Dieyi came in, only footsteps behind Xiao Si and the master of ceremonies.

"Put on your makeup," he said curtly.

"Can't you see I'm busy right now?"

The master of ceremonies tried his hand at persuading Xiaolou.

"Please, sir. Please do us all a favor and come back to the theater. The military police are coming to the show tonight, and we can't afford to offend them. Please help us!"

"Just putting on a painted face won't do any good," Xiaolou said, his attention already back on his cricket cup. In a burst of anger, Dieyi swept the cup off the table. It went flying and shattered to pieces on the floor.

The master of ceremonies attempted to pacify the two men.

"You gentlemen are both reasonable men. I'll go ahead and get an understudy to fill in until you can get there yourselves. Please hurry. We'll all be waiting for you, sirs."

Dieyi tugged urgently at Xiaolou's sleeve.

"What are you doing here?" he hissed.

"I'm trying to make enough money to get my costumes back from the pawnshop. I've had to pawn everything."

Dieyi called impatiently to Xiao Si, who hurried to his side. After whispering a few instructions to him, Dieyi handed the boy some cash. Xiao Si nodded and ran out.

"Duan Xiaolou!" Dieyi spat. "You've really gotten yourself into quite a mess! I'm sure the pawnbroker is more than happy to give you plenty of spending money. You'll never run out of nice things for him. If you take him something today, somebody else can always redeem it for you tomorrow!"

"Who cares about tomorrow? If the Japanese destroy us, there won't be any tomorrow!"

"Maybe you don't have a future, but I do!"

"You have a great future!" Xiaolou said sarcastically. "Every day you loll around, smoking that garbage. It's ruining your voice, not to mention your looks. You've been looking pretty dull recently. Do you call that a future?"

"You spend money as if it were water," Dieyi countered. "But when the well runs dry, who'll take care of you? When we go our separate ways, who will redeem your costumes for you?"

"What makes you think you'll always be richer and more successful than I am? If you don't start taking better care of yourself, you're going to lose your voice. And if you let yourself go, it won't be you who leaves—it'll be me. I won't want to be seen on stage with you!"

Hearing this made Dieyi shake with anger. He thought back to that day by the riverbank, a decade ago, when Xiao Shitou had protected Xiao Douzi from the other boys. "Don't pick on him!" he'd said. "Leave him alone!" What had happened to them?

"Let's go our separate ways, then!" Dieyi said with resignation.

Xiaolou was speechless; but before things could get any worse, Xiao Si returned with Xiaolou's costumes. Xiaolou stepped forward.

"Dieyi—before you go on, you ought to put on some extra powder to cover the grayish cast of your skin. Yu Ji still has to look like Yu Ji. As for me, I'll just swagger on and strike a pose. It'll bring down the house. With the pair of us top-notch actors up there together, we can't go wrong."

The backstage area had been completely transformed. There was now a gambling table where patrons could amuse themselves after the show, in addition to an area set aside for opium smoking, and a small room where men could take prostitutes.

Xiaolou was putting on his makeup. He had already forgotten his argument with Dieyi and was trying to cheer him up.

"It looks like most of tonight's audience is here to see you play Yu Ji."

"I'm not sure they can tell the difference between me and her."

"You're probably right. Some of those guys come in shouting for Yu Ji; but it's you they want. You can be sure of that."

"There's something else I have to say," Xiaolou added gravely. "I think you should quit smoking opium. It makes you lethargic, and it's bad for your lungs. If you keep it up, your voice is going to get scratchy. I'm saying this for your own good."

Dieyi looked at Xiaolou.

"I—" he faltered.

"Juxian suggested I talk to you about one other matter," Xiaolou went on. "Remember what she said the other day about your getting married? Have you given it any thought? Maybe you could let her know what you think. Juxian—"

Dieyi had only been half listening. He was inspecting the costumes Xiao Si had brought back from the pawn shop, but when he heard the name "Juxian," he started to pace uneasily. It irritated him that he and his best friend couldn't have even the simplest conversation without having her barge into it.

"Little Bean," Xiaolou sighed. He saw Dieyi start at the mention of his old nickname.

"You'd be better off pawning your wife than your costumes!" Dieyi snapped. "They've all been ruined—the mice in the pawnshop have chewed them up. I went to the trouble of redeeming them for you, and now it turns out that they're all full of holes!"

With that, he went back to putting on his own costume. The drums and cymbals of the orchestra were reaching a crescendo. The show was about to begin.

Farewell to My Concubine was approaching its dramatic climax. The sound of the songs of Chu came from backstage. The Han army had surrounded General Xiang Yu's forces and their singing threw them into confusion. Xiang Yu was filled with homesickness:

"Our fields lie fallow—we must return,
—We've followed the army these many leagues—
But for whom?"

"All around us we hear the songs of Chu. Has Liu Bang already captured our kingdom? My powers are spent!"

Even his stallion, Wuzhui, could not escape the siege at Gaixia.

Just as the opera reached its most beautiful and moving point, a group of Japanese soldiers filed into the theater. All of them wore crisp uniforms and leather boots that clicked out of time with the music onstage. One contingent led the way, while another group brought up the rear for a high-ranking officer, Marshal Aoki. His breast was paved with shiny medals, and he carried an elegant sabre in addition to the regulation pistol. The sabre hung from a golden sash that glowed faintly in the gloom of the house. Aoki's starched uniform was stiff and unwrinkled, and his spurs shone like moonlight on snow.

He glanced around, looking for empty seats; ushers quickly appeared and began to set up his seat of honor. First, they had to chase away the Chinese people who were already occupying those places. Those who were displaced dared not object.

There was a commotion in the front rows and a few muffled cries of pain. Some of the Chinese patrons had not moved out of the way quickly enough and were being driven off with kicks and blows. The crowd seethed with silent anger. When Xiaolou saw what was happening, he stopped singing and jumped down into the audience.

"The show's over! This damn theater is full of devils!"

The curtain quickly fell, but the orchestra kept playing, in an effort to keep the show going. The company manager, the theater manager, and the master of ceremonies were all aghast.

"Master Duan! Get back on stage! If they're offended, you'll have to face the consequences! Please."

"You're a man of the world, Master Duan. Nobody can argue with the military police, you know that. You can't beat them. Please go back and sing—"

"I'm one man who won't sing for devils!" Xiaolou said adamantly. "Maybe I should be in a different line of work."

"Xiaolou," Juxian broke in. "This is no time to lose your temper."

But it was too late, and Xiaolou rushed out with a sweep of his long silk sleeves. Juxian was right behind him, followed by the rest of the audience.

Dieyi hadn't moved. He had let others speak for him. Now he was alone, while Xiaolou and his wife faced the future together.

Xiaolou intended to go straight home that night; he was arrested by the military police the instant he stepped outside the theater.

Xiaolou's captors beat him, kicked him, whipped him, and struck him with pistols.

"So you won't sing?" they taunted him. "This bastard won't sing for the Imperial Army!"

He was quickly losing awareness of his own body. All he knew was pain, and a wave of dizziness overcame him, making the room spin. Refusing to beg for mercy, he struggled to stay standing but fell backward to the floor. He kept trying to crawl back up. The more brutally they beat him, the more determined he became.

No one would be able to survive that kind of beating for long.

* * *

Dieyi was still asleep, although it was late in the day. He had nothing in life except the opera. With the theater closed, he had nowhere to go, so he slept on as darkness fell.

Juxian was pleading with Xiao Si at the front door of Dieyi's house.

"Is he awake yet? Please, wake him up. It's an emergency."

"I believe he just woke up. Come in."

Dieyi wondered if he was dreaming. It seemed his soul had rounded the corner of a mountain path and come abruptly face-to-face with his enemy. What was she doing in his dream? He blinked.

"Younger Brother, please save Xiaolou!" she begged.

He eyed her coolly. She was drawn and pale and seemed to have aged several years overnight. He had never seen her like this before, looking as worn as a wadded-up old handkerchief. She must be in serious trouble.

"Don't call me 'Little Brother,' " he sneered. She was not his elder. "My name is Dieyi. What's happened to my brother?"

She let the insult pass.

"He's been arrested by the military police. I was hoping you might be able to intercede and get him out of prison before it's too late. There's no telling what they're doing to him in there. If we wait too long he'll be dead. He's probably making the guards angry right now. I know better than anyone how bad his temper is—"

"You don't know him any better than I do," Dieyi cut her off. "You haven't known him all that long, really."

"Please help him, Dieyi," she pleaded. "If you do, I'll be in your debt forever."

Although he was also anxious about Xiaolou, Dieyi kept his composure. He had an opportunity to exact his toll from her, and this might be his last chance. After a long pause, he broke the silence.

"Since it concerns my brother, I'll see what I can do."

He stared at her coolly. At last she spoke.

"What are your conditions?"

Dieyi reached out and gently brushed away the tears that rolled down her cheeks. In an almost sisterly gesture, he stroked the stray hairs at her temples back into place.

Xiao Si was spying on them from behind the doorframe. Completely misunderstanding the situation, he tactfully slipped away.

"Xiaolou and I have been performing together for more than ten years. We've been close since we were children. You must know how hard it is to find a good partner. You have him; but what do I have? I'm afraid he's lost all desire to sing. He's very confused right now."

Juxian began to sense what he was hinting at.

"Dieyi," she asked cautiously. "What is it you're trying to say?"

"Marriage!" he spat, but his anger was for show. "Honestly! He married you without having the faintest idea what he was doing!"

"Do you want me to leave Xiaolou?"

"It might be a good idea."

Dieyi was satisfied. It was she who had said it and not himself.

"You and I both want what's best for Xiaolou," he said smugly. "He's been held back—one of the greatest talents of our time. It would be a terrible loss to the theater if he quit singing."

Juxian folded her arms across her chest. Her mouth had a stubborn set.

"I see. If you get Xiaolou out of prison, then I am to go somewhere far away. Or, if all else fails, I can always go back to the House of Flowers. Is that right?"

All of the guests seated on the tatami matting were Japanese. Many were officers from the military police; but there were also some Kabuki actors. The Kabuki performance had just ended, but the actors were still in costume and makeup—matte white foundation, touched with red under the lower eyelids and a half-moon for the lower lip. There were characters from *Chūshingura, Benten Kosō, Yotsuya Kaidan,* and *Sukeroku,* as well as a wise king, a devil, a red-haired lion, and a white-haired lion. The most striking figure was that of the egret maiden, Oshimusume, who was dressed from head to toe in pure white.

As with Peking opera, all Kabuki roles, both male and female, were played by men.

Everyone in the audience sat cross-legged and straight-backed, in attitudes of respectful appreciation. They seemed to hold their breath in awe as they watched the Peking opera performance Dieyi had prepared for them.

Marshal Aoki of the Kwantung Army was a great connoisseur of the Peking opera. His translator, Xiao Chen, was a gifted amateur. Aside from Xiao Chen and Dieyi, there were no other Chinese guests at this gathering.

Dieyi was not wearing makeup, and he had put on

simple, understated clothing—a long Chinese gown with a muted pattern on a gray background. His voice was clear and pure as he sang the famous aria:

> "The flowers of spring should be blooming here, crimson and violet,
> But in their place are broken wells and ruined walls.
> When will a fair day dawn again?
> Whose family will know joy?
> In the morning the birds fly away,
> Evenings they fold their wings.
> I watch the sunset clouds from a painted balcony.
> Thin filaments of rain blow down on gusts of wind.
> Waves rock the painted boats out on the lake.
> Nature seems a pale imitation of the landscape painted on the screen."

Dieyi lost himself in the song, oblivious to his surroundings. It was always that way for him when he performed. He didn't care who was watching or what he was singing. Dieyi was infatuated with the opera.

> "It's all been for you, beautiful as a flower.
> The years rush past like flowing water."

He put his entire soul and years of training into this performance. It was all that he had to give to repay the debt of kindness he owed Xiaolou. Xiaolou had protected him many times when they were children, and now it was his turn to protect his friend. That was why he was there.

Aoki was a burly fellow. His eyes had a single fold, and they were long and narrow, in contrast to his bushy eyebrows, which tilted upward in a way that made him look fierce even when he was smiling.

"Bravo!" he shouted out in Japanese. "Chinese opera is superb. An absolutely first-rate performance!"

When Xiao Chen translated, Dieyi half rose to express his appreciation.

"Tonight we'll speak only of opera—nothing else," Aoki said earnestly. "His Highness's war shall have to take second place. You know, when I was a student at Imperial University, I memorized all of *The Peony Pavilion*."

"You are a true connoisseur, sir," Dieyi said delightedly. Aoki was speaking in Japanese.

"Art is the most exalted thing in this world. It is pure and beautiful like a cherry blossom as it opens. There must be someone there who can appreciate it fully at that glorious but ephemeral moment. Otherwise, it will have blossomed in vain."

Dieyi waited uncomprehendingly for Aoki to finish speaking so that the interpreter could translate. Only then did he know that the serious tone of Aoki's pronouncements had been in praise. Dieyi wondered if he had found a foreign soul mate. Or was Aoki just an enemy who happend to be in a good mood tonight?

Aoki motioned to a servant, who pulled back a painted shoji screen depicting a scene of Mount Fuji. A sumptuous banquet had been laid out in the adjoining room. Everything on the table was the best that money could buy. There were delicacies of all descriptions, fine wines, and fresh seafood. There was sashimi, sliced paper-thin, some of the fish pale and pearly, some of it deep red.

The long table had been laid carefully and decorated with seasonal motifs. Set beside every hot pot was a bright red maple leaf, like the tiny crimson hand of a young woman, with intriguingly pointed fingernails.

Aoki beckoned to his guests, including the Kabuki actors and Dieyi.

"The snows of winter, the cherry blossoms in spring, the rivers in summer, the leaves of autumn—these are the beautiful scenes we revere."

Dieyi listened to Xiao Chen's translation and pondered a moment before replying.

"Our country has always been very beautiful. Yet, so much has changed since you arrived."

"What does that have to do with art?" Aoki laughed. "We can all live together and prosper together!"

They may have been living side by side, Japanese and Chinese, but everyone knew that the prosperity wasn't shared equally between them. But here in the lion's den, Dieyi was in no position to press his point. Remembering why he had come, he bowed his head deferentially. He was still nothing but the evening's "entertainment," an actor joining his host for a brief meal.

Looking over the platters spread with raw fish, Dieyi smiled condescendingly.

"We Chinese aren't accustomed to eating our fish raw."

Eaten raw, he thought. That was how it felt to be invaded. China was being sliced up like a fish by the Japanese Army.

"Excuse me, Marshal Aoki, sir," he said with an obsequious bow. "Might I ask you a favor? I wondered if I could trouble you please to release my costar from prison? I would be extremely grateful to you, sir."

"No." Aoki's face hardened. "You still have to sing one more piece. Sing *Yang Guifei Gets Tipsy*."

"What an excellent choice," Dieyi said, swallowing his pride. "This is one of my specialties."

After dinner, he sang again.

"Just like Chang'e coming down to earth,
Cold and lonely in her palace in the moon.
The chilly palace of the moon."

Opening a golden fan painted with red peonies, he hid his face behind its faint beating. He was a languid and seductive Yang Guifei.

"Precious Consort" was what the name meant, and Dieyi was only valuable when he performed.

Night had fallen like a heavy curtain by the time the prisoner was brought out.

Dieyi waited by the massive prison gate at Military Police Headquarters, a building at the edge of a wood. He could barely discern the vague outlines of trees and remote hills in the gloom. He was just another shadow among many. The stars and the distant autumn moon all seemed to have slipped behind an inky curtain.

A few minutes elapsed, but it seemed like an eternity.

At last, Xiaolou emerged from the darkened gate, supported on either side by soldiers. Bruised and exhausted, he stumbled out. He saw Dieyi.

"Brother," Dieyi said. "Everything is all right."

He stepped forward to help him, ready to forgive every past insult.

But When Xiaolou spoke it was as though he were trying to spit out a fly.

"Did you get down and grovel and sing for those devils?" he rasped angrily, his eyes glittering with contempt. "You're spineless!"

He spat, and Dieyi felt as though a nail had just been driven into his face. The barb burrowed its way into his flesh and blood, boring in too deeply to be pulled out.

He felt someone wipe the spittle away with a fine handkerchief. There was something familiar in the way the hand moved gently, gracefully. It was Juxian.

She gave Xiaolou a light pat and fixed Dieyi with a brief but meaningful look. Then she led Xiaolou away by the elbow towards a ricksha that was waiting near where the road emerged from the wood. It had been there all along. She had been there, too, biding her time. She must have planned this from the first! he thought angrily. She had broken her promise to him.

Dieyi would never forget the look she gave him. You could never trust a whore, Dieyi thought.

He had endured humiliation, all for the sake of his friend. But nothing hurt him more than Xiaolou's contempt. He felt at once deeply wronged and deeply ashamed.

The moon slipped out from behind the clouds, shining down rays of cold, clear light. Suddenly, Dieyi heard the sound of voices and footsteps, followed by harsh shouts.

"Get going!"

"Down with Japanese devils! Down—"

The cries of resistance were muffled as gags were forced

over the prisoners' mouths. There was the sound of a struggle and the sound of someone being beaten.

Then there was a gunshot. It was followed by another, and the woods reverberated with the deadly reports.

Realizing he was standing near the execution ground, Dieyi panicked and ran into the woods. Crashing through the underbrush, he strained his eyes to see where he was going. He might as well have been dead. There was no escape. He hurtled forward, overtaken by blind terror.

At last he staggered forward and fell to his knees. Watery moonlight illuminated his limp form, a form that seemed to have no bones to support it.

Dieyi heard a rumble, followed by a loud clap. Then it grew perfectly still and quiet again. For a long time he knelt in the clearing, head bowed in despair. A man is tiny and insignificant in the universe, a lonely, solitary creature. Everything was finished.

☰☰☰
6

T he music on the gramo-
phone droned on, at
once tinny and gloomy. Aside from this, Dieyi had no other
company.

His room was a treasure trove of curios and objects of
art, all of them the finest that money could buy. Just as one
gives a child a new toy to distract him from some frustration,
so Dieyi bought trinkets for himself with a passion.

Assorted mirrors seemed to lie in ambush on every
available wall. There were large ones, small ones, round
ones, squares, and oblongs. Dieyi liked to admire himself in
these mirrors and practice the stylized gestures of Peking

opera. Pointing gracefully at an imaginary companion, he indicated "you." Touching his heart with the middle finger of the right hand was "I." "He" was an elaborate flourish with both hands, first left, then right, and ending with an arc.

He practiced flirting in the mirror, too. His expressive eyes seemed to dance—he was beautiful. What man could resist him?

Costumes were draped around the room, like a field of brocade flowers shot with gold. Xiao Si was shaking them out and carefully hanging them up, a wardrobe of women's clothing—skirts, jackets, cloaks, short capes, chain mail, shawls, and pleated skirts. In contrast to the brightly colored garments were the inner robes, with flowing sleeves as white as snow. They brushed against each other in the breeze whenever Xiao Si walked by.

Dieyi was surrounded by shades, the empty garments of long dead beauties. No one came to visit, and the beaded curtains to his room hung motionless. Let everyone stay away, Dieyi thought to himself. Xiao Si would stay by him.

He grunted lazily, and mumbled:

"People say the flowers in Loyang are like brocade,
But I have been imprisoned so long, I don't know when
    spring is here."

Xiao Si put on one of the costumes. Even more elaborate than most, it was the one worn by Du Liniang, the heroine of *Wandering in the Garden, Waking from a Dream*, in the scene when she chances to meet the young student.

Xiao Si delicately picked up a fan, and the subtle scent of sandalwood wafted through the air.

"Xiao Si," Dieyi said with a weak smile. "Tear that costume for me."

The young man obeyed, and Dieyi leaned back and savored the sound of tearing silk.

"Tear up that one, too."

Xiao Si began ripping up a second garment. The cloth was thick and heavily embroidered, making Xiao Si's job difficult. He had to find a hole or a tear and then pull with all his strength before it would give. The damaged fabric made a loud grating sound, and Dieyi closed his eyes in a mixture of pain and pleasure.

Lucky, his opium-addicted cat, had been lying docilely at his side. But, startled by the sudden noise, he raised his hackles, ready to fight or flee. When Dieyi extended a hand to stroke him, he scratched unexpectedly.

The scratch wasn't deep, but it stung. Even his own cat, so loved and pampered, had betrayed him. Dieyi looked at the mark—a bright red hairline, almost invisible.

Xiao Si was still trying to cheer him up, and he put on his finery to sing to him.

"It's all been for you, beautiful as a flower,
The years rush past like flowing water.
I've been idle and lonely,
Pining here in my lonely chamber."

Lulled by the sweet, sad melody, Dieyi let his mind wander. He felt a tender, almost pitying affection for Xiao Si.

"You'll never be famous, Xiao Si, not in ten or even twenty years. You weren't cut out to be an actor."

Dieyi drifted off to sleep, and Xiao Si quietly put away the costumes. Another day had ended.

★   ★   ★

Winter gave way to spring, and it was June in Peking. The summer sun beat down, and people's houses became unbearably hot. Driven outside by the stifling heat, the citizens of Peking whiled away the hours sitting on wooden benches and bamboo stools carried from indoors, fanning themselves to keep cool.

Dieyi rode throught the hot, crowded streets in a ricksha. He had not seen the sun in a long time. He sang opera at night and slept all day. His face had become so white that sometimes it appeared as though he had forgotten to wash off his makeup. He sat in the ricksha, a cardboard box between his feet. It contained a new costume.

As the ricksha rolled through a street market where all the stalls sold fruit and snacks, Dieyi heard a clear and strong voice shouting out with the singsong rhythm of Peking opera:

"Get your big, juicy watermelons—they're all pulp,
We sell them by size not weight,
Big sweet pieces of melon,
Sweeter than candy—"

Dieyi knew that voice.

Beneath the spreading branches of a locust tree was a flatbed tricycle. Set on the bed was a large wooden tub holding a block of ice, against which several green-skinned watermelons had been set to cool. The vendor was wearing a sleeveless T-shirt and had an apron tied around his waist. He looked exactly like Xiaolou.

As the ricksha eased past the melon stand, Dieyi motioned the driver to stop. He watched in amazement as a modestly dressed woman laid out a clean indigo cloth and arranged some melons on it in neat rows like soldiers. She sprinkled a little ice water on them. Xiaolou picked out a good melon, set it in front of him, and, with an elegant sweep of his cleaver, sliced it in two. Then he cut the halves into smaller pieces to be sold individually. Juxian covered the fruit with a domed screen and fanned the flies away with a large bamboo fan.

The watermelon seller continued his chant:

"Who will come try one of my watermelons?
Green skins, juicy red flesh, and sweet as honey—"

Dieyi was about to motion the ricksha puller to move on when Xiaolou spotted him and broke off in midsentence.

"Brother! Brother!" he shouted to Dieyi.

Dieyi climbed down from the ricksha and went over to his old friend. Wiping his sticky, juice-soaked hands on his apron, Xiaolou pulled Dieyi to him. He seemed unembarrassed by his circumstances.

"I wasn't fair to you, my friend," he confessed. "I was angry and spat on you as though you were my enemy. It's been a long time, but I want to apologize to you."

"I've forgotten all about it!" Dieyi looked him up and down. "You're not singing anymore?"

"All of my costumes are in the pawnshop. Who can think of art at a time like this? We're at war and fighting for our lives. But what have you been doing with yourself?"

"The opera is still my life. I can't do anything else."

Juxian approached them. The coarse, plain clothes she wore only enhanced the beauty of her rosy complexion, and her eyes sparkled warmly as she came up to them with a good-sized watermelon.

"This melon is the pick of the crop," she said. "It's not quite ripe, but it should keep for a few days without spoiling."

"I'm glad to see you two are settled into your new life," Dieyi said with an insincere smile.

"How can anyone be settled in bad times like these? We're just doing our best to muddle through."

Xiaolou put his arms around Juxian protectively.

"She's right. We just do what we can to get by."

Dieyi still felt bitter toward her, and seeing them together made him angry at them both. No matter how much he suffered privately, the two of them would go on in blissful ignorance. He despised Juxian, for she had no shame. She had gone back on her word and stolen Xiaolou away from him by trickery.

Dieyi's eyes traveled from the melon to Juxian's belly. There was a slight bulge there—she must be several months pregnant. No wonder Xiaolou was so protective of her.

Dieyi felt the shock like ice water being poured down his back; and when he took the cold melon in his arms, he felt even colder inside. He held the big, round fruit like a false and secret pregnancy.

"You're not singing anymore?" he asked again.

"That's right. I've quit."

One of the best opera stars of his generation had thrown away a brilliant career to become a common melon vendor. To Dieyi, this was incomprehensible and an insult to their teacher. Master Guan's efforts had all been wasted.

★ ★ ★

The Master had grown older, but he was still an intimidating figure. He called the two men forward and ordered them to kneel, giving each a sharp slap. The Thirteen Greats of the late Qing gazed down on them as Master Guan admonished his former students with a shaking finger.

"I wasted ten whole years on you two good-for-nothings!"

They bowed their heads in shame. He had been their teacher, and they owed him lifelong obedience. The opera lyrics they had sung every day honored this precept of Confucian morality.

"I taught you about teamwork, made you set high standards for yourselves and trained you hard. I wanted you to be outstanding," Master Guan fumed. "Missing just one day's practice slows your reflexes—and here you are, going off on your own. Giving up and becoming a watermelon seller!"

The old man snorted contemptuously. He choked and had to take a few labored breaths before he could speak again.

"How could the two of you, who trained together, grew up together, and graduated together, become enemies overnight? Don't you have any consideration, any respect for me, your teacher?"

He was getting more and more excited. The children who were his current pupils watched in awe from behind the door as he upbraided the two full-grown men.

"There's an old saying I learned a long time ago. 'Brothers can build a wall together to keep out their enemies; but if brothers fight between themselves, then the enemy can conquer them.' Do you recognize those lyrics? That's what's happening right now. Japan is about to destroy us, but you two go on bickering! Now, get out of here! I want to see you back here in a month, with a brand new company. I'd like you to put on a performance for me."

With that, he sent them away. But Master Guan would not live to see their reunion.

The students were doing their daily leg stretches at the old and scarred wooden bar. Master Guan sat on a low stool, counting in a loud voice: "seventy-six, seventy-seven, sixty-three, sixty-four, forty-four, forty-five . . . forty-six . . ."

The boys groaned under their breath and exchanged exasperated looks, but there was nothing they could do. They had to keep stretching until the Master reached one hundred. Lately his memory had become less and less reliable, and he often lost count, starting again at a lower number. The numbers grew ever more random, and his eyes started to mist over. Finally his white head dropped forward. The students thought he was dozing, and they pulled faces at each other; but Master Guan never raised his head again. He had died quietly, in the courtyard of his school, under the oblique rays of the setting sun.

It was a long time before any of the children realized what had happened.

Xiaolou rushed over to Dieyi's house. It was four in the afternoon, and Dieyi had just finished two pipefuls of opium. Xiao Si was peeling a pear for him. The fresh sweetness of the fruit would cleanse Dieyi's mouth of the drug's burnt residues.

The telephone lay dormant on its table beneath the window, covered with a fine film of dust that looked like a coating of face powder. Nobody had called for a long time.

Xiaolou hurried into Dieyi's room, looking distraught.

"The Master—"

"I know he's concerned, but as long as we practice our old duets, we'll be fine," Dieyi said, rousing himself. "After all, we are old partners—"

"He's gone!"

Dieyi sat up and the pear tumbled from his hands to the floor.

"Gone?"

"He's dead!"

"Dead? He can't be!"

"The school will have to be closed. The children have nowhere to go. We two should raise some money to help them."

"Just a few days ago, he was scolding us," Dieyi moaned. "Didn't he say we had a month to organize our company? Didn't he?"

Dieyi would have gladly endured a beating if it would have brought the Master back. Xiaolou bowed his head and fought to keep from sobbing. Dieyi and Xiaolou had been reunited.

Master Guan's young students helped out backstage at the benefit performance given by Xiaolou and Dieyi. They raised enough money to give the Master a fine funeral, and there was plenty left over to distribute among the children. They were like monkeys scattering when the tree they've made their home has been chopped down.

"Hataman! Five Fifty-five! Twin Sisters!" A cigarette vendor called out the names of the brands he had for sale. He had set up his stall in the mouth of the lane outside the theater.

Inside, on stage, the armor-suited hero Xue Dingshan and the heroine Pan Lihua were standing face-to-face. Xiaolou and Dieyi had put their own troubles out of their minds. They had the ability to forget themselves and make the play new every time they performed. When the two main characters saw each other for the first time, even the performers felt it was a chance meeting.

The romantic couple was flirting as the music swelled. Just then, there was a deep rumble and a series of loud cracks outside.

"Is that gunfire?" Dieyi whispered apprehensively to his costar, but kept his composure.

Xiaolou listened carefully without losing time to the music.

"I don't think so. That's odd."

Suddenly the audience was in an uproar.

"We've won! We've won!"

"The Japs have surrendered!"

"Our boys are coming home!"

Jubilant shouts shook the rafters. The explosions they'd heard had been celebratory firecrackers, and the rumbling was the sound of people beating on tin basins. The audience was overjoyed, and everyone rushed outside. There was a wild, carnival atmosphere, and sparks from fireworks flew everywhere.

"Victory! We've won!" roared the crowd. People took whatever was at hand—hats, towels, coats, teapots, chairs, melon seeds, candies, or cigarettes—and tossed them high in the air.

"The war is over!" Dieyi whispered exultantly in Xiaolou's ear.

"Maybe. But the show must go on."

The crowd cheered and the show went on.

Juxian stood watching from the wings, tears rolling down her cheeks. An eight-year-old boy from the opera school clung to her side.

The performance ended, and they added up the day's receipts, distributing the money among the children.

It was drizzling lightly outside the theater. Tattered pieces of paper from burst firecrackers had bled into the runoff, which formed red meandering streams and puddles that looked like intermingled blood and tears.

Juxian held a blue cloth sack filled with silver coins while the former pupils lined up patiently, each awaiting his share. The oldest among them were all of fourteen; the youngest ones were eight years old. One by one they came forward to Xiaolou, who gave them an admonition along with their share of the money.

"The school is closing, and you are going your separate ways. Be decent and good men." He handed each one two silver coins, and they thanked him; but he knew the money wouldn't last them very long. For a moment, he couldn't think of anything else to say.

"Be honest and work hard," he added.

The children stepped into the street. Mist obscured the road, but the sky overhead was clean and fresh, washed by the rain. The boys felt as though they had been cut adrift, and they missed Master Guan. If he had still been there, he would have protected them, giving shade like a giant tree; now they were on their own.

Where were they going to go? One of them began to cry, and two others hugged each other and started to weep.

They would probably never see each other again.

Dieyi opened up a large oil-paper umbrella with a frame of black bamboo. He held it over Xiaolou's head, and it sheltered both of them from the rain, which made a muffled patter on the oil paper. Xiaolou was back, and Dieyi deferred to him as the elder, just as he always had. Any ill feeling had been forgotten, like a bad dream.

Juxian stood holding the cloth sack, now emptied of its contents, and put a hand on her belly. She felt content when she touched the small bulge there.

"We're just like family," Dieyi said, smiling smugly at Juxian. "It wasn't easy, but we survived the war, and we're still together."

"Yes, we are like a family," she replied. "By the way, when our child is born, what should he call you?" She pressed close to her husband and asked silkily, "What do you think? Should he call Dieyi 'Uncle'? Or should he call him 'Godfather'?"

Xiaolou thought for a moment.

"I think he should call him 'Godfather.' My friend here has wanted to raise a child ever since we were children ourselves."

"Is that so?" She nodded triumphantly. "Then he'll have a family of his own someday, and lots of children, I'm sure! But then again," she laughed, "you are so very accomplished. Perhaps you're not interested in such commonplaces."

The Japanese emperor announced his nation's surrender in a radio broadcast. The war was really over, and the Japanese troops withdrew. The year was 1945.

A pair of matched verses hung over the archway to the

theater. The words were caked with dust and soot from artillery fire.

> Rank and wealth, all spent for nought,
> Insignia of jade, and black caps of office,
> In a blink a millennium's labors are lost.
>
> Union and parting, sorrow and joy, all are but dreams,
> The hero and his lady, the handsome and the fair,
> In an instant a century has passed.

The manager stood off to the side while his workers took down the Japanese flag that had flown over the arch and threw it to the ground. They replaced it with the Nationalist Chinese flag, a white sun on a field of blue. The red rising sun of Japan lay abandoned in the mud, to be trampled by anyone who passed by—soldiers, wounded veterans, and barefoot and filthy beggars.

In the uncertain economic climate that followed the Japanese surrender, business fell into a slump. Economic recovery was a long way away, and there was civil unrest. Students held strikes and lit bonfires in protest.

For a time, the Nationalists held sway, and Nationalist soldiers did as they pleased, eating and drinking wherever they chose without paying. Inflation was so serious that a box of matches cost tens of thousands of yuan. Unable to fill their theaters to capacity, most owners disbanded their opera companies and turned the theaters into dance halls. Soon after that, costumes began appearing in the windows of pawnshops. There were exquisite phoenix headdresses and fancy embroidered skirts of silk gauze, all of them for sale.

No matter how much difficulty he was in, Dieyi would

not pawn his costumes. He would rather have gone hungry. He loved the opera with a passion few outsiders could have understood.

Unable to leave Peking, he performed whenever he could. The theaters that remained open were always quite full, but most of the patrons didn't have tickets. Slogans hung on either side of the stage, next to the Nationalist flag:

"SALUTE THE NATIONALIST ARMY!"

"WELCOME OUR TROOPS BACK TO PEKING!"

"GREETINGS TO OUR SOLDIERS!"

A handful of hoodlums and demobilized soldiers straggled into the theater. With nowhere else to go, men like these had to sleep outside bathhouses or small restaurants. Sometimes they banded together and forced their way into small theaters without paying. They weren't there to watch the show, however; they were simply looking for a place to rest their feet and let off a little steam. Sprawled aggressively across the benches, they alarmed the more timid patrons, who left as fast as their feet would carry them.

Dieyi was singing a sweet, sad aria from *Farewell to My Concubine*. An old soldier started to weep in a corner of the theater. He had lost one of his legs and was tapping the ground with his cane.

Suddenly the blinding beam of a flashlight shone in Dieyi's eyes, causing him briefly to lose his balance.

"Stop singing and fight! Fight to the death!" the soldier wailed miserably.

All at once, the theater was thrown into an uproar.

"What's wrong with Yu Ji?" a one-eyed man howled. "Is she on the rag?"

Raucous laughter followed this remark, and Xiaolou

stopped singing to come to Dieyi's defense. Although his fists were clenched, he bowed politely to the old soldier.

"Gentlemen, this theater does not permit flashlights. Please return to your seats and watch the show—"

An ear-splitting shriek silenced him.

"I fought in the resistance for eight years! If it hadn't been for me, you and your ilk wouldn't be prancing around up there and singing. You're a bunch of spoiled brats! You would never have made it without us!"

Others joined the chorus.

"While we suffered at the front lines, you stayed behind and enjoyed yourselves. Have any of you third-rate street singers ever shouldered a gun? How many Japs have you killed? Have you ever bled for your country?"

Somebody threw a flashlight at Xiaolou, and it struck him squarely. Angered, he kicked over a small table and hurled it at the old veteran. It landed with a loud crash that whipped the crowd into a fury. As Xiaolou fought his way down from the stage, Dieyi rushed to defend him, but he was not equal to the task and took several blows to the chest. Someone brought a board crashing down on his head, and he staggered and almost lost consciousness. He was bleeding. Xiaolou seized the culprit by the hair and butted his head with his own. He was Xiang Yu, the general of ancient times, taking on a ragtag band of modern soldiers in a final battle. But he was outnumbered, and his enemy was armed with benches and canes. Juxian watched from the side, but when she saw a blow aimed at his back, she rushed in to protect him and took the blow for him. In the melee she was struck again, and again. The third blow struck her full in the belly, and she collapsed to the floor in agony.

"Juxian!" Xiaolou cried.

Blood was seeping out from between her legs. She felt as though a knife were being twisted inside her, tearing out her heart. She writhed in pain, but any motion only made the blood flow faster.

Xiaolou went berserk, attacking wildly.

"My child!" he shrieked. "Juxian! My child!"

"Someone's been killed! Let's get out of here!" shouted one of the troublemakers. Fearing the police, the mob fled.

Dieyi covered his bleeding temple. He hadn't been able to sacrifice anything for Xiaolou, and he desperately wished it were he lying bleeding on the ground. Dieyi's pain was in his heart, and while he felt pity for Juxian, it was for Xiaolou he truly ached. He had been the cause of his friend's misfortune; because of him Juxian had lost Xiaolou's child.

There would be no child to draw Xiaolou and Juxian closer together, no child to come between Xiaolou and himself, Dieyi thought. Another thorn had been plucked from his side. It was divine retribution, yet he still felt somewhat disappointed. She had been punished now, but she wouldn't be punished anymore.

While his bleeding had slowed, there was blood covering a corner of his eye. His satisfaction—at knowing that Juxian was suffering more than he—was blunted by the fact that Juxian's suffering hurt Xiaolou as well. For Juxian was the person Xiaolou cared for most in the world. Dieyi buried his head in his hands.

The police arrived and waded through the mob, crunching shattered glass underfoot. They made an arrest, on a charge of treason. The detainee was Dieyi. Cheng Dieyi, the actor who had sold his services to the Japanese, was being accused of treason. The last thing Juxian saw before she lapsed into unconsciousness was Dieyi being dragged away.

After her miscarriage, Juxian lay unconscious for a day and a night.

She awakened to find Xiaolou sitting beside her sickbed. He could barely keep his eyes open, and bruises and scratches covered his body, but he had been fighting all of his life. His deepest wound was the loss of his child, but he was also suffering because his childhood friend, who was like a brother to him, had been arrested as a traitor. Those accused of treason always got the worst treatment from the authorities; and the more departments they were examined by, the worse it was for them. Because they were the most despised of prisoners, it took only one misstep, one imagined insult, to send the accused to the firing squad. Xiaolou was brooding over this when Juxian awakened.

Her face was pallid, and she looked emaciated. The loss of the baby had greatly diminished her. Only days before, she had been two people. Now, once again, she was only one. She awoke with a start and called to Xiaolou.

He put his arms around her. Though he held her tight, his mind was still preoccupied with rescuing Dieyi. When he told Juxian of his plans, she was furious.

"If that's how you feel, Xiaolou, then go ask that fake Yu Ji to bear you a child!"

"I have to help him. He's as good as dead unless I can intercede. Traitor, indeed! I have to save his life!"

"Dieyi did the things he's accused of, Xiaolou. He'll have to be punished, but I'm sure they'll let him out after he's served his term. There's really nothing you can do—you know how the authorities are."

"He hasn't killed anyone," she persisted. "There's no blood on his hands. I'm sure the authorities will be easy on him. What could you possibly do to help?"

"Dieyi sang for the Japanese all for my sake. And now he's being accused of collaborating with the enemy. It's ridiculous!"

She thought back to Xiaolou's release from prison and remembered the deal she'd made with Dieyi. She had gone back on her word. She had felt Dieyi's jealous eyes boring into her back like daggers as she led her husband to the ricksha that waited at the mouth of the woods. They had turned their backs on him, both of them. Perhaps now was the time to make it up to him. She might be safe if their accounts were settled.

"Let's go plead for him," she said, tugging on Xiaolou's hand. "If we can get him out of this trouble, then we won't be beholden to him for anything anymore." She tried to sit up. "Let me take the sword—"

Dieyi stood in the defendant's box. He faced his interrogators haughtily. He felt it was not a crime to sing Peking opera for a group of Japanese people at a private party. His only crime was his passion for Peking opera.

"Nobody forced me," he said stubbornly. "I did it of my own free will. I love the opera; and I'll sing for anyone who appreciates it. Art does not recognize the limits of nationality, and Marshal Aoki is a connoisseur. For all we know, a man like him might spread the art of Peking opera to the distant shores of his country."

Unrepentant and unremorseful, Dieyi was headed straight for the executioner's gun.

Juxian dressed up and put on makeup, rouging her cheeks and painting her lips bright red. It was like going on the road with a theater troupe. Summoning back her wiles, she made ready to play the part of the coquette, of the ingenue. She would lead her man along, waiting until the time was ripe before asking for her favor.

Her plan was to arrive at Yuan Siye's house with Xiaolou at her side and the sword in her arms. The sight of the sword would bring back pleasant memories to their host, who would then be favorably inclined to accept the sword as collateral against a loan of enough money to bribe Dieyi's jailers. She also hoped that by getting rid of the sword, she would deprive Xiaolou of one more reminder of Dieyi.

Yuan Siye received them condescendingly. Although Juxian looked exquisite, having lost none of the charm or beauty that had made her a great courtesan, Yuan reserved his attention for Xiaolou. He chastised the younger man for his ingratitude, but Xiaolou held his tongue, enduring the humiliation in the hopes of saving his friend.

In the end, their efforts were wasted. In the midst of his trial, Dieyi had been escorted from the courtroom. Nobody knew where he had been taken, and he hadn't been released, although he had been pardoned. People became suspicious, and there was speculation that he had been working with the Nationalists all along.

In fact, the soldiers had escorted him to another private party, this time for a senior officer in the Nationalist Military

High Command. As a welcoming tribute on the official's visit to Peking, the local authorities had decided to present him with the "gift" of a special performance by a famous Peking opera star. The letter of the law was meaningless. Dieyi had been saved.

The evening's highlight was *Wandering in the Garden, Waking from a Dream*. He was singing an aria:

"The flowers of spring should be blooming here, crimson and violet,
But in their place are ruined wells and broken walls.
When will a fair day dawn again?
Whose family will know joy?
In the morning birds fly away,
Evenings they fold their wings.
I watch the sunset clouds from a painted balcony.
Thin filaments of rain blow down on gusts of wind.
Waves rock the painted boats out on the lake.
Nature seems a pale imitation of the landscape painted on the screen."

The century-old lyrics still had meaning. They told of the rise and fall of a dynasty, and yet they could have been describing the fortunes of the Nationalist government. China was locked in a civil war.

Juxian convalesced slowly and spent her days in bed, seemingly unable to regain her strength. Her poor health gave her a kind of power over Xiaolou, and it was hard to tell how much of her weakness was feigned and how much was real.

Dieyi no longer spoke of the past, preferring to try to get along with them, at least for the time being. He had come to visit and was watching Xiaolou spoon-feed a tonic to his wife. Xiaolou's face was covered in stubble, and his brows were creased with concern.

Dieyi had mixed feelings as he handed a sack bulging with paper money to Xiao Si. The money was for Juxian's herbal medicine, which Dieyi was having his servant buy as a gesture of forgiveness.

"Don't dwell on it," he said compassionately to Juxian. "If your child had been born into this unhappy world, he would have had a miserable life. Now, get some rest. If you don't take better care of yourself," he added, "you'll never recover. You could easily get tuberculosis. And then where would you be?"

Juxian smiled tightly.

"Someday, I'd like to give Xiaolou a nice fat little baby girl. That's what we women are here for!"

"Who said you weren't?" Dieyi snapped.

"Your medicine isn't warm anymore," Xiaolou put in. "Do you want it or not?"

"Being waited on hand and foot by the famous actor, Duan Xiaolou, is such a treat. I'm not sure I'm deserving. It's like patching a homespun shirt with silk brocade."

"You're right about one thing—I'm completely attached to you. Just try getting rid of me!" he teased her.

Aware that he was the odd man out, Dieyi was becoming acutely uncomfortable. Fortunately for him, Xiao Si returned from the herbalist's shop just then. But he still had the same net bag full of money that he'd left with.

"Did you buy the medicine?" Dieyi asked.

Xiao Si flung the bag aside.

"The manager at the pharmacy said that this would have

been enough money at yesterday's rate. But it's not enough today."

Xiaolou turned the sack upside down, and loose bills fluttered in the air.

"Damn government money! It's not even good enough to wipe your ass with. People always want the government to fix things for them; but whenever it does get involved, everything goes to hell!"

Xiao Si had to bear the brunt of Xiaolou's anger, but he was used to it. An orphan taken into Master Guan's care, he had first endured the Master's harsh discipline before becoming Dieyi's personal servant and the company's errand boy. Xiao Si stayed by Dieyi day and night, serving him devotedly. He would have done anything to please him. Although he was bright, Xiao Si became a scapegoat—nobody had ever treated him any differently. He didn't expect to be nurtured or cherished. Even his beloved Dieyi had spoken unkindly and told him, "You'll never make an actor!"

As he stood listening to Xiaolou's tirade, most of it directed against himself, Xiao Si's eyes swept over the all but useless bills that littered the floor. It was all he could do to stop himself from simply walking out then and there. But where could he go? It was even worse outside. Despite the daily abuse he had to endure, he at least had clothes on his back and a full belly. Pride was a luxury he could not afford.

He scanned Xiaolou's front room for anything of value that they might be able to pawn. There was nothing.

Then he spotted the sword hanging on the wall. Following his gaze, the others saw it, too. It ought to be worth something. Juxian and Dieyi both looked at Xiaolou.

"We can't sell that!" Xiaolou said emphatically.

Dieyi sighed with relief, but Juxian's eyes flashed angrily. She wanted nothing more than to cast that old relic into the depths of hell. Xiaolou was heading out the door, muttering under his breath.

"I'll go have a talk with that damn pharmacist. He's supposed to help save people's lives. How can he be so heartless?"

Dieyi was at his heels.

"Xiaolou, I have some extra cash."

"Xiaolou! Come back soon," Juxian called after them, with more than a trace of desperation. "Please stay out of trouble."

With the economy in a shambles and inflation spiraling out of control, lawlessness and civil unrest were on the rise. If you walked down the street with anything to eat, a hungry beggar might snatch it from you. Carrying a quantity of money was even riskier.

The Good Fortune Theater had long since been turned into a dance hall, but nobody had time to go dancing anymore. People spent their days standing in long lines, waiting for essentials like grain or cooking oil. There was a lot of jostling and shouting as people pressed forward with fearful faces.

"Give me a pound! I'll pay twenty thousand!"

"I've been waiting all day!"

"Do you take silver coins?"

One by one, the shopkeepers closed their doors. They couldn't afford to restock their shelves because of the inflation.

Somebody was trying to trade a whole trunkful of paper

money for only two silver coins. But nobody trusted paper money anymore.

An old man, faint with hunger, moaned feebly. None of the passersby noticed when he fell silent and stopped breathing.

In the distance, a bonfire was burning. Students were demonstrating again.

"We want democracy, not dictatorship!" they chanted.

"Stop the civil war!"

"Stop hunger!"

"Don't kill your countrymen!"

The Nationalist gendarmes set up fire hoses and began to spray the marchers. Hopelessly overpowered, the band of students scattered. But they were the lucky ones. Any Communists who were arrested by the Nationalists would be paraded around in public and then led to the execution ground. Sometimes they would be beheaded; sometimes they were killed with a single gunshot to the head.

Dieyi and Xiaolou found themselves in the midst of the crowd of fleeing students. Water from the fire hoses rained down on them. Dieyi had hidden himself away for so long that he was unprepared for such chaos, and he ran, pulling Xiaolou after him. They didn't feel safe until they had run down another street and turned the corner onto a quiet road. Their clothes were sopping wet.

On one corner was a tobacco stand with all its wares laid out in the open air. Squatting next to the stall like an exhausted old silkworm was an old man with silver hair. He seemed as dead to the world as a caterpillar inside its cocoon. Xiaolou handed him a stack of wet bills for a box of matches.

Dieyi peered down at the old man and gave a start. It was old Master Ni.

"Sir? Do you remember us, sir?" he asked tentatively.

Master Ni raised his clouded eyes and squinted at the two men. One of them had once been the young Yu Ji he had held on his lap and fondled.

He shook his head vigorously and lowered his eyes.

"We were little children when we sang at the party at your mansion. We sang *Farewell to My Concubine.*"

"I've never seen either of you in my entire life! And I've never put on parties, either!" he said, as he handed Xiaolou the box of matches with shaking hands.

Just then, a few routed students came running their way. They knocked over the tobacco stand, scattering cigarettes and matches everywhere. Old Ni dropped to his knees and started to gather up his wares, muttering to himself.

"The Manchu people ruled China for three hundred years before they were vanquished. But it's taken only thirty years for the Nationalists to be ruined. Now the Communists are coming. I say let them! Are you Communists?"

Neither Dieyi nor Xiaolou responded. They walked away slowly and continued in silence for a while.

At last, Dieyi looked up and saw a kite sailing in the sky overhead. It was shaped like a centipede, each leg several yards long. With its body and legs undulating in the breeze, the centipede looked down on them, seemingly carefree. Dieyi remembered that day long ago, when he and Xiaolou and all of their classmates had posed for their class picture.

"Brother," Xiaolou asked nervously, breaking Dieyi's reverie. "What the hell is communism, anyway? They say the people will share their fields, share their labor, and share their produce. Will we also have to share our wives?"

Dieyi glanced at him without answering. When he looked up at the sky again, the kite was gone.

"How could it have vanished without a trace?"

"What?"

"Nothing. Let them come!" he whispered to himself. "The Communists will want to see operas, too, won't they?"

The war against Japan had ended, only to be replaced by a bloody civil war that raged all over China. Ordinary people went about their business as best they could, concerned only with putting food on their tables. What did they care who ruled? They simply stayed close to home and minded their own business; but actors grew stale if they stayed in one place for too long. Even a star as great as Mei Lanfang had to tour with his hits. Dieyi and Xiaolou couldn't stay in Peking indefinitely, and they were forced to go on tour again. Unlike former times, they had to keep ticket prices low, despite their fame. Otherwise nobody could have afforded to see them. With fighting breaking out everywhere, travel was limited, and they planned only to play a few large cities. First, they went to Shenyang, and then on to Changchun. They had only been there a day when the city was surrounded by the People's Liberation Army. Soon, Changchun was liberated; and then, piece by piece, the rest of China.

7

It was 1949, and theaters and opera houses all over Peking were thriving once more. The Tianle Theater at the Bridge of Heaven was festooned with gold-flecked scarlet banners announcing the program in bold black characters: "FAREWELL TO MY CONCUBINE." A barker outside the box office called to passersby.

"Come on in! See Peking's two greatest pre-liberation opera stars in Peking performing their most famous opera! Buy your tickets now—they're going fast!"

Tickets were only ten cents in the new currency of the People's Republic of China.

The Party held opera performers in high esteem. Special performances were held all over town, in honor of the soldiers of the People's Liberation Army. Little red flags waved from every building, balcony, and awning, turning Peking into a sea of scarlet.

Even in the New China, people still liked to watch the old operas. They flocked to see General Xiang Yi sigh in defeat as the lady Yu Ji committed suicide. At that moment of catharsis, right before the curtain fell, the drums and gongs of the orchestra grew loud and frenzied. Yu Ji collapsed to the floor, and the general cried out in grief. But unlike former times, the audience was discouraged from cheering and shouting "Bravo!" Instead, they were supposed to applaud politely. They did this with enthusiasm, but the even rhythm and clear beats lacked spontaneity, as though the audience were being conducted by some invisible hand.

Dieyi looked out on the house. It was filled to capacity with PLA soldiers, cadres, and Party secretaries. They all wore uniforms of olive with red patches, a color combination that was at once monotonous and jarring. Dieyi missed the days before liberation and the elemental din of unreserved cheering. He longed for the chaotic warmth of the past.

The government launched the movement for Suppression of Counterrevolutionaries, and executions took place daily. Meanwhile, the opera flourished. Theaters were nationalized, and Dieyi and Xiaolou started to receive lavish monthly salaries of five hundred yuan. Their lives had become serene and dreamlike. The Communist Party had promised everyone a "new life," and the two actors soon found themselves promoted to performers of the first rank. They had faith in the Party.

When he heard of their new status, Xiaolou was incredulous.

"Are you sure? Do you think we'll be able to live decently, at last?"

"I sure hope so. I haven't been able to set aside any money in ages."

"Our salaries are relatively low, I think. I heard the highest-paid singer is Ma Lianliang."

"How much does he get?"

"One thousand seven hundred."

"That much?"

"Yes. Even Chairman Mao doesn't get that much," said Xiaolou, duly impressed.

"My salary is plenty for me."

"Well, I have a wife to support, and I have to think about the future."

Dieyi felt slightly irritated at him. Xiaolou had become so steady and dependable, so ordinary. What was he worried about? At thirty he already had the gravity of the patron saints, Dieyi thought. It a shame that his protective benevolence was directed at someone else. Love was like gambling—if one stayed at it long enough, one was bound to lose eventually. Life was like bean flour, he thought ruefully—faintly sweet, and of an ambiguous but warm color.

Radical changes were taking place in the world around them. As the theaters became the stage for revolutionary activities, the stages themselves had to be taken out to make room. The new program was heralded on bright red banners as before, but now it read: "MEETING TO PRONOUNCE JUDGMENT ON THE OLD TYRANTS OF THE PEKING OPERA, IN CON-

JUNCTION WITH THE MOVEMENT FOR SUPPRESSION OF COUN-
TERREVOLUTIONARIES."

More than a half-dozen people were assembled on stage,
arms bound behind their backs, and torsos wound with elaborate knots. Cardboard signs on poles were attached to their
backs. These were the targets of the movement. At the center
of this group was Yuan Siye.

Cheng Dieyi and Duan Xiaolou were sitting in the
audience for a change, in the front row. The chairman of the
meeting was addressing the hall.

"These counterrevolutionary elements, Yuan Shiqing,
Ding Heng, Zhang Shaodong, and their ilk, all held high
positions, with three counterrevolutionary governments. Yuan is especially guilty. He served under the former warlord of
North China, collaborated with the Japanese, and was a
lackey of the Nationalists. The accused consistently used
every cruel and evil means that the Old Society put at his
disposal to swindle, exploit, and blackmail those who toiled
in the theater to make their living. His guilt is incontrovertible."

Dieyi felt his face flush. He stole a furtive look at the
man who knelt silently, head bowed. Yuan had been the first
man he'd been with. With his broad shoulders and piercing
black eyes, he had once radiated vigor. Now, his hair was
unkempt and his face dirty. He had clearly been beaten sav-
agely, for half of his face was swollen, and he was drooling
uncontrollably from one corner of his torn mouth. Dieyi had
trouble imagining that this puffy-eyed, broken man was the
same one who had taken him not so many years before, in a
room the color of his bruises. Imprisonment had aged him
quickly.

The leader was reading out the verdict.

"In the name of the Bureau of Public Security and the Military Control Committee of Peking, we hereby sentence the criminal to death. The sentence shall be carried out immediately."

The sentence came as no surprise to Dieyi, but he blanched. Just then an enthusiastic young man crossed to the center of the stage and began shouting slogans. It was Xiao Si. He stood in the limelight, all eyes upon him. His time had come, and he was riding the wave of progress into the new era.

"Uphold the campaign to put down counterrevolutionary bosses in the theater!" he exhorted the crowd and everyone shouted after him. "Down with reactionaries! The people have risen up! The downtrodden have become the masters!"

The people in the crowd all waved their arms excitedly.

Xiaolou watched the spectacle with a surprised expression, and a brief look of understanding passed between him and Dieyi. Yuan Siye still knelt abjectly on the stage, a once rich and powerful man brought low, while the newly elevated Xiao Si strutted about before him. The Party had the power to change anything. It had the power of life and death.

Yuan Siye was escorted from the stage under a barrage of angry shouting. Dieyi lowered his eyes as he passed by, not daring to look at him. He was just one of the many "enemies of the people" doomed to be annihilated, along with landlords, members of wealthy families, patrons of the arts, and rightists.

Dieyi's head was swimming when he looked back at the stage. What strange sort of show was this? And why had he given up the starring role to Xiao Si, who was such a poor actor? He began to wonder what the Party had in store for him.

One of the Party's first goals was mass literacy, and Xiaolou and Dieyi dutifully donned Mao suits and attended classes. Workers, peasants, soldiers, and members of the lumpen proletariat who had risen from the streets to become actors were all beneficiaries of the Party's literacy program, which included classes in history and culture.

Dieyi's and Xiaolou's teacher was a young woman who wore a Lenin jacket. She had just written the character for "love" on the blackboard.

"What is love?" she asked her pupils.

"To be nice to people," answered an old woman.

"I've never loved anyone," said an old army general. "I don't really know what the word means. Besides, I always get this character mixed up with the character for 'endure,' because they look so much alike."

She turned to Dieyi.

"I don't know either," he mumbled. "Love and 'endure' look the same to me, too."

The teacher burst out laughing.

"How can 'love' and 'endure' be the same? 'Endure' means to suffer hardship. In the Old Society, before liberation, all anybody could do was endure. But now the People have risen up, and 'love' is everywhere."

"Endure" looked like "love" without any heart, without any feeling, Dieyi thought to himself. The teacher was still babbling on about different kinds of love. There was the love between parents and children, brothers and sisters, close friends, and men and women; but none of these could compare with the love of the Party and Chairman Mao for the people of China.

Having finished her lecture on love, the teacher wrote another character on the blackboard: "Loyalty."

"This is 'Loyalty'," she explained. " 'Loyalty' means an unwavering devotion to a person or a cause. Loyalty cannot be distracted by any hardship, no matter how extreme. This is what we mean when we talk about your loyalty to Chairman Mao and the Central Committee of the Communist Party. Another kind of loyalty is your devotion to improving your minds by studying hard."

As he sat busily copying the character, Dieyi's mind was on loyalty, but not in the sense the teacher meant. He was thinking back to his struggle to break his addiction to opium.

During the Japanese occupation, Dieyi had become addicted to the drug. Although he had wanted to quit, he was afraid to go to the clinics for addicts, as these were operated by the Japanese. It was common knowledge that those who went to the clinics to be cured came out with an even more serious addiction than before. After liberation, Dieyi renewed his efforts to fight his dependence.

He remembered how hot it had been that first summer after liberation. Peking was as blisteringly hot as a steel factory, and everyone in town spent as much time as possible out of doors to escape their furnacelike rooms. But Dieyi lay shivering under his quilt, feeling as though his bones were being broken apart, never to be fitted together again. It had been five days since his last pipeful of opium.

The first few days had been the worst. At times the urge for the drug became so powerful that all he could do was writhe on the ground like a madman, shouting himself hoarse. Xiaolou had locked the door to his room from the outside. Although he scratched at the door, bit at the rug, tore his hair, and broke every mirror in the room, still the door did not open. He had never known such suffering in his life, and it showed in his sunken eyes, pale face, and shrunken body. Hearing his anguished, almost inhuman moans, Xiaolou had to harden his heart and leave him to his suffering.

There was no other way to cure him, and he nearly gave up several times.

"If I don't make it," he whimpered to Juxian one day, "please try to remember what was good about me."

Moved by his misery, Juxian held him until he became calm.

"Don't be silly," she admonished him. "You're going to be fine!"

He looked up at the face of the woman leaning over him and saw his mother, a vague shadow in his delirium.

"Mother!" he called out, embracing Juxian suddenly. "I want to die!"

"You're going to be fine," Juxian repeated gently.

At other times, her jealousy got the better of her. Xiaolou walked in one day to find her standing outside Dieyi's door with a basin of water.

"Why haven't you taken that in yet?" he demanded.

"I was just waiting for him to calm down. Otherwise he'll just get angry with me."

Xiaolou took the basin away from his wife and went in himself to tend to his friend. Lifting him up, he helped him off with his jacket, and mopped the sweat from his body with a towel.

"It's very difficult at first, but you're already over the

worst," he said soothingly. "Once you've overcome your addiction, you'll be a new man."

"I have been waiting for you to force me to quit." He smiled ruefully.

Dieyi felt that he and Xiaolou were fighting his addiction together, in a shared struggle that brought them closer. There were times when Dieyi wondered if he hadn't started smoking just to arouse his friend's sympathy.

The pain of withdrawal was more than offset by Dieyi's joy at being close to Xiaolou once more. Xiaolou was patient and firm, and he looked after Dieyi devotedly. That was what "loyalty" meant to Dieyi.

Accustomed to seeing Xiaolou in heavy makeup, Dieyi was surprised one day to see how coarse his friend's skin was.

"The skin on your face is so rough," he remarked.

"Is it?" Xiaolou said absently. "Every day I have to put on layers and layers of heavy makeup. And then I have to wipe it all off afterward with coarse tissues. Even though they're dipped in vaseline—"

"With that kind of treatment," Juxian called sweetly from the doorway, "even the most delicate skin will end up looking like an orange peel." As she spoke, she set a lunch box down by Dieyi's bed and started to lift out the trays. "It wasn't that way before. But now it has become so rough the palms of my hands are going to be sanded right off!" she joked.

"That's not the point," Dieyi replied, short of breath. "Xiaolou's skin was always coarse. He even had mange on his scalp when he was a boy. You didn't know that, did you?"

Juxian looked surprised, and Xiaolou shot Dieyi a quizzical look.

"You always bring up the most embarrassing things—things I'd rather forget."

"Back then," Dieyi rambled on, "he fought with the other boys at the school. He protected me and taught them not to pick on me. But once he fell onto some sharp rocks and cut his forehead open. He still has a scar above his brow." He regarded the other two meaningfully. "That's the kind of thing that stays with you for life."

Juxian touched the mark on Xiaolou's temple and laughed.

"How heroic!" She turned to Dieyi. "I would never have known if you hadn't told me."

"There are many things you don't know about him. You haven't known him very long, really. There is probably a great deal he hasn't got around to telling you. Who knows what's going on inside his head?"

Juxian felt pushed to the limits of her patience. When was Dieyi going to give up? The past few days had been especially trying—her husband and Dieyi had been practically inseparable. She was tired of pretending to like Dieyi for Xiaolou's sake. Expressionlessly, she began to serve lunch.

"Dieyi," she said. "These lotus seeds are good for purifying the blood. I made you some congee with lotus seeds and fancy salted vegetables from Liubi Delicatessen. Here, try some."

"What's this?" Xiaolou asked her, looking down at the dish.

"It's dried fruit. I bought it for Dieyi." Her voice was silky. "Sweets for the sweet! These are from—"

Xiaolou reached out to take a piece of fruit, and she slapped his wrist.

"Hands off, you naughty boy!" she said, laughing. "Don't touch those with your filthy paws! Here, open wide!"

Dieyi watched helplessly. She hadn't bought the dried fruit for him at all, he thought jealously. She'd intended to share these delicacies with her husband all along. He couldn't listen to any more of their banter. Xiaolou was chewing dispiritedly on a piece of dried apricot when he noticed a pile of dirty clothes and mattress pads that had been heaped in the corner.

"Maybe you could wash those," he said apologetically to Juxian.

When she didn't answer, Xiaolou started singing operatically.

"If I might trouble my virtuous wife—"

"Since you're asking so nicely, I suppose I will." She flashed a triumphant smile at Dieyi and picked up the laundry basin.

"I'm having my period, Xiaolou, and I'm feeling a bit tired. Do you think you could carry the laundry out for me?"

Left alone, Dieyi sipped his lotus-seed porridge and let his eyes run back and forth over a large blue vase. It was a good piece. The glaze had fine hairline cracks running through it—the type that develop on their own and are not the result of the vase being struck. He noticed that the clock in the room had stopped, but he had long since quit caring about the time.

After recovering his health, Dieyi returned to the stage with Xiaolou, this time at the Middle Harmony Theater on Qian-men Avenue. It was right after liberation, and people were still filled with an intoxicating optimism.

Performances of Peking opera had been supplemented with Yangge folk musicals, at the behest of the "comrades" at the Bureau of Culture.

Stepping backstage for the first time, Dieyi and Xiaolou were greeted by a crop of new faces. Xiao Si was among them. He seemed to be thriving in the New Society. All of these young actors and actresses were about twenty years old and were dressed in the same gray uniforms and cloth shoes. Seeing the famous actors walk in, one of them came up and greeted the pair.

"We're all from liberated areas. None of us has had any formal training; but, as Chairman Mao says: 'Don't pretend. Admit what you don't know.'"

"We're here to be close to the working people," added their leader. "We're here to serve the people, and to entertain them. We're here to learn from you comrades, too."

"You flatter us!" Dieyi replied.

"You have both training and experience," the leader countered.

Xiao Si stepped forward officiously.

"In the Old Society," he put in, "these two held themselves aloof from the common people. Singing stars can't help being arrogant."

Despite this interruption, everyone shook hands and exchanged flattering compliments.

"We are united to serve the same goal," the group leader was saying. "Our job is to serve the People by spreading propaganda for the Party. Let's learn as much as we can from each other."

Their novel props and costumes gave the Yangge operas brief popularity. The Yangge troupe performed plays like *The*

Married Couple Learns to Read, Hatred for the Oppressors, and *Brother and Sister Pioneers.* The performances were crude but lively, with lots of singing and dancing. In *Brother and Sister Pioneers,* for instance, a young man and woman dressed as peasants competed with each other to see who could work harder. They sang a duet:

"Brother is walking swiftly ahead."

"Sister is rushing to keep up."

Then the chorus came in:

"Learn from the heroes of production!
Learn from the heroes of production!
Speed up production, and work very hard!"

"What on earth are they doing?" Xiaolou whispered to Dieyi as they watched this performance. "There's no emotion, and no moral, either!"

"You're right. And the lyrics are just awful!"

"It's a good thing we're only supposed to exchange views and not trade places. I couldn't possibly writhe around the way they do. Look at the contortions they're going through—all that effort just to pretend to be planting crops. It makes about as much sense as a two-legged chair!"

"Aren't they 'serving the people'?"

"No, they're just an appetizer! Once they've warmed up the audience, we'll give them what they're really hungry for."

"You'd better be quiet! Here comes a comrade."

What one said and did in public was very different from what one said or did in private. Dieyi enjoyed this sense of having shared secrets with Xiaolou. They were intimate friends, who could confide their dissatisfactions to one another without fear of betrayal. Not only would a true friend never betray you, he would even accept punishment in your place, Dieyi thought as he gazed fondly at Xiaolou.

Dieyi's makeup for that night's performance was too heavy, and it made him look cheap, like a harlot. With society decaying from the inside out, it was all one could do to put an a false face. Xiaolou was the only real person in his life—the most important man in his life, and the only thing that kept him afloat.

The two friends retired to Xiaolou's house after the show. Xiaolou pulled up a chair and sat down with Dieyi. He had a lot on his mind.

"Juxian, pour us some tea. Serving the People is thirsty work."

Juxian snorted derisively.

"I spent my entire day with a group of women, taking care of other people's children and cleaning up after other people's messes. I'm tired, too. We were *really* serving the People!"

"Who were you looking after?"

"Our worker and soldier comrades," she replied sarcastically.

"I thought they also served the People. They can't be the People."

"Well, who are the People?"

Dieyi began to recite a list of different types of people.

"We singers aren't the People. Women aren't the People. Workers and soldiers aren't the People. Nobody is the People, but everybody seems to be serving the People. Who are the People? Who's left?"

"Chairman Mao?"

Juxian clapped her hands over Xiaolou's mouth as fast as she could.

"Are you out of your mind? Are you trying to get yourself killed?"

Xiaolou broke away from her.

"I'm just having a quiet conversation in the privacy of my own home. What is there to be afraid of?"

But fear had become contagious, like a lingering flu nobody could shake. Politics was a matter of life and death, and people learned not to discuss certain subjects if they could help it. Even a silkworm sealed inside its cocoon would have been wary of uttering a sound. Despite its high-minded goals, the revolution was crude in its methods; but people had no choice but to go along with Party policy.

The opera performers found their spare hours filled with new activities like political study. Instead of practicing new songs and dialogue for new operas, now they met to recite quotations from Chairman Mao. Nonetheless, Peking opera performers fared relatively well. With their companies nationalized, they received high salaries. It was a time of transition, and the revolution had not really touched them yet.

One morning several workers took down the couplet that had framed the stage for over a century, and they replaced it with political slogans that read: "All the people of the nation unite! Smash the vicious forces of feudalism!"

Xiao Si was accompanying the opera company's Party secretary, Liu, on an inspection of the theater. The inspection included an inventory of the props and costumes left over from before liberation. As he made his rounds, Xiao Si ran into Dieyi and Xiaolou.

"Comrade Duan. Comrade Cheng."

"Comrade?" Dieyi was momentarily confused. He still wasn't used to this term, although he'd heard it many times already.

"We've all heard Secretary Liu's speech calling us to join in the effort to preserve valuable props and costumes for future generations. Many performers from the old days have already donated their things to the government. Some have even donated costumes that are two hundred years old."

When Dieyi didn't respond, Xiao Si smiled and continued.

"If you don't participate fully in this movement, people will question your dedication and sincerity. As I recall, your costumes were very beautiful and lavish. Many were embroidered with silver and gold thread."

Dieyi didn't like the idea of being forced to donate his costumes to the government. They were a part of him. How could he give them up?

That night, alone in his room, he opened up one of his trunks. Admiring the fine and costly garments, he ran his hands over them, stroking the fabrics. Suddenly something caught his eye. It was the corner of a torn piece of paper.

As he bent down to lift the costume carefully out of the trunk, the intense odor of camphor rose up to him. The scent seemed to burrow its way into his brain like a bunch of tiny serpents, making his head spin.

He picked up the paper and felt his face flush. The red dye of the paper had faded, but the black of the ink had not. Written on that piece of paper was Xiaolou's first signature. His characters were awkward but sincere, and they conveyed to Dieyi a kind of childish delight. The first time he had sung opera. The first time he had signed his own name. The years had passed so quickly.

Dieyi had kept that piece of paper for over a decade. The sight of it sent him into a reverie. The image of Xiaolou concentrating hard as he first learned to write came into his mind. He smiled sadly and wondered what he could have done to make Xiaolou love him.

He came to his senses abruptly and put the paper back into the trunk. Then he set about wrapping up his hair ornaments and putting them into small boxes. These he placed inside a square wooden casket of yellow pearwood, which he locked up before setting it into the large trunk that now held his entire collection of costumes and ornaments. At last, he closed the lid and locked it with a brass lock.

Thinking he'd found a safe hiding place, Dieyi pushed the trunk under his bed. It would be secure there, like his own Forbidden City. Even in the privacy of his room, he didn't feel entirely safe. Glancing furtively from left to right, he caught sight of himself in the mirror and saw his own hunted expression. In the dim light of the room, he had the sensation of having come face-to-face with a ghost. Fear and loneliness had aged him, and although he was barely past thirty, he looked like a man in his forties. His eyes filled with tears, but he dabbed at them gently with his fingertips before they could fall, much as one of the heroines he played on stage might have done. There was even something theatrical about the redness around his eyes, which resembled stage makeup more than anything else.

The honeymoon period with the new Communist government didn't last long, and soon Peking was engulfed by successive waves of political movements. There was no time for contemplation—the revolution was unending.

By the mid-1960s, ideologues were saying that art was decadent and corrupt, and that it only existed to manipulate people's feelings. If people were led astray by unsavory influences, production would be adversely affected; and material production was paramount in the New Society. Emotions were merely a kind of poison.

Peking opera was a tool of the ruling classes of the old China, the Party theorists said. It was populated by feudalistic characters like emperors, noblemen, generals, and officials, in addition to reactionary Confucian scholars and frivolously outmoded beauties. The opera was just a way to infect the People with the crippling disease of feudalistic ideology.

As a consequence of these ideas, the status of performers sank to a new low. At the prompting of leaders in the Central Committee of the Communist Party, opera houses became movie theaters, or stages for spoken dramas. A few theaters were shut down altogether, leaving the performers at loose ends.

The grassy meadow at Taoranting Park was soaked from an early morning drizzle, and the air echoed with singing. Dieyi was practicing his scales. The oppressive gray sky trapped his voice like a glass dome.

He felt depressed, for while he tried to keep in practice, he no longer had a place in the world. He had tried hard to be politically active, but he didn't fit into the New Society. He finished practicing and left the park, slowly walking back into town.

He came to an old, abandoned building. When he

pushed open the side door, his shadow fell inside a thin wedge of sunlight on the wooden floor. This neglected building, sepulchral in its quiet, was the theater in which he had first made a name for himself. Choking on the dust, he stepped cautiously forward, and the boards sighed beneath his feet. Placards still hung on the walls, the writing still legible, but the concepts outmoded. "PROSPERITY BECKONS," read one. Another extolled, "BEAUTY EVERLASTING," while two others proclaimed, "WONDROUS MUSIC HAUNTS THE SOUL," and "FAIR FLOWERS BLOSSOM IN THE GARDEN OF ART."

Cheng Dieyi was over forty. Like the middle-aged man that he was, he tucked his umbrella under his arm, put his hands behind his back, and slowly mounted the rickety stairs to the balcony seats. Standing in one of the boxes, he looked down on the stage and imagined he saw himself there as Yu Ji.

> The moon is at its loveliest,
> But the sad sounds of autumn fill the fields,
> Leaving me desolate and afraid.

The audience listened with rapt attention, devouring his image. But it was all transitory, a beautiful nightmare, and the audience was an audience of ghosts. Looking down on the whole scene were the portraits of the Thirteen Greats of the late Qing, those same faces that had watched him critically for more than thirty years. Each one was depicted in his most famous role—be it statesman, empress, warrior, or beauty. The original colors had long since faded, leaving one to imagine what they might have been. Only black outlines and deep red seals remained.

Dieyi lingered there a long time, until the spell was

broken by the sudden crackling of a loudspeaker.

"The Great Proletarian Cultural Revolution is a great revolution that shakes people's souls!" The words echoed: "shakes people's souls! . . . souls!"

Dieyi shivered, and the swallows that nested in the beams startled and took flight, as though their very nests were being threatened. Dieyi's umbrella clattered to the ground. Picking it up, he went outside again. It was only about three or four in the afternoon, but the sky was already growing dark.

As the Great Proletarian Cultural Revolution got under way, Dieyi saw his life altered beyond recognition. In the past, when times had been hard or the political situation was unstable, the opera company only played to full houses on holidays, like Chinese New Year, the Dragon Boat Festival, or the Moon Festival. The singers had been forced to look for odd jobs to supplement their incomes, pulling rickshas, working as day laborers, taking in embroidery, or helping out part time at small businesses. But in 1965, the Party found a new job for the old singers. That year, the model Peking opera was created as a means of spreading propaganda. Every aspect of these works was subordinated to this goal: the music and dance, the story, the costumes and sets, even the lighting. Everything was dictated by formula.

Cheng Dieyi and Duan Xiaolou were given roles in these model operas, but they weren't the starring roles. These were not tales of heroic scholar-gentlemen and fine ladies. The sole theme was class struggle, and the operas had names like *The Red Lantern, Taking Tiger Mountain by Strategy,* and *The Red Detachment of Women.* In place of rehearsals, the actors attended political study. Political texts replaced music and scripts, and the actors had to memorize their lines after they went home at night.

The lines proved difficult for Xiaolou to learn. He was trying to recite them for Juxian, but he kept stumbling.

"Tens of thousands of mar—mar—what was it?—martyrs—sacrificed their lives for the People. Oh, let us raise high their banners . . . tread on the soil stained with their blood—"

He stopped short and hit his forehead.

"Shit! I forgot again! Why can't I get this stuff into my head? I've spent most of my life memorizing things! What's wrong with me?"

"Remember what your teacher always said," Juxian said encouragingly. "Recitation is the foundation of good singing. Try it again."

I'll try it again, Xiaolou thought to himself. I'll just pretend I'm singing real opera, and I won't try to understand it. He began again:

"Let us raise high their banner,
And march forward over the soil stained with their
    blood!
Arming ourselves with Mao Zedong Thought,
We'll fight the evil winds and dark waves
With our unwavering spirit of struggle!
Erect a glorious model!"

He laughed out loud. It had worked. He had memorized one more section.

"Bravo, Xiaolou!" Juxian said fondly.

Xiaolou's pleasure was short-lived.

"What's the point of these revolutionary model operas? Dammit! There's no real passion, and no real moral, either. They're as dry as dust!"

"There you go again. Hush! You have to be more careful about what you say. Do you talk like this anywhere but home?"

"Not much."

"What kinds of things have you said?"

"Nothing. Just a little grumbling. You can't stop eating simply because you're afraid of choking."

"Who do you tell things to, Xiaolou?" she persisted.

"Xiao Si, and people like him. They're always asking me for my opinion. I have to be honest, don't I?"

"How many times have I warned you to be careful? When you're at home, you can say anything you like; but the instant you walk out that door, you have to watch your step! Please, don't make trouble for yourself."

"All right," Xiaolou said heavily. "I'll do my best, if only for your sake. If something happened to me, I don't know who would look after my wife—I mean my 'lover'. I just can't get used to all this new jargon!"

"Xiaolou." Her tone was mildly reproachful, but she embraced him and said, "I'm all yours. All I want is for you to be safe. Don't say things that people can use against you later on. You don't have to be a hero. All I want for us is a quiet and peaceful life."

Safety was the most anyone could hope for. Although every political campaign was launched in the name of the People, it was the common people who suffered the most.

Juxian felt afraid. It was important to keep a low profile.

She had even come to regret that her husband had portrayed a general onstage and been a star instead of a bit player. She shivered.

"Are you cold?" Xiaolou asked her.

She shook her head.

A soft rain began to fall outside the window. Xiaolou raised his head and saw the sword hanging on the wall. Pushing Juxian away, he rose and took it down. He unsheathed it and gave it a few random sweeps, reciting a few lines from the old opera:

"But the times are against me, even my horse cannot
    advance,
My horse cannot advance, what shall I do?"

He sighed and hung his head. Juxian took the sword without comment and hung it back on the wall, next to a portrait of Chairman Mao that gazed down on them benevolently. Juxian glanced out the window.

"It's done nothing but rain these past few days," she said dispiritedly.

When the weather cleared, renovations on the opera house were completed. It had been completely remodeled and redecorated. On either side of the stage hung a new set of couplets, written in white paint on a red background. The one on the left read: "The arts should serve the workers, peasants, and soldiers." The one on the right read: "Art should serve the goals of socialism." The verses were clumsy and did not attempt to match the poetic quality of the lines they had replaced. Four large characters ran across the top of the stage: "Up with the proletariat, and down with the bourgeoisie."

It was 1966, and the company was giving a performance of the model opera *Taking Tiger Mountain by Strategy;* they had reached the scene entitled "Entering the Tiger's Den." Xiao Si had been cast as the hero, Yang Zirong. Clad in a PLA uniform, he stood above the rest of the characters, trying to project revolutionary spirit. He clenched his fists and opened his eyes wide. It looked as though his eyeballs were about to pop out and roll across the stage in a frenzy of devotion to the Party. Puffing out his chest, he recited the many crimes of the class enemy.

Cheng Dieyi, Duan Xiaolou, and a handful of traditional actors filled out the cast, performing their tedious duty. Duan Xiaolou was cast as a villain, one of the Eight Bodyguards. The hero, Yang Zirong, was denouncing him:

"The Eight Body Guards are nothing but a bunch of filthy rats, unspeakable—"

"Kill that bastard!" bellowed Xiaolou in his inimitably martial style.

The audience applauded with the familiarity and warmth of someone meeting up with a long lost friend.

"Bravo! That's real opera!" someone called out, forgetting the new etiquette.

"That hit the mark!"

The roar of the audience drowned out Xiao Si's next line, and a shudder of dismay crossed his face. Neither Dieyi nor Xiaolou noticed his expression, and Xiaolou plunged on, excited by the cheering. He was a performer—his only job was to please his audience.

Juxian watched apprehensively from the wings. When her eyes met Xiao Si's, her heart froze.

That night, she persuaded her husband to be a "conscientious revolutionary." They tore up all of his old scripts, masks, and outlines and threw them into the fire. They would surrender all of his props and costumes to the authorities, hoping that they would be safe as long as they went along with the Party's policies. There were only two kinds of people in China anymore—victims, and victimizers.

As they went through their things, Juxian came across her most prized possession, her wedding dress. Xiaolou noticed her holding it and saw how her eyes lingered on it. He snatched the dress away from her.

"What do you think?" she asked tentatively.

"I don't see why we should turn this in, too," Xiaolou replied, taking out a sheet of plastic. "Here, wrap it up in this and hide it under the water barrel. It's just a wedding dress. I'm sure nobody will notice. I know how important it is to you."

"I'm afraid, Xiaolou."

"Don't worry. Everything will be fine."

"You'll always want me, won't you?" She looked up at him briefly as she folded the dress, and her eyes were moist with tears.

Xiaolou didn't respond, but he picked up a jar of spirits and poured out a bowlful. Taking a big gulp, he threw the bowl down onto the table, spilling some of the wine. Juxian stood, picked up the bowl, and took a drink.

"Of course I'll always want you—just as I do right now!"

"Xiaolou, I've really been worried lately, worried about

you, and afraid for myself, and—" Her mind was not on what she was saying. She and Xiaolou were feverishly unfastening each other's clothes.

"I want another baby," she said urgently. "Maybe it's too late, already. I don't know."

Driven by fear as much as by passion, they clung to each other, as if hoping to find refuge in each other from the dangerous times that lay ahead.

Juxian and Xiaolou arrived at Dieyi's house, and Xiaolou knocked on the door.

"Brother, it's me. Open up!"

"Dieyi," Juxian said. "There's something we need to discuss with you."

Dieyi had laid his props and costumes out to dry in the courtyard. They had already been there for several days, and as he wandered among the rich, bright fabrics he had the sensation of walking through his own glamorous past. Soon, it would be too late for him to turn them in voluntarily.

He heard Xiaolou and Juxian rapping at his door.

"There's a new political campaign being launched," Xiaolou said urgently through the door.

What campaign was that, Dieyi wondered. He felt ill equipped to cope with these successive political movements. The old operas had been banned, and he no longer had a script by which to live. His costumes were merely relics. Either the authorities would come to dispose of them, or he could destroy them himself.

Ignoring the couple waiting outside his door, he strolled across the courtyard, scissors in hand, and picked up a pair of embroidered shoes. He cut them to pieces. One at a time he cut apart all of his shoes. Then, very methodically, he took the scissors to his costumes, letting the strips of fabric slip through his fingers like little pieces of the past. In time, the courtyard was littered with a confetti of silks and satins.

Waiting outside the front door, Xiaolou grew increasingly agitated; but he could do nothing but listen to the faint sound of snipping that came over the wall.

Several hours later, Dieyi built a small fire and threw in the scraps of cloth. They imploded like withering faces, and Dieyi watched this mass cremation of decades of personae while the bitter smoke scratched at his already raw throat. He felt he was killing off parts of himself, but this was far better than letting the authorities do it. He knew that Xiaolou was concerned for him, concerned that this act of disobedience could cost him dearly; but he refused to let him inside. Perhaps if he had come alone, Dieyi might have included him in this ritual cremation; but he had not come alone.

The whole company had assembled for a political study session on the topic of Chairman Mao's instructions in the field of arts and letters. With every member of the company attired in the same Mao jackets, there was no longer any distinction between stars and bit players. Everyone sat in earnest silence, their books of Chairman Mao's quotations held up in both hands. This, and a small notebook, were their new props.

The Party secretary was giving an impassioned speech.

"Our company performs revolutionary operas, not old-fashioned operas. We must use different methods from those used in the Old Society. The old ways spread superstitions that poisoned people's lives; and the old style encouraged actors to be self-aggrandizing." He shot a glance first at

Xiaolou, and then at Xiao Si. Xiaolou didn't react, but Xiao Si looked smug. The secretary went on with his lecture.

"Recently, someone has been going on about the virtues of individualism. He was assigned to play a bandit, but his recitation was so loud that he upstaged the revolutionary protagonist. This amounted to direct opposition to the proletarian party line that we in the arts must uphold. The incident in question took place during a performance of *Taking Tiger Mountain by Strategy*, a play that Comrade Jiang Qing was revising personally at the time." He took a breath.

"Duan Xiaolou!" he thundered.

Xiaolou started and broke into a cold sweat.

"Do you realize that you have a serious problem? What motivated you to act as you did? Tell us."

Everyone looked at Xiaolou. Dieyi was stunned. He had expected himself to be the target of today's criticism.

Xiaolou stood up, filled with righteous indignation.

"Any opera singer worth his salt knows the key to a lively performance is interaction with the other players. I was just trying to interact with Yang Zirong and be a foil for him. The stage is like a plot of tilled earth—you have to grow lots of different crops. What's wrong with that?"

"Have you ever worked in the fields, Duan Xiaolou? Are you a peasant? Is that your class background? What qualifies you to make that remark?"

Xiaolou stood dumbly as cold sweat ran down his back. Although he was a tall man, he suddenly appeared to be half his height.

䷇
8

As the Cultural Revolution gathered momentum, actors were transformed into revolutionary workers in the arts, charged with fighting evil tendencies and armed with Mao Zedong Thought. Dissent was violently suppressed, and the latest movement preached "Down with the Four Olds": feudalism, old culture, old customs, and old traditions.

The loudspeakers came on with a screech, and an announcer began reading the guiding principles of the Cultural Revolution. The volume was so high that the party secretary felt the sound rumble through his body, and he halted his speech midphrase. He looked up, a wary expression flickering across his eyes. He had only just begun to exercise some power himself, and already it seemed precarious. Anyone could become a victim, even he.

Xiaolou and Dieyi exchanged fearful glances.

"A revolution is not a dinner party, or writing an essay. It is not painting a picture or doing embroidery. It cannot be so refined. It cannot be so gentle or leisurely; it cannot be so soft or polite. Revolution is a violent action by which one class overthrows another."

The announcer's voice boomed through the meeting hall.

Sound had always been a powerful force in China. In peacetime there were bells tolling the hours. In wartime there were dirges when a hero lost in battle. Now, when a political movement was launched, loudspeakers created an air of authoritarian unity. Ever since liberation, loudspeakers had been the Party's most powerful and irresistible tool for propaganda. A loudspeaker never got tired of talking, never wanted to take a day off. The constant haranguing was imprinted indelibly in people's minds.

The ground shook with the thundering broadcasts, but people often couldn't make out the words because of the distortion created by the tremendous volume. All that came through was a series of emotions. The voice ranged from charming to violent, from flattering to earnest, by turns passionate, sorrowful, or agitated. It resembled nothing so much as the shocked cries of a crowd.

"Be Chairman Mao's good student!"

"Always follow in Chairman Mao's footsteps!"

These were the chants of Chairman Mao's "little generals," the Red Guards. With any adult a potential enemy of the revolution, children had become the only true revolutionaries. Classes were suspended so that students could search people's homes for anything associated with either Western culture or traditional Chinese culture. Sometimes they engaged in "criticism" and "struggle sessions." It was all very novel and glorious, and the children were excited simply to be a part of such an important, revolutionary movement.

The Red Guard leaders were all in their teens. Some were from Peking, while the rest came from every other part of the country. They entered houses, descending in large groups like swarms of locusts. They smashed and looted as they pleased, all in the name of the revolution, and so-called black elements were criticized and their families were made to sweep the streets. The terrifying power of the mob had been set loose, while the adults who had brainwashed the little generals hid safely behind the walls of Zhongnanhai.

How this sweeping movement started is not altogether certain. Some say that one day a small-character poster appeared on the bulletin board of the middle school attached to Qinghua University in Peking. It said: "LONG LIVE THE SPIRIT OF REBELLION!" Soon, the entire nation was in rebellion. Even traffic lights were reversed, with green signifying "stop" and red standing for "go forward." The world had been turned upside down.

The nights were strangely quiet. All day long Dieyi and Xiaolou endured "criticism" of their political attitudes and past actions. At night they went home to write "self-criticisms," and when they were finished with these, they had to copy Chairman Mao's poems as a penance.

Dieyi didn't understand much of the poem he was copying, which was about the taking of Nanjing by the PLA. But as he wrote, he came to a familiar word, one for which he felt a special affection—the two characters for "general" reminded him of Xiaolou. "Don't be like the old general who strove for empty fame," the poem exhorted the reader. Dieyi's fountain pen made an irritating noise as it scratched over the coarse paper, but with Xiaolou sitting beside him, writing out the same poem, Dieyi felt oddly at peace. Juxian was not there.

The school was deserted, and the classrooms had been turned into "confession rooms." Dieyi and Xiaolou were once again sitting side by side, writing out confessions and copying poems. At forty-nine, Xiaolou had become an old "general," but he would always be in his prime in Dieyi's eyes. As they grew tired, they started to make mistakes. The characters were wrong, and the confessions were lies. Everything was wrong. They seemed to have walked into the wrong play.

Whenever the men's attention wandered, the little Red Guards stationed behind them struck them or kicked them, yelling, "Keep writing! Tell all about your counterrevolutionary activities! Don't think you can hide anything from us! If you don't pay attention, we'll take you out and make you kneel on a bench in the hot sun."

On the spur of the moment, the children dragged them out into the street. There was some sort of farcical parade going on, with lots of banging on drums and gongs as a cavalcade of old-fashioned performers snaked down the road. It looked like a carnival, with all of the players in makeup and costumes, but they had had to make up in a hurry, and their faces were crudely drawn masks of red and white. They looked just like the monsters the Red Guards accused them of being.

Xiaolou's hands had been shaky, and the lines on his General's face were crooked, with black and white paints smudged together. Dieyi had on white base and rouge, and he had drawn his eyes and eyebrows very precisely, so that it appeared that the shadows of a pair of peach leaves lay across his eyes, protecting him from visions of the world.

The skin of his hands and face was no longer supple and had lost its healthy glow. Nonetheless, he could still summon up a serene stage presence. This parade promised to be just another performance.

At the last minute, he reached out for Xiaolou's makeup brush. As he looked at Xiaolou's scarred brow, Dieyi had the momentary impression that nothing had changed in over twenty years.

"Let me touch it up for you."

Xiaolou did not respond.

The parade of old-fashioned opera characters was beginning. Statesmen, beauties, peasants, temptresses, wise judges, the General, and Yu Ji marched down the street, led by a propaganda truck and flanked by Red Guards beating gongs and drums. The actors couldn't take even two steps without being abused by the Red Guards.

"Keep twisting your body, or we'll twist it for good!"

"Show us your 'orchid hands,' you stuck-up clown!"

"Keep singing! Now moo! Moo like a cow!"

It was a hot August afternoon, and the blistering sun beat down on the actors; sweat mixed with greasepaint rolled down their cheeks, thick as porridge. The ground radiated heat like the bricks of a kiln.

"Down with poisonous weeds in the arts!"

"Pull them out by the roots!"

"Long live the Cultural Revolution!"

"Long live Chairman Mao!"

The shouting was almost deafening, but suddenly there was an even louder commotion up ahead, which was followed by a very loud thud that shook the ground.

A woman had jumped from a building. The impact had broken off one of her legs and sent it bouncing over to the base of a wall. Her head had cracked open, spreading brains across the pavement like bean curd. Blood and flesh were splattered everywhere. Something tiny had landed near Dieyi's foot, either a tooth or a finger; but he was too exhausted and numb to care.

Red Guard little generals from Peking's Number 15 Girls' High School had gone to the home of an old writer to search for and confiscate so-called reactionary materials. This had been their third visit in a row. The old gentleman had a reputation for being mild and cultivated, and he was scarcely strong enough to lift anything more than a pencil; but today he had picked up a large cleaver without warning and had started hacking at the Red Guards like a madman. After this initial frenzy, he dashed downstairs and attacked a twelve-year-old "little revolutionary" with a knife.

"The enemy is on the offensive!" shouted the leader of the Red Guards. "Comrades in arms, attack!"

The children surged toward the old man and twisted one of his arms behind his back until it broke with a series of sharp cracks. The writer's wife became hysterical and tried to fight off his tormenters with a broom, but she was no match for the gang of adolescents. They chased her up many flights of stairs until she reached the top floor. There, with no hope for escape, she jumped. Her husband did not witness this horrible event, having lost both of his hands and fallen unconscious.

Dieyi and Xiaolou passed by this spectacle on wobbly knees, and Xiaolou sighed and recited a few lines of verse under his breath.

"It was fate that destroyed my kingdom of Chu,
For we fought valiantly indeed."

Dieyi responded softly:

"Victory and defeat are the way of war,
Let it not trouble you."

A Red Guard saw the two whispering to each other, and he struck both of them with a brass-buckled belt that knocked one of Dieyi's pearl hairpins to the ground. Without thinking, Dieyi reached down to retrieve it, but another Red Guard stepped on his hand. Several girl generals spat on his face and cursed him.

"Keep moving, ghoul! You're forbidden to pick it up!"

Seeing his friend in trouble, Xiaolou shielded Dieyi with his body. The spittle landed on his face and dribbled down, and he wiped it away with his sleeve in disgust, which irritated the Red Guards. Crowding in, they twisted his arms behind his back, kicking and beating him.

"Brother!" Dieyi cried out.

Xiaolou warned him off with his eyes, and Dieyi could only watch in horror as they tormented his friend. Were they human beings, or not? They were as savage as animals.

Maybe they had been abandoned as children, he wondered. Perhaps one of them was the newborn infant he had seen years before, dead and reincarnated, bent on revenge. But though he searched among the faces of these children, he found none that resembled the foundling. Heedless of his friend's advice, Dieyi pushed forward again and took several blows before he fell to the ground.

He reached for the hairpin, but it had already been crushed underfoot.

It was early that evening when Juxian returned home, a large placard still hanging from her neck. It read, "MEMBER OF COUNTERREVOLUTIONARY CONSPIRATORS' FAMILY." She had been out sweeping the streets, and she still held a broom in her hands.

"Xiaolou!" she cried, when she saw him.

He was covered in blood, which had dried in places, caked like deep red mud. She couldn't simply peel off his shirt, for the cloth was glued to his skin, which forced her to cut it away very carefully. As she washed his wounds with hot water, Xiaolou noticed that she was crying.

"It's just a scratch, nothing serious," he said comfortingly. "What really hurts me is the fact that they don't treat people like human beings. They were being cruel just for fun. They were riding on Dieyi's head as though they were going to shit on him—and he's too weak even to wrestle with a chicken!"

"You've got to start looking out for yourself! You're going to get yourself killed," she said resentfully. "You can't afford to get them angry." She took a breath before continuing her diatribe. "Can't you think of anyone but him? What would have happened to me if they'd beaten you to death? Did you think of that?"

She rubbed hard at his sores, making him wince. She touched him tenderly.

"If it hadn't been for you," he whispered, "I would have killed a few of them!"

"Please, don't—"

She was cut short as a group of Red Guards forced open the door and came crashing in. They were earlier than usual—night had not yet fallen, but the sound of doors being pounded on and broken down filled the building. No household would be spared. Whatever was smashed or broken was later taken out and burned—with the exception of articles the rebels coveted. These would become rebel property.

After locking all the doors and windows in the apartment, the Red Guards held up their copies of the *Quotations of Chairman Mao* in a show of solidarity. Their leader was all of fourteen, but he had a powerful presence and fierce eyes. He led his group in reciting from their books.

"Reactionary materials are like dust. You have to sweep them away with a broom—they won't disappear by themselves." He barked out an order: "Come here, comrades. Let's sweep up!"

They started to turn the apartment inside out, upending trunks and knocking down cabinets, destroying everything in sight. The most satisfying experience by far was breaking glass. Both the sight and sound were terrifically impressive, and they had the desired effect of intimidating the "class enemy."

This family did not have any classical Chinese paintings or calligraphy, nor did it have antiques, books, or letters. The young activists were disappointed not to find anything of value, but they smashed everything in sight, nonetheless, as Xiaolou and Juxian watched helplessly, hand in hand.

Suddenly, one of the Red Guards spotted the sword hanging on the wall next to the couple's obligatory portrait of Chairman Mao. The tip of the sword was pointing directly at the chairman's head.

The Red Guards turned their eyes on Xiaolou. They were filled with righteous indignation and not a little excitement, for they had found the evidence they were looking for. Their earlier disappointment was replaced with irrepressible glee, and they began to speak excitedly.

"Whose sword is this?"

There was no answer. It had grown completely dark outside.

Two of the Red Guards were suddenly seized with an inspiration, and they gathered the group for a whispered conference. Shortly afterward, they hurried out.

Minutes later they returned, with Dieyi in tow.

The three of them, Dieyi, Xiaolou, and Juxian, were ordered to line up in front of their accusers, and they obeyed mutely. They could only wait nervously to see what lay in store for them.

"Confess!" barked the leader. "This sword is clear and incontrovertible evidence of counterrevolutionary activity. Everybody here is a witness to the fact that it was pointed directly at our great leader, Chairman Mao, where it was poised to slash him to pieces."

Xiaolou glanced at Juxian, and Dieyi looked at Xiaolou. All three of them went pale, the color of dead, dried-out silkworms. They felt as though their feet had been nailed to the floor. Everyone knew that this was a very serious crime.

"Whose sword is this?" the leader repeated sternly.

"It's his!" Juxian cried, pointing her finger right at Dieyi. "It isn't Xiaolou's. It's his!"

Xiaolou straightened his back.

"No, it's mine," he said softly.

"Why did we keep that sword, Xiaolou?" Juxian was frantic. "We haven't had a moment's peace since it came into this house!"

One of the Red Guards slapped her in the face, but she didn't back down.

"Dieyi, please don't do this to Xiaolou!" she begged. "Please don't destroy our family!"

"What family?" he asked contemptuously. He had never truly recognized her as Xiaolou's wife. He smiled coldly. "Where were you when I gave that sword to my brother?" He turned to the Red Guards. "I was the one who gave it to him, but she is the one who hung it up," he told them solemnly, pointing at Juxian.

"Stop fighting!" Xiaolou cut in. "I said it was mine!"

"Is that so?" One of the Red Guards tilted back his head and looked down his nose at Xiaolou. "You want to be a hero, do you?"

Some of the Red Guards brought in some large bricks and pushed Xiaolou to his knees.

"It's common knowledge that this 'general' has a very loud voice and sturdy bones. When he was young, he was known for breaking bricks on his head."

"Let's see if he can still do it," said the group leader.

Seizing a brick, he smashed it against Xiaolou's forehead.

"Xiaolou!" Juxian screamed. "No! No! It was me!"

Dieyi was horror-stricken. Xiaolou was nearly fifty, and his bones were not as strong as they had once been. He was no longer a "little rock," untouched by hardship. He had been battered by the wind and rain.

Xiaolou's expression remained calm, but a bright red trickle of blood began to run down his face. He seemed to sway slightly but made no sound. The brick was still in one piece.

Seeing his friend had been hurt, Dieyi fell to his knees, and Juxian held her breath. Xiaolou looked at his friend in dismay. Had Dieyi lost all self-respect?

"I confess! Please, little revolutionary generals, I beg you to let Duan Xiaolou go free."

Walking forward on his knees, Dieyi picked up the sword and gave it one last fond caress.

"I'm the guilty one!" he said, throwing it to the ground, certain he had just signed his own death warrant.

"Thank you, Dieyi," Juxian whispered.

"I did this for him, not for you," he said without looking at her. Xiaolou was so agitated he couldn't even breathe. Then he shouted out with fierce power. It was as though he were performing on stage again—but these were his true feelings and his true nature.

"Why are you making up these stories?" Xiaolou's voice resonated. "Are you trying to deceive the Party? I accept full responsibility for my actions."

He limped from the room, his injured body dwarfed by the hearty children who escorted him out. They were taking him to be interrogated by the self-styled revolutionary "rebels" in his work unit. He was just one more bad element.

* * *

The room was cold and dark, like an empty stage. Suddenly a pair of spotlights converged on the man in the wooden chair, shining in his eyes. He felt like the disoriented soul of someone newly dead first entering the netherworld.

A harsh and disembodied voice came from somewhere above him, as though the Emperor of Heaven himself were interrogating him. But there wasn't just one inquisitor. They were taking turns haranguing him so that each voice would retain its intimidating force. He had to reveal every transgression he had committed since he'd first entered the opera school. He told them about his old evil habits of frequenting brothels and carrying on shamelessly with prostitutes. They demanded names. They demanded dates. They wanted to know every trivial detail of his behavior. He felt they were stripping away his psyche, layer by layer.

Xiaolou was exhausted in both body and spirit. If only they would let him sleep and return to the world tomorrow as an obedient nobody, a faceless member of the crowd.

On the third day, the spotlights were moved in closer. They blazed hotly on his haggard face.

"Did you not say you were opposed to the Eighth Route Army?"

"No."

"Think carefully."

"No. I can't remember."

"Didn't you say you wanted to fight the Eighth Route Army?"

"Absolutely not!"

"You've always loved to play the hero. Are you telling me you're not disobedient!"

"I am grateful to the Eighth Route Army for liberating us."

"What about Chairman Mao? Aren't you grateful to him? The truth is that you've opposed him at every turn!"

"How could I?"

"You sabotaged the model opera and committed the crime of Heroism! And you plainly harbored murderous intentions toward Chairman Mao, intending to kill him in effigy with that sword. The Chairman teaches us not to put ourselves above others. 'Don't be self-aggrandizing,' he tells us. But not only are you self-aggrandizing, both you and your wife are counterrevolutionaries!"

"I didn't—"

Dozens of spotlights flashed on with the suddenness of an ambush, and Xiaolou was blinded momentarily by the stabbing light. The heat was intense.

And then they set upon him, armed with belts and planks, beating and kicking him without mercy. Phantasmagoric shadows twisted and arched across the walls.

"Confess! Do you refuse to confess?"

Xiaolou crumpled to the floor. They had brought him down in the name of the Party.

"I admit it," he said hoarsely. "I am a poisonous weed. I am a monster. I have made ideological mistakes and have disappointed the Party. I have wronged Chairman Mao. . . . I—I am guilty. I am guilty!"

He stared up at his accusers in fear.

"I am no better than a dog."

At last they were satisfied.

★ ★ ★

It was quiet in the classroom. Like every classroom in every school in the nation, this one had become a confession room. Pencil shavings caught in the crevices of desks and floorboards were the only tangible reminders of another time.

Several members of the Women's Propaganda Team, the director of the Neighborhood Committee, and a handful of cadres were lined up in chairs behind the teacher's desk.

Juxian sat motionless before them, biting her lips.

"This is going to be good for him, and for you, too," a middle-aged female cadre said expressionlessly. She turned and gestured at someone in the doorway.

A minute later, Dieyi was escorted in, and the cadre instructed him to sit down, facing Juxian. The pair of them looked like elementary school students, with their hands folded obediently in their laps. They were both rather pale.

"The organization has invited me here to persuade you to draw a clear line between yourself and Xiaolou," Dieyi said. "We . . . are . . . poisonous weeds in the field of the arts. As counterrevolutionaries, we should be criticized. Staying married to Xiaolou will do you no good."

Dieyi realized that he was walking a tightrope. He wanted to destroy Xiaolou's marriage, but he didn't want to destroy Xiaolou. His fear was mingled with a curious kind of elation as he watched Juxian, waiting for her reaction.

"Juxian," the cadre admonished her. "You must decide. All the necessary facts are here before you. If you don't make a clean break with Xiaolou now, it will be that much worse for both of you in the future."

"It seems that there are some problems with your attitude!" the director of the Women's Propaganda Team said disapprovingly.

Was the government going to do what he had never been able to do for himself? If the destructive force of the Cultural Revolution were to break up Xiaolou's marriage to Juxian, then all of the violence and suffering would not have been wasted. Despite all that he had endured himself, he felt oddly grateful and had to suppress a fleeting smile.

"I won't leave him," Juxian said calmly.

"Are you saying that you stand in willful opposition to the wishes of the Party organization?" Dieyi said flatly.

"I am grateful to all of you for your concern, but I intend to wait for Xiaolou." She straightened herself and went on with composure. "I won't divorce him, and I'm willing to accept the consequences. I am his true wife."

When he heard the words "true wife," Dieyi winced, but the room remained as still and quiet as the unruffled surface of a pond. He read the slogans pinned to the wall behind Juxian's head: "LENIENCY FOR THOSE WHO CONFESS. SEVERE PENALTIES FOR THOSE WHO REFUSE."

Juxian and Dieyi stared at each other intensely.

"If you are stubbornly determined to oppose the Party, so be it!" the cadre barked at Juxian. Then she turned to Dieyi: "Cheng Dieyi. Tomorrow night you must draw a clear line of your own."

The opera company had assembled in the courtyard of the temple to the founders. The old actors were all in costume and full stage makeup for their roles in a new kind of ritual performance, the burning of the Four Olds. Costumes, headdresses, publicity stills, props, makeup, art directors' sketches, and sheet music were all piled high like a colorful pagoda.

One of the leaders set the heap of articles on fire, and the flames shot up into the night sky like the tongues of so many hungry wolves. The silhouettes of a cavalcade of historical figures were thrown against the walls of the compound while the actors looked on numbly, feeling like husks of their former selves. Each one was forced to commit his own belongings, his own treasures, to the roaring blaze. Satins and brocades, sweat stains and smudges of greasepaint—everything was transformed into smoke and cinders, which floated up and away, vanishing forever.

The flames crackled and the strains of the "Internationale" filled the air:

"The old world has been completely smashed.
But don't say we have nothing.
We are the masters of the new world.
The Internationale shall be achieved!"

The leader of the Red Guards stood up and made an announcement. It was time for the two former stars to "peel each other's scars" and "criticize" each other. The crowd of supporters applauded thunderously, and the leader had to raise his hand to silence them.

"We want to expose these two poisonous weeds in all their ugliness and corruption."

Young children wearing olive-green army uniforms with red kerchiefs and arm bands kicked Dieyi and Xiaolou down until they knelt on either side of the bonfire.

"You!" roared the leader, pointing at Xiaolou. "Give us an account of him first!"

A black robe with an embroidered serpent appliqué writhed in the flames. Xiaolou had worn it as the General, Xiang Yu.

"Speak!" yelled the leader.

When Xiaolou didn't respond, one of the Red Guards kicked him hard in the back. He had to say something, so he tried to think of something relatively harmless.

"When Cheng Dieyi was a little boy, he was rather girlish; and . . . on stage, he was also a bit effeminate and . . . pretentious."

It was Dieyi's turn.

"The first time Duan Xiaolou had to have his head shaved, he didn't want to," Dieyi mumbled. "He ended up with a ring like a toilet seat around his head. And he was shifty-eyed and didn't have a good attitude."

"This is nonsense!" the leader shrieked. "Tell us something important."

Xiaolou looked at Dieyi and told himself that his friend would understand what he was about to do.

"Cheng Dieyi never had any self-discipline. Popularity made him lazy, and he slept in late every morning."

"Now you," said the Red Guard, indicating Dieyi.

Dieyi looked apologetically at Xiaolou.

"He gambled and bet on cricket fights. He indulged himself in luxury and didn't concentrate hard enough on his performing. He also liked to visit whorehouses."

He felt the brass buckle of a leather belt strike his head. Xiaolou felt its sting next; but neither of them flinched or moved to avoid the blows.

"What kind of confessions are these? If you don't draw a clear line between yourselves, you may not get out of here alive. Now, speak!"

Xiaolou thought hard.

"His name was always written in bigger characters than anyone else's on the marquee advertising the operas he appeared in. He was a prima donna, often ignoring others and never thinking about anyone except himself. He was arrogant, but he stooped to perform opera for anybody, no matter how despicable they were."

The Red Guards were somewhat mollified.

"Was he a collaborator? Did he ever entertain Nationalist troops?"

Xiaolou said nothing at first, but then he remembered the party's promise of leniency if he cooperated and harshness if he resisted.

"He sang for a private party of Japanese—he was a collaborator. He also sang for wounded Nationalist soldiers, reactionaries, capitalists, rich landlords, society matrons, and even the big opera boss, Yuan Shiqing!"

A Red Guard unsheathed the sword and swept it in front of his face.

"Did he give you this sword? Where did he get it?"

"It was—he got it from Yuan Shiqing, the most hated man in the theater . . . in exchange for . . . sexual favors."

"Xiaolou!" screamed Juxian. She was standing with a group of relatives of bad elements. Xiaolou had gone too far.

"Yu Ji's filthy sword is even filthier than we thought!" the little general laughed coldly.

With that, he threw the sword into the fire; but before the flames could engulf it, Dieyi rushed into the fire like a spirit fleeing the underworld and retrieved it. Smothering the fire with his hands, he hugged the blade with its singed tassels to his chest, just as he had many years before. It was the only thing in the whole world that was truly his.

"I have something to report!" he said desperately. "Duan Xiaolou is no better than an animal. His mistress was a cheap whore! She and her cohorts flattered him shamelessly while she distracted him from his work with her seductive wiles and constantly pawed him in public!" The more he talked, the more worked up he got. Years of resentment were boiling over. "She's a two-faced whore!"

Two Red Guards picked her up and dragged her over to the bonfire.

"You slut!" Dieyi spat at her. "You deserve to be trampled to death. You're just a barren, stinking prostitute—and a liar, too!"

"She is not a liar!" Xiaolou said passionately. "Please, let Juxian go. I'll do anything you say."

Dieyi renewed his attack.

"He's even willing to give up his life for that whore! He thinks he's General Xiang Yu, always playing the hero, the big man! All he's ever cared about is power and prestige. This bourgeois scum has always looked down on the masses. He has no respect for the law, no spirit of struggle—"

"What are you talking about?" Xiaolou cut in fiercely. "Your precious Yu Ji is the real bourgeois scum! During the war against Japan, when our nation needed him most, did he go to the front to fight? Was he willing to sacrifice anything for his country? No! He stayed where it was safe and sang and danced to decadent music!"

"Bravo!" chorused the Red Guards. They were enjoying the show now.

"I am not Yu Ji!" Dieyi protested. "I am not the Yu Ji the General loves. I am not the kind of woman a decadent counterrevolutionary like him could love. His Xiang Yu was a travesty. He turned Xiang Yu from a pure and honest peasant into a sentimental, antiparty individualist. He is a threat to our very way of life, a poisonous weed, one of the dregs of society! He has even made fun of our glorious Party. Once he asked me, 'What is the Communist Party about, anyway? They share everything—do they share wives, too?' "

Xiaolou stared at Dieyi with incomprehension, no longer able to recognize either his old friend or the man his friend was describing. They had become strangers.

The other members of the company watched in horror as Dieyi continued his denunciation.

"As for this filthy creature," he said, pointing at Juxian. "She has no respect for anyone but herself. She doesn't respect the Party, and she viciously attacks Mao Zedong Thought. The organization has tried to raise her consciousness, but she refuses to be helped. She'll never change—till the day she dies!" He shook with anger. "We must uproot this immoral woman and her husband. We must struggle against them without mercy, to the death!"

Abruptly, he fell silent. He had seen Xiaolou's face through the curtains of flame and dancing ash, wearing a complicated expression he could not read. Although the two were only a few feet away from each other, they seemed to be separated by an unbridgeable and unfathomable distance.

Dieyi's head was pounding. What had he said? Struggle

to the death? He had destroyed everything. It was too late.

Juxian was speaking now.

"Although I used to be a prostitute, I have been faithful to one man. Even in the old society, no one could force a wife to betray her husband or abandon him. Dieyi is right about one thing, Xiaolou. I'll never repent—I'll never change my mind, even until the day I die."

The Red Guards shouted her down.

"Down with the class enemy!"

"If the enemy refuses to surrender, we must exterminate her!"

"Let's give her a yin-and-yang haircut!"

One of them took a knife and grabbed her by the hair. He shaved off the hair on one side of her head, which resulted in black hair on one side and bare skin on the other, like the symbol for yin and yang. There were bloody nicks on the bare skin from his crude cutting.

"Tomorrow she is to be sent down to the countryside for reeducation through labor! Now take her away!" ordered the leader.

"No!" Xiaolou cried desperately. "I am to blame for everything. I want to make a clean break with her. I'll divorce her right now!"

Dieyi felt a mixture of joy and sorrow when he heard Xiaolou's words. Chairman Mao had once said: "Nowhere in the world is there love without reason. Nor is there hatred without a cause." But he had been wrong. Love was by its very nature unreasoning, while hatred has a thousand causes. The great revolutionary didn't understand this at all.

Juxian looked back at Xiaolou in shock.

"I don't love this whore! I want a divorce!"

Her eyes went dead, and she stared at him as at a stranger.

"Don't let her go!" Dieyi cried. "Struggle against this slut. Struggle to the death!"

A black shadow emerged from the crowd.

"Cheng Dieyi," came a voice. "Save your breath. You say that prostitutes are scum, but you singers are no better than whores yourselves. I'm telling everyone here, Red Guards and little generals, that this singer sold his body to our old oppressors so that they would show him favor. He lounged in his boudoir all day, smoking opium and thinking indecent thoughts. Nobody knows his corruption better than I. He treated me like dirt! He's rotten to the core!"

Although Dieyi craned his neck, he couldn't see the face of the speaker. But he knew that voice. It was Xiao Si.

"How did he gain favor with our enemies? What did he use? His asshole! He was always the big star, keeping younger singers down, refusing to give us a chance. He treated me like shit. I was his servant, and I had to wait on him hand and foot. Still, I tried to avoid him whenever I could. He is the true criminal, the true scum. We must struggle against him to the death."

This was his proof of loyalty to the Party, and he was making quite a show of it. Tears streamed down his face, as though his misery had been the greatest of all and his hatred were the deepest.

The crowd applauded and set upon Dieyi, kicking, scratching, pummeling, and taunting. Like a cricket that had been thrown into the fire, he felt its fierce heat along with the sting of the blows. It crackled in his ears. The beating seemed to go on forever, and he was sure he was going to die, until he fell back in exhaustion. The flames had burned themselves out. There was nothing left but a heap of ashes.

"You lied to me! All of you!" he cried with what remained of his strength. But the Red Guards drowned him out as they shouted in unison:

"Long live the Great Proletarian Cultural Revolution!"

Xiao Si snatched away the sword that Dieyi still clutched in his arms and submitted it to the Red Guards.

"Little generals, this sword is hard proof that he is a counterrevolutionary."

The leader raised his arms and exhorted the others.

"This is our evidence! This shall be the cornerstone of our struggle against these monsters! Let this be a lesson to them!"

The unruly mob became more and more savage.

"Long live the Great Proletarian Cultural Revolution!" they chanted. "Long live the Great Proletarian Cultural Revolution!" The angry voices all blended into one.

Dieyi and Xiaolou were led to the "cowshed," where there were temporary holding cells for monsters like them. Their solitary cubicles stank of urine and excrement—they had never been cleaned—but the prisoners no longer noticed. The deafening noise of gongs pounded in their heads. Tomorrow, there would be another struggle session, and their captors had announced that such sessions would take place every day. Would there never be an end to it?

Dieyi peered around his dark and grimy cell. There was a bowl of brackish water, and nothing else but the four walls and dirty floor. He was too shaken for sleep.

Thick, inky blackness enveloped him. He could no longer see any future. Like Yu Ji, he felt he had lost his mainstay. His General had been brought low—where could he turn? What was the point of living? He seized the bowl and hurled it against the wall. Then, picking up one of the shards, he started to slash at his neck. But the broken crockery wasn't sharp enough to cut deeply, and the skin of his neck had grown loose with age. It was like trying to carve a piece of meat with a dull knife. He couldn't make a clean cut. With a great deal of effort, he finally managed to draw a little blood, but he felt almost no sensation.

Remembering the little bat, he realized that the wound on its neck had been fatal because the little knife had been quite sharp. Blood had spurted from its jugular and dripped down into the pot of boiling broth, spreading into clouds of bright red. When all the creature's blood had drained into the soup, Yuan had ladled him out a bowl of soup. "Drink this," he'd said. "It's good for the blood." He had endured this just for Xiaolou.

The more he dwelt on the past, the angrier he became. He had to think about something else, but his mind was starting to drift.

"What's going on in there?" someone shouted through the door.

A crowd of voices chorused, "He's slit his throat! He's trying to kill himself!"

Five Red Guards on night duty dashed in, their eyes lit up with excitement. Death was theirs to mete out—no one else had the right. One of them took away the pieces of broken bowl while another brought in a handful of old newspapers and stanched his wounds with them.

"Do you think you can take the easy way out by dying?

Don't you want to put on another show for us tomorrow?"

"You ungrateful wretch! The Party and the People are trying to help you, yet you refuse to be helped!"

"You may want to die," the leader said sternly, "but we can't allow that."

"Long live the Cultural Revolution!" chanted the others as they wiped at Dieyi's cuts.

Dieyi crawled over to a corner of the room, shaking violently. He had lost a fair amount of blood, but his life was not in danger.

"I have no culture," he moaned. "Leave me alone! Just leave me alone!"

He had failed where his heroine Yu Ji had succeeded. Life in the opera was more fulfilling, indeed. All one had to do was sing, up to the glorious finale; and the curtain always fell, right on cue. Onstage, Yu Ji was able to tell her lover that just as a virtuous minister does not serve two princes, so a virtuous woman cannot marry twice; then she asks for his sword so that she can end her life in his presence. This was her way of demonstrating her love for him, and her acceptance of his boundless love for her. But in real life, Dieyi's love was unrequited.

Xiaolou was being sent down to the countryside for reeducation through labor. He would have to take everything he owned with him, since nobody knew when he might be allowed to return. He trudged through the darkness, escorted by two Red Guards, the wooden board that announced his many crimes still hanging from his neck. It was pitch-black when he entered his apartment to collect his few belongings.

Someone switched on the light. There, dangling in the

air in front of his face, was a pair of white-stockinged feet. They twisted slightly back and forth. Startled, Xiaolou fell back several steps and looked up. Juxian had hanged herself.

She had put on her bright red wedding dress, and it looked incongruously festive. With half of her hair shorn off, she had a somewhat comical appearance. She had pinned a red flower into what was left of her black hair. Only a bride could wear that crimson blossom.

"Juxian!" Xiaolou cried heartrendingly. The Red Guards beside him were too stunned to reprove him.

Juxian's heavy makeup concealed her forty years.

Xiaolou remmbered their wedding night. Half-burned wedding candles had thrown gentle light on the bride's flushed face as she showed off the fine workmanship of the wedding dress to her new husband.

"This peony is embroidered with seven different colors of silk thread. The phoenix has eleven colors, and this—"

Xiaolou had grabbed her firmly around the waist and thrown her onto the bed.

"You temptress—" he whispered impatiently.

"Stop, you're wrinkling it! Let me keep it on just a little longer!"

She pushed him away. She wouldn't be forced, but she narrowed her eyes flirtatiously.

"It's so beautiful, I can't bear to take it off yet. Have you ever seen anything like it?"

"You're too much," Xiaolou said, as he hurriedly unfastened her collar. "I've seen more than my share of fine embroidery! My brother's trunks are full of pretty costumes! Don't make me wait any longer!"

"Costumes and wedding dresses aren't the same thing at

all. A wedding dress is meant for a solemn and sacred ritual."
She winked at him. "Do you know when I decided to buy
myself this dress? The madam thought I was leaving empty-
handed, but I'd been planning this ever since I first met you."

Juxian had always gotten what she wanted. She had
charm, beauty, and intelligence. She had wanted Xiaolou,
and she had bought her freedom. Now she had chosen her
own death.

Xiaolou felt like a drowning man watching the last life
preserver slipping away from him. His love had slipped from
his hands. He could no longer touch her; she was now like
flowers in a mirror, or the reflection of the moon on water.
His good intentions had gone awry. Instead of protecting her
by divorcing her, he had driven her to this. He collapsed
heavily to the floor.

Dieyi stood in the doorway behind him, thin and pale as
a wraith.

"What are you staring at?" demanded a Red Guard,
banging the door shut in Dieyi's face.

Dieyi and Xiaolou had given up their places at center stage to
a new cast of monsters. Today's victim was a playwright.
With his hands pulled back behind him, he looked like an
airplane poised for takeoff. His head was bent far forward, as
though pointed toward a crash landing against a mountain-
side. The position was painful and difficult to maintain, and
his face had turned a swollen purple. Kneeling around him
were several dozen others, all targeted for criticism.

After this group had been criticized and struggled
against, a new group would be hauled in. It was seemingly
endless work, like winnowing newly harvested grain in a

bumper year. Would they never run out of victims?

All of the "monsters" had packed up their things. Each had a bag containing all of his belongings—quilts and sheets, a towel, a toothbrush, soap, and a cup swinging by a string from the outside of the knapsack. They walked like zombies in a long line, once-respected scholars in their seventies trudging along like schoolchildren shouldering heavy book-bags. They were all bound for remote parts of the country.

"Protect Chairman Mao until death!" shouted the green-uniformed children who were their keepers. "Protect Vice Chairman Lin Biao and the Cultural Revolution Group of the Central Committee! Protect Comrade Jiang Qing to the death! Fight to expose the class enemy! Fight to the death!"

The exiles were herded onto a half-dozen trucks. As Dieyi clambered up into the back of one of them, he stopped short. He had seen Xiaolou.

"Bro—"

Xiaolou had the haggard and defeated look of someone who has been reduced merely to surviving. Before he could respond to Dieyi, one of the guards shoved him onto another truck.

Once all of the trucks were full, they drove off in different directions. They might never have a chance to see each other again. "UNTIL DEATH" read the slogans on the sides of the trucks. China is so vast and populous that a person could be swallowed up anywhere. But all over the world, nothing is immutable. Even the seas must become fertile lands, and fertile lands must be swallowed up by the sea.

9

The city of Fuzhou is set in the vast delta of the Min River, in Fujian Province. Many northerners like Xiaolou had been sent there, to China's Far South; while southerners were relocated to the Northeast. The policy was one of dispersion.

There were all kinds of people among the mix of counterrevolutionaries at the cadre school—whether bright or dull, beautiful or ugly, here they were all treated the same. It reminded Xiaolou of his childhood at the opera school, with all of the bald-pated little boys crowded together on one big kang.

Xiaolou worked hard every day, pulling carts, making bricks, building sheds and houses. Sometimes he toiled in the fields, planting beans, rice, or vegetables. The soil was poor and difficult to work, alternately baked hard or sodden and muddy, and mixed with sweat, blood, urine, and other by-products of labor. In addition to performing manual labor, the prisoners attended political study sessions mornings, after-noons, and after dinner. Xiaolou's stamina, the result of years of diligent training in the theater, stood him in good stead; but while he was able to withstand the hours of backbreaking labor, he was no longer a young man.

He'd heard that Dieyi had been sent to Jiuquan in Gansu Province, in the arid Northwest. Jiuquan meant "Wine Springs" and was a small town on the Silk Road. Wine Springs and Silk Road were very poetic names, but Dieyi spent his days there doing the tedious work of polishing stone wine cups called "night-light cups." Although he thought of Dieyi often, Xiaolou had no news of him. He could only imagine that Dieyi was also growing old.

Fuzhou was a poor and isolated place, with harsh and rugged terrain. Xiaolou found the food strange. Everything had a cloying taste, but he was too hungry to refuse it. At New Year's, every family received a ration coupon for poul-try and ten eggs. The lines for pork were discouragingly long, and the meat had to be pounded for hours before it became tender enough to eat. After it had been pounded to a pulp, it was mixed with dough, which was in turn wrapped around chopped vegetables. These were called "meat swallows," and it was a dish Xiaolou could never get used to. Why waste all that extra time preparing it when you'd already spent so much time waiting to buy it? It didn't make sense to him.

People were also given rations of something called "old chicken spirits." This bitter, carnelian-red concoction was made from a live chicken that had been drowned in wine. After prolonged soaking had dissolved much of the meat and bones into the liquor, it was ready to be drunk. The people were too poor actually to eat the chicken, so they saved it for the next batch, even though by then it had lost its flavor. But it was better than starving.

Xiaolou often reminded himself that he was lucky to be alive. His loved ones were all gone—Juxian was dead; and there was no news of Dieyi. Still, he was alive.

He had long since forgiven Dieyi. He realized that Dieyi had turned on Juxian out of concern for him. Otherwise he would never have spoken against him. Everybody had said things they later regretted, himself included. Where was Jiuquan, he wondered. Perhaps someday he would go there. Or maybe he would never get the chance. Knowing that he would never see Dieyi again made him forget the bad and remember only his friend's good points; they had been like brothers, after all.

Xiaolou and his companions were very diligent. First thing every morning, they bowed three times before a portrait of Chairman Mao. Then they would shout, "Long live Chairman Mao! Long life! Good health to Vice Chairman Lin!" This ritual was called "asking for morning instruction."

In the evenings, they repeated this ritual before giving a full report to Mao's portrait of all that they had done that day. They told the Chairman of their ideological progress and of their careful attention to what was said during political study meetings. This was called the "evening report."

People became accustomed to doing as they were told

without asking questions. There was even an official way of holding Chairman Mao's book of quotations. Thumbs had to be pressed tightly to the open pages, while index, middle, and ring fingers had to be pressed tightly to the open cover. The three fingers that held the cover symbolized the "Three Loyalties": loyalty to Chairman Mao; loyalty to Mao Zedong Thought; and loyalty to the revolutionary path of Chairman Mao. The little fingers lay across the bottom of the book, symbolizing the "Four Extremes": limitless love for Chairman Mao; limitless belief in Chairman Mao; limitless faith and loyalty to Chairman Mao; and limitless worship of Chairman Mao.

One night they were all sitting in the courtyard on the little folding stools they carried there for regular study sessions and films. Everyone was watching a revolutionary movie when an old man collapsed to the ground, dead. He had been the best violin player in Peking opera.

Several men, including Xiaolou, carried his body out and took it to the foot of the mountain for burial. When they were finished, the soil mounded over the grave looked like a smashed and rotten bun, but it would nourish the earth, at least. Far below, the political study meeting continued. The dim yellow light looked like will-o'-the-wisps.

Suddenly, they heard a scraping sound. Someone was digging in the earth nearby, in the plot where they grew yams.

"Someone's stealing our yams!" shouted one of Xiaolou's companions.

"We've been working hard on those. It's a good crop. Every time they get big enough to eat, somebody comes and steals them."

The thieves had taken flight, but Xiaolou and his companions soon caught up with them. The pilferers turned out to be a ragged child and a pair of teenagers, aged sixteen or seventeen. They all wore torn and filthy clothes and looked to be half-starved.

"Where do you live?" demanded Xiaolou. "Where are your parents?"

The youngest one shivered.

"My father . . . and my mother . . . both went to political study school, to struggle with selfishness and criticize revisionism. It's been over a year since there's been anyone home. I'm hungry."

The other two looked like students, but they were still wearing red arm bands on their shabby sleeves, with the characters for "Red Guard" written on them in yellow. Red Guards no longer ran everything, and these children had obviously run away from a "reeducation camp" somewhere in the countryside.

In the early days of the Cultural Revolution, Red Guards had traveled all over the country for free so that they could participate in the political movement. So many had converged on Peking that the situation got out of hand, and the State Council issued a directive that stopped the policy of free travel and ordered them all back to their schools and work units. Once they had outgrown their political usefulness, many of them had nowhere to go, and in the end, many were sent down to the countryside to be reeducated by the poor peasants. Some of the Red Guards never made it to the countryside, falling victim to bloody factional fighting. Others, like these two, were simply runaways.

One of the teenagers reached into his pocket and took

out a handful of Mao buttons, which he offered to Xiaolou.

"Uncle," he begged. "Pick any one you want. Please, just let us have some yams. We haven't eaten anything in days."

The young people, formerly the masters, were now begging the "monsters" for a few scraps of food.

Ten years passed.

In 1976, Chairman Mao died. Chairman Hua stepped up to replace him but soon stepped down. The Gang of Four was overthrown.

The decade-long disaster was over, but what of the people who had perpetrated the crimes of that time? What of their victims? Nobody cared to remember. It was too painful.

Xiaolou saw the show trial of the Gang of Four on a television displayed in an electronics shop in Tinlok Lane in the Wanchai district of Hong Kong. He had fled to Hong Kong by sea from Fujian. Unlike General Xiang Yu, he had chosen to live. His life was not a play. In the play, Yu Ji had coaxed her lover, the General, into giving her his sword; and she had committed suicide right in front of him. Xiang Yu had fled to the banks of the Wu River, where an official was waiting to escort him across to his home on the opposite bank. But he had lost all of his men in battle at Kuaiji, and ashamed to face his people, he chose an honorable death.

In real life, Xiaolou, the General, crossed the water to safety, refusing to die for a country that didn't want him. Nonetheless, like an old soldier who has nothing left to fight for, he was living out the remaining years of his life.

As he stood before the television set, his mind wandered.

The final lines of *Farewell to My Concubine* were going through his mind.

> Summer fades and winter comes; spring turns to fall,
> The sun sets in the west, and the river flows ever east-
> ward.
> Where is the General's fine steed today?
> Grasses and wildflowers spread desolately across the land.

"Hey, you! Do you want to buy a television or not?" The salesman had noticed Xiaolou staring into the set, completely absorbed. Xiaolou was blocking the doorway.

"I'm sorry. I just wanted to watch," he said diffidently, as the salesman herded him out. He had no real right to be there.

The trial was the most exciting and important event in many years, and everyone in Hong Kong followed it closely. Consequently, Xiaolou had only to walk a few blocks before he came to a teahouse where there was a television on. He joined a crowd of curious viewers, searching the screen for familiar faces. There she was—Jiang Qing! Her trial ended up being the highest-rated program in Hong Kong for the year of 1981.

Fully aware that the world was watching her, Jiang Qing strutted into the courtroom with her head held high. She proudly recited the slogans for which she had been famous all through the trial.

"Revolution is the violent action taken by one social class in an attempt to overthrow another class."

"I shared the difficult times with Chairman Mao, and I was the only female comrade with him during wartime. I was at the battlefront, and I stood by Chairman Mao for thirty-eight years. Where were you all hiding then?"

"All I have is a head. Take it if you want."

"I was Chairman Mao's running dog. I was ready to bite anyone he told me to."

When questioned closely, she said, "I can't remember! I don't know! I don't know anything!"

The show had obviously been rehearsed and the tapes edited.

Jiang Qing was sixty-six at the time of her trial. If not for her and the great man behind her, many people of her generation would have been enjoying their old age and playing with their grandchildren. But the two of them and their followers had destroyed everything they touched and all but ruined the nation.

The people of Hong Kong, separated from China by the sea, had been protected from the bloody turmoil on the mainland. Jiang Qing had not made them suffer, so when they saw her on television, a fearless and hotheaded old lady, they applauded.

"What a tough lady!"

"Would you want to be married to her?"

"No, thanks! You can have her for yourself."

None of the other onlookers noticed Xiaolou slipping away. He was an unremarkable, gray-haired man in his sixties. An out-of-service streetcar clanked by, and Xiaolou remembered his first job in Hong Kong had been with the streetcar company, working long hours through the night. Reeducation camp had strengthened his body, so he had no trouble with the extended hours.

Hong Kong was a beautiful city at night. The streetlights had just winked on, and tramcars slid lazily from Central District to the racecourse, the clanging of their bells echoing in the lonely night. The tracks seemed to go on forever, with no end in sight, but crossing was dangerous.

Back at the terminal, the trams sometimes had to switch tracks. This wasn't done mechanically. Rather, a worker had to use a long pole to move the cables. That had been Xiaolou's job. He wielded the pole like the General on the Peking opera stage, all strength and confidence. But it was hard work, and by the time the tram pulled away, lights shining and bells ringing, Xiaolou was shaking with exhaustion. Ultimately he became too old and weak to do the job at all and was fired.

Lately, he'd been apartment sitting for the son of a former coworker, a streetcar operator. The son had successfully applied for a rent-controlled apartment, which he planned to sublet at a profit without reporting it to the government. In the meantime, he was paying Xiaolou a tiny stipend for living there, which supplemented his social welfare income of six hundred Hong Kong dollars per month. Xiaolou could not report his extra income, as the authorities would have automatically canceled his welfare payments. While he was ashamed of his dishonesty, he felt he had little choice if he wanted to survive.

Hong Kong was filled with ordinary men and women who resorted to a host of ploys and scams simply to scrape by. Housing was one of life's biggest worries. Like insects living in holes underground, people occasionally poked their heads up into the fresh air, seeking a better way, but they always burrowed back down into the mud. One was lucky even to have a cramped and dingy little dwelling. There were just too many people living in the city.

Xiaolou walked back to his own cramped nest. It was near Tinlok Lane. He liked that name, Tinlok. It meant "Heavenly Bliss." Back in 1949, the year of the Communist takeover, he and Dieyi had performed in an opera house near the Bridge of Heaven. The opera house had been called the Heavenly Bliss Theater. He remembered the gold-speckled red banner, with four big characters emblazoned on it: "FARE-WELL TO MY CONCUBINE." In those days, the Bridge of Heaven had been full of magic shows and storytellers. Stalls sold herbal medicines and tonics, or little pictures of faraway places, which children bartered and bet for. There were stands selling soy milk, rice cakes stuffed with dates, figurines of spun sugar. But Xiaolou had lost his voice the day of that beating in 1966; he had had nothing to do with the opera again after that. Today, the name Heavenly Bliss brought out a rueful smile in him.

When he reached his building, there was a policeman out in front, checking people's identification.

"Sir," he addressed Xiaolou in English. "Your ID, please."

Xiaolou fumbled for his papers and presented them to the officer respectfully.

"See, it has a green stamp on it."

The Hong Kong government had started to crack down on illegal immigrants in 1982, in an effort to stem the tide of people flooding into the city. Discovery by the authorities now meant immediate deportation. When Xiaolou had come to the colony, regulations were less rigid, and he had a green stamp on his papers to prove that he was legal.

"Shanghai man," called out the fat little boy who was banging on the metal grille in Xiaolou's doorway. The child was his neighbor's son, a fourth grader who liked to visit Xiaolou and play with Xiaolou's pet turtle. Today, the turtle was nowhere to be found.

"Shanghai man, where is the turtle?"

"I am not Shanghainese!" Xiaolou said emphatically in his poor Cantonese. "I've told you over and over, I'm from Peking!"

"What's the difference?" asked the boy.

Xiaolou was at a loss, and simply repeated himself.

"I'm from Peking, not Shanghai!"

"Where's the turtle?"

The tubby child looked around the sparsely furnished apartment. Aside from an old rattan chair, there was no other furniture, save an old wooden cot with one broken leg. Xiaolou had put the turtle under the bad leg to prop it up. It didn't look any the worse for wear, and Xiaolou had taken the trouble to place a saucer of rice and water in front of it.

"What do you think you're doing?" the little boy yelled. "He's going to die!"

What did this child know about death, Xiaolou wondered. He had seen more death than he cared to recall during the Cultural Revolution. Two hundred of the five hundred people with whom he journeyed south to Fuzhou had died on the way, thirty of them from an outbreak of some disease—Xiaolou didn't know what. Xiaolou had watched Red

Guards cut off people's legs off with saws during the endless struggle sessions. He had seen people beaten so badly in the face that they lost all of their teeth. Often, death had been a merciful release.

China had known too much suffering in this century, Xiaolou thought to himself. From the last years of the Qing dynasty to the Nationalist Revolution in 1911; through the Japanese occupation; the civil war between the Communists and the Nationalists; liberation; the land reform movement; the Korean War; the "Three-Anti" Campaign; the "Five-Anti" Campaign; the Antirightist Campaign; the Great Leap Forward and three hard years of drought and famine; all the way down to the Great Proletarian Cultural Revolution—it was nothing but suffering. A hundred million dead. A decade wasted. And for what? The people had laid down their bodies to prop up their rulers' thrones. But when one died there was always another to replace him. They were an ever-renewing resource.

Xiaolou looked at the little boy. Maybe he had a future, but Xiaolou felt relieved that his own death could not be far away. Still, he hoped to savor what remained of his life.

"I'm bored. There's nothing to do here. Bye!"

Xiaolou pondered the child's rude spontaneity. He was lucky, indeed. If he had been born in Peking, his life would have been completely different. There, after the ousting of the Gang of Four, he had heard that children threw rocks at straw effigies of Jiang Qing during physical education classes. They were completely carried away by this game. But what would happen if, years down the line, Jiang Qing's case were to be reversed? Would these innocent children be accused of wrongdoing?

Adults often took advantage of children's naive enthusiasm and used it to channel their own feelings of anger and frustration. His neighbor's boy had a favorite computer game that he brought over to teach Xiaolou. The character in the game was a foolish man who existed only to get into a tiny room. As he struggled to get in, a whole range of hard objects kept raining down on him—water buckets, hammers, saws, and the like. If one of these things hit him in the head, he would die; but he had to die three times before he was out of the game! Just like the Chinese people—stubbornly clinging to their lives.

Xiaolou's fingers were clumsy, and his games were over quickly.

"I can always tell you've died again from the music," the boy laughed.

This miniaturized, mechanical music was the only music Xiaolou heard anymore. He often felt he had lost everything that had ever been important to him. But he had gained his freedom.

In Hong Kong he was free to ride the trams wherever he wanted, for as long as he wanted. He liked riding the tram because it was a cheap way to pass the time. The rhythm of the trams was like the droning of the Chinese violins in Peking opera. It reminded him of his days on the stage, when he felt he commanded the world like General Xiang Yu. "It was heaven's will that destroyed my kingdom, And not that we fought badly." The mournful music of the humming tram surrounded him on all sides, like the songs of Chu. It was raining hard, and raindrops slashed across the glass of the windows, in melancholy chaos.

In the mood to kill a little more time, Xiaolou caught a

streetcar from Wanchai to Shau Kei Wan. Passing the New Light Opera House at North Point, he noticed a worker putting up new posters outside. Another touring company was coming to Hong Kong.

He didn't give it much thought, but on the way back to Wanchai, he happened to look out the fogged-up windows of the car again. The posters were up now, and three characters jumped right out at him: CHENG DIEYI.

10

Xiaolou had never learned to read very many characters; but those three characters were among the first he had learned, and they were etched permanently in his mind.

Cheng Dieyi. He couldn't believe his eyes. Maybe his eyesight was failing—he was over sixty, after all. He must have been mistaken. As the tram hummed past the opera house, he turned around to take another look at the marquee, but it was too far away for him to read the characters clearly.

Determined to find out, he forced his way off the tram, even though it was between stops. The conductor cursed him, saying he was the kind of person who would stop the earth in its orbit if it suited him. But Xiaolou paid no heed.

Standing on the sidewalk across the street from the theater, he looked up and saw a sign reading "CAPITAL PEKING OPERA COMPANY." The marquee posted a long list of performers' names and scheduled performances. Prominent billing had been given to the senior art advisor. Next to that were the words "FAMOUS *DAN* OF THE 1940s—CHENG DIEYI."

Xiaolou stood with his mouth hanging open for quite some time. His heart was pounding, and his dull eyes were once again filled with fire. He never imagined he would meet his long-lost friend on this tiny speck of land in the middle of the sea. Hadn't Dieyi been sent down to Jiuquan, Wine Springs?

Whenever Xiaolou opened up a newspaper and saw advertisements for Chinese wine, he always searched for any characters he might know. Sometimes there were lines from Tang poems in the ads, like "Fine grape wine served in a cup that lights the night." This always reminded him of Dieyi, who he'd heard was making and polishing stone cups called night-light cups. His friend, Dieyi, who had very nearly had him killed.

Xiaolou smiled sadly. Neither Yu Ji nor her lover, the General, had died after all. They had simply gone their own separate ways.

The rest of the verse ran through his mind:

Fine grape wine, in a cup that lights the night,
I went to drink and the strains of a lute came to my ears.
Don't laugh at me, lying here drunk on the battlefield,
Tell me if any of the soldiers have found their way home.

Xiaolou paced back and forth for a long time in the lobby of the New Light Opera House. He had looked over every color poster and glossy publicity still, but none of them had been of Dieyi. None of the stars' names was familiar. They were probably the vanguard troops of China's "Four Modernizations"—sent out to earn the hard currency needed to support the motherland. These sons and daughters of the New China had names like "Facing East," "Facing Red," "Progress," or "East Wind." Xiaolou was happy for them. Although their names were silly, they were politically safe.

As dusk fell outside the theater, workers began to set up the stage, busily carting around heavy trunks full of props and costumes. Occasionally, the curtains flapped open, revealing a piece of the stage.

When Xiaolou worked up the courage to approach the stage, an usher stepped up to him.

"Can I help you?"

"I—I'm looking for someone."

"Who would that be?"

"Cheng Dieyi."

The usher looked him over skeptically.

"How well do you know this person?"

"We're as good as brothers. We went to opera school together. Please tell him Xiaolou is here. It's been many years, but he and I—"

"Xiaolou, right? What's your surname?"

This man had never heard of him. No one remembered him anymore.

The usher led him to a dressing room. The area backstage was thronged with actors and stagehands getting ready for the performance. Long rows of mirrors reflected a line of faces, all painted red and white. But the faces belonged to strangers.

Xiaolou kept looking around, afraid that he wasn't going to find his friend. Maybe it had been a trick, a lie. Suddenly, he caught sight of a pair of graceful hands. They were withered with age, but they were unmistakable in the way they moved lightly over the face of a young actress, applying the final touches to her makeup. An old man peered intently at his work, and even though his head was lowered, Xiaolou could still see several scars on his neck.

Xiaolou gently patted the man's frail shoulder, and he half turned and nodded absently. He hadn't recognized him.

"Brother!" Xiaolou said beseechingly.

Dieyi turned around to face him squarely. He searched Xiaolou's face, finding the once-familiar eyebrows and eyes. The scar at Xiaolou's temple was the only feature that time had not altered.

For a long time they looked at each other mutely. Neither of them really knew what to say.

Dieyi went back to making up the young actress, but his hands were shaking now and he ruined the job. The actress waited awkwardly for the senior art advisor to dismiss her or finish the job, but Dieyi simply stared at his frustrated efforts. At length, she made polite excuses and slipped away. Dieyi didn't notice her leaving. Seeing Xiaolou again was unbearably painful.

He had been drifting along for many years, like a lonely boat on a river, or a fallen leaf. He had grown used to living without feeling; to speak of the past meant only pain. He could still feel the weight of Xiaolou's hand on his shoulder, as though he had not taken it away, as though it had always been there. He shivered.

"How are you?" Xiaolou asked.

"Fine. And you?"

There was another awkward silence, this time broken by the crashing of gongs from the stage. The performance was starting, and they walked over to watch it from the wings.

The company was performing a program of experimental Peking operas, in this instance a scene from *Lady Li Huiniang* in which the heroine drifts around the netherworld.

"My righteous indignation reaches the heavens,
I am a wronged ghost, burning with anger at my unjust
   death.

.   .   .   .   .   .

Looking heavenward, I protest:
Why must people suffer so much?"

Lady Li was telling the Bright Mirror Judge of the underworld about the crimes of a man named Jia Sidao. While his spirit guards did acrobatics, the judge breathed fire, through some special effect. There was also a lot of smoke swirling around, an effect achieved with quantities of dry ice, while costumes and fans changed colors beneath the lights. It was a spectacle that bore little resemblance to the Peking opera Xiaolou remembered.

Dieyi spoke.

"Since my rehabilitation, I haven't appeared in any full-length operas. It's just been repertory."

"Well, it takes too much time and energy to do an entire show, anyway. But I'm glad to hear that you were rehabilitated. It's a good thing."

"I suppose so. But you can't bring back the past."

Only then did Xiaolou notice that Dieyi was missing one of his little fingers. His stage career really was finished. He had once had the most beautiful hands in the theater, but now they were better suited for light manual labor, like making night-light cups.

These cups were carved from stone quarried in the Gobi Desert. Some of the cups were long-stemmed, while others had no stems. Many had designs carved into them—human figures, lotus blossoms, landscapes, trees and flowers, feather or animal motifs. During the long days of dull and exhausting work, Dieyi had comforted himself by reciting the lines from the scene in which Yu Ji offers Xiang Yu a goblet of wine. He imagined Xiaolou picking up one of the glasses that he had polished and saying, as in the play, "Bring me some wine."

A good cup was as valuable as jade, as thin as paper, and as shiny as a mirror. That was what people said, but Dieyi had never seen one of the cups at night, so he didn't know if they actually shone in the dark.

"I hardly knew you, at first," Xiaolou was saying.

"Really?" Dieyi asked thoughtfully. "Is that right?" Xiaolou's remark distressed him. Had he lost everything, then? He had lost his little finger, his thin waist, his shapely legs. His eyes had lost their almond shape, his eyebrows were thin and ragged, his lips sagged. His beauty had faded. He had no mother, no teacher, no brother. There was nobody left. Xiaolou was still talking, but Dieyi wasn't listening.

"What are you thinking about? You're just staring off into space."

"I miss Peking." His voice was barely audible over the clanging drums and cymbals.

"If I said I missed Peking, that would make sense. But you still live there. How can you miss it?"

"The longer I'm there, the more I miss it. Brother, the Bell Tower doesn't even ring anymore."

"What's not ringing? What Bell Tower?"

He looked at Dieyi quizzically. His memory was failing.

The Capital Peking Opera Company's Hong Kong performance run was a success, and the troupe held a press conference while they were there. Dieyi and the other members of the group met the press wearing their new Western-style suits, which were nicely tailored and made of good-quality fabric. Some of the artists performed selections from famous operas, but few of the reporters knew anything about Peking opera. Recent college graduates who were new to journalism, they had only to take copies of the program back to their editors and finish the story at the office to complete their assignments.

"See how skinny and dried up that old man is?" one of them quipped to another. "It's hard to believe he was a *dan* in the 1940s. Who'd want to see him?"

"Don't ask me. I wasn't even born in the 1940s. I wasn't even born in the fifties!"

Dieyi excused himself from several rounds of public obligations to spend a half-day with his childhood friend.

Xiaolou took him out to a Peking-style breakfast at a small stand in a crowded lane in North Point. They ate soybean milk and fried crullers; but the soy milk was thinner than the soy milk in Peking, and the crullers were not as crisp, nor were there any crisp sesame cakes that day. Nonetheless, Dieyi enjoyed the meal, despite the fact that he only had ten of his own teeth left.

The day was fading, and getting grayer by the moment. In another fifteen minutes, the streetlights would wink on. Faces were becoming indistinct. Dieyi glanced at Xiaolou, letting his eyes linger when the other did not acknowledge him. Suddenly, he remembered something and reached into his pocket and took out a leather wallet. Slipping out a somewhat singed and smoke-stained old photograph, he placed it in Xiaolou's hands. Xiaolou squinted at it closely. It was the group portrait taken in front of the shrine to the founding fathers. A sea of earnest faces gazed out at him under clean-shaven heads.

The two old men leaned their heads close together, trying to make out friends from long ago.

"This is Xiao Zongzi, isn't it. Whatever happened to him?" Xiaolou asked.

"He died in a 'cowshed' during the 'Clean Up Social Classes' campaign."

"Here's Xiao Heizi!"

"He died of illness sometime after he was sent down."

"How about Xiao Sanzi? He was the spunkiest kid there!"

"I expect he died quietly. Both his legs were broken while he was being tortured, but he lived on for many years after that. He took to drinking and died of hepatitis."

"What about Xiao Meitou?"

"I heard he became a paraplegic. He fell off a beam once

when he was setting up the lights for a performance in a factory."

Dieyi smiled gently as he put away the photo. He felt sad but also lucky.

"Stop asking questions. Let's just count our blessings. At least we're alive and well."

"What happened to Xiao Si, our old nemesis?"

"He was accused of being a follower of the Gang of Four and was put in prison in a water cell—you know, those cells they fill with water up to the shoulders. Someone told me he went crazy, and for all I know he could be dead by now. It frightens me to think about it. You can't escape from politics—and it's always life or death, kill or be killed. I don't want to talk about it anymore."

Xiaolou changed the subject.

"What do you think of Hong Kong? Do you like it?"

"No."

"I don't really like it, either. But it never occurred to me that we might be rehabilitated. Who came up with this rehabilitation business, anyway?" he muttered. "Well, never mind. I want to show you something."

They came to Nathan Road. Across the wide street, at a three-way intersection, was a public bathhouse. It had been there longer than anyone could remember, and all of the old Shanghainese and Pekingese in Hong Kong knew it well. The name of the bathhouse was *Yude* Pool—"Bathing in Virtue Pool."

Someone on the street handed Dieyi a piece of paper. Written on it was the English word "Passport." Dieyi held it gingerly, until Xiaolou took it. He couldn't read it either—it was all in English. But it was printed to look like a Hong

Kong passport, down to the pair of lions flourishing their great tongues at the crown they were guarding. The only word in Chinese was "Linguaphone," which was printed in a prominent spot. It was a brochure for a language school, where people could learn English so they'd be better equipped to leave Hong Kong someday.

"What kind of phone is it talking about?" Dieyi asked.

"It's not worth hanging onto. They send these out every day. They've become quite common." Xiaolou was making things up as he went along, for he had no idea what the flyer was for. "Besides, it's not big enough to use as a table mat, either."

Dieyi was satisfied with Xiaolou's nonsensical explanation. As long as the flyer wasn't advertising megaphones for political demonstrations, there couldn't be anything in it that could possibly trouble him. He had had enough of revolution.

The bathhouse was filled with steam. Xiaolou and Dieyi sat naked in the hot water together, face-to-face, a pair of old men with soft muscles.

"Everything is in the past, now," Xiaolou said with comfortable resignation.

They peered through the steam. The place was filling rapidly with customers. They came for massages, manicures, pedicures, or shaves. Dieyi wondered if the other patrons came there to relax in their free time, or if they simply had too much time on their hands and came to the bathhouse so that they could appear to be busy.

The two friends soaked so long that their skin turned white—as colorless as the bodies of the drowned.

"We've grown too old to fret about the past anymore, haven't we?" Dieyi said.

"You're right. People really lost their heads during the Cultural Revolution. I hadn't thought you were capable of getting that angry."

Dieyi felt embarrassed.

"There is a little boy who lives in my building," Xiaolou was saying. "He's very naughty and likes to make fun of my cracked voice. He'd never guess what a fine voice I used to have!"

"Did you remarry?"

"No."

"I see. I have a spouse, now." He paused. "During the two years when I was being struggled against, I scarcely spoke a word. I just kept my head down every day and went about my business. By the time I was released, I had all but lost my voice. Years later, when I was rehabilitated and returned to Peking, the Party leaders showed a great deal of concern for me and introduced me to my spouse. We could hardly refuse the kindness of the organization. She works in a tea shop."

"Really?"

"Yes."

"Really?"

"Really."

Xiaolou smiled at Dieyi.

"I expect that you get to drink a lot of very good tea, these days."

"Sure, but it always leaves me hungry."

"We spent our childhoods feeling hungry, didn't we?"

Dieyi's expression lit up.

"My favorite sweet was sticky pudding—the kind

steamed in a bowl. It tasted so good dipped in sugar. I used to just stuff myself with—"

"Remember the time I said we should save our money so we could spend it on a feast of pudding? I've never saved even a penny in all these years. Not that I'd be able to spend it on sticky pudding here. Nobody in Hong Kong has heard of it."

"When you come right down to it, there's nothing that special about sticky pudding."

"We only think it's special because we can't get any."

"That's true. We always want what we can't have. It's so disappointing."

"Back to Peking opera," Xiaolou said. "Now that it's no longer banned, who are the stars?"

"Hardly anybody wants to sing Peking opera nowadays. The most promising tenors want to be pop singers or work in karaoke bars. Peking opera companies aren't good for anything except earning foreign currency." He frowned. "Liulichang has completely changed, you know. The restaurant that specialized in lamb and mutton has been remodeled, and a Hong Kong investor is building a big, fancy hotel nearby. And did you know that ballroom dancing is back? It was even broadcast on television this past New Year's. Remember how Red Guards used to make people do that kind of dancing just to humiliate them, during the Four Olds campaign? Now people go to dance parties; and there are dance hostesses, and prostitutes—"

Dieyi stumbled over the word "prostitute."

Xiaolou's face stiffened, and Dieyi cursed himself.

"I've been wanting to ask you . . . ," Xiaolou said tentatively.

Dieyi's heart was pounding.

"Brother, there's something I want to ask you about—no, I mean I'd like you to do something for me. Could you find Juxian's ashes and send them to me here? I'd like her to rest in peace. Please?"

Dieyi felt like a drowning man. He wished he were dead.

"Brother," Xiaolou said haltingly. "There's something else. I wonder if I should talk to you about it or not?"

"Go ahead."

"Whatever there was between her—her and me—is in the past. It's over and done with. Please—please don't judge me too harshly."

Dieyi was speechless. So Xiaolou had known all along. Xiaolou could have let the moment pass without saying anything, but he'd chosen not to. Xiaolou looked exhausted by the effort, but relieved. Oddly, it reminded Dieyi of the old Party cadres who had suddenly awakened to the brutality of the Party. "Several decades of revolution, and we're right back where we started," they would sigh heavily.

Dieyi did not want to face the truth. Who would want to? It was too shocking. He wished that this meeting had never taken place. He wanted to live out the rest of his days enjoying the solitary pleasure of his secret. Xiaolou threatened to shatter his fragile world. He had to keep him from saying anything more, before it was too late.

"What are you talking about?" Dieyi said breezily. "Judge you for what? Never mind. You know the saying—always sing on an empty stomach! Let's sing something."

"I've forgotten the words."

"I'm sure you haven't!" Dieyi smiled. "It'll all come

back to you once you start. Really. The show must go on! Come on." He added, as if to himself: "I've always wanted to be Yu Ji."

It was the evening of the Capital Peking Opera Company's last performance. The show was over, and the performers were gone. All the props, sets, and lights had been taken down, and the stage was completely empty.

There was no one in the theater except Xiaolou and Dieyi. They were backstage, putting on their makeup, preparing to play for the empty house.

They fell back into their old ritual. First Dieyi spread vaseline over the whole area to be made up. Then came a white base, followed by red paint, which had to be blended in. Next, he drew his eyebrows and lined his eyes with black. After dusting his face with powder to set it, he did the touching up. There was more eyebrow paint, an application of lipstick, fine powder for his neck, hands, and forearms. Lastly, he rubbed rouge into his palms to conceal their true color.

Once his face was done, Dieyi pulled the skin of his temples and forehead back so that his eyebrows slanted upward at an angle. Then he wrapped a cloth around his head and combed his hair up. He put on decorative combs and hairpins, some made of silk, some opalescent.

Xiaolou was putting on his makeup with unsteady hands. He began with a dot of white base on his nose and then hesitated. Characters who die in middle age have the symbol for longevity written on their faces. What about those who live to old age, Xiaolou wondered. Was that symbolic longevity meant to be a consolation? As he resumed his work, Xiang Yu reemerged once again from his hands. Dieyi gave him an appraising look, and he wasn't thoroughly satisfied, but this was his General, his Xiang Yu. He felt he had stepped back in time.

Dieyi brought out the old sword and fastened it around Xiaolou's waist without a word. Its singed tassels hung somewhat stiffly. The authorities had confiscated the sword as evidence of Dieyi's revolutionary activities, but after his rehabilitation, it had been returned. He stepped back, then adjusted Xiaolou's black halberd and took him by the arm. They were ready to go onstage.

Age had taken away much of his strength and flexibility, but despite the fact that he had lost much of his range of movement, Dieyi was still full of spirit.

"Pray, my lord, take a cup of wine."

Xiaolou drank down the proffered cup and cast it over his shoulder with a vigorous shout. Then he sang with his broken voice:

"My strength can uproot mountains, and my vast spirit
    reaches every corner of the land.
But the times are against me; even my horse cannot
    advance;
My horse cannot advance, what shall I do?
Yu Ji! Yu Ji!
What shall I do?"

Taking up the sword, Dieyi began to dance, singing in accompaniment.

"Pray, take this cup and let me sing you a song,
I'll dance to ease your sorrows.
Evil Qin has ruined the empire,

Forcing brave men everywhere to take up arms.
Remember the old saying, for it is true:
Victory and defeat, flourishing and dying—all pass
　　within the blink of an eye.
Pray rest here a while and drink your fill."

Dieyi danced stiffly to the mournful aria. He couldn't
bend his back, even slightly. Yu Ji was trying to comfort
Xiang Yu; but who would comfort Yu Ji?

"Enemy troops surround us,
Singing the songs of Chu, they mock us.
My lord is doomed,
I have nowhere to turn."

And then it came to him.
He brought the sword to his throat and drew it across.
Xiaolou rushed to Dieyi's side and tried to stop the
blood that flowed from the wound. Held in his embrace,
Dieyi stared up into Xiaolou's eyes.
"Dieyi!"
As the blood oozed from his body, Dieyi felt a kind of
satisfaction spreading through him. It was like applause. This
was the last act, the perfect climax.
"Brother! Xiao Douzi!" Xiaolou was shouting. It
sounded like he was practicing his scales, the way they did as
children at Taoranting Park. The stage seemed to echo with
children's voices.
"Brother!" Xiaolou was shaking him. "The play is
over!"
Dieyi returned to his senses. The glittering tragedy was
over. It had all been a fake. He would not die for love. It had

merely been a joke, an elaborate joke, but a joke just the same.

It was with great difficulty that he at last managed to stand up. Dusting himself off, he smiled enigmatically.

"I always did want to be Yu Ji!"

He had given it everything he had. It was his farewell performance.

A few days later, Dieyi returned to mainland China with the opera company.

One evening, around dusk, as Xiaolou was walking down Nathan Road, he noticed a long line of people snaking like a dragon around the front of the Home Affairs Department. There was quite a hubbub. It seemed everyone was there to pick up a copy of the Joint Declaration that had been signed between China and Great Britain on September 26, 1984. They wanted to know how much freedom they were going to have after Hong Kong was returned to China in 1997.

Xiaolou had no interest in this question. He would be dead by then, anyway. What did he care about politics? Or about matters of the heart? The most pressing problem in his life was his apartment. The owner had told him that he wanted the place for himself now. Soon, Xiaolou would have nowhere to go. All of China and all of Hong Kong had abandoned him.

He decided to drop by the bathhouse and have a long soak. But when he got there, he saw that the sign over the entrance had been changed from BATHING IN VIRTUE POOL to read FINLAND BATHS. There wasn't even any refuge in virtue anymore.

Discover more about our forthcoming books through Penguin's FREE newspaper...

Penguin
Quarterly

It's packed with:

- exciting features
- author interviews
- previews & reviews
- books from your favourite films & TV series
- exclusive competitions & much, much more...

Write off for your free copy today to:
Dept JC
Penguin Books Ltd
FREEPOST
West Drayton
Middlesex
UB7 0BR
NO STAMP REQUIRED

READ MORE IN PENGUIN

In every corner of the world, on every subject under the sun, Penguin represents quality and variety – the very best in publishing today.

For complete information about books available from Penguin – including Puffins, Penguin Classics and Arkana – and how to order them, write to us at the appropriate address below. Please note that for copyright reasons the selection of books varies from country to country.

In the United Kingdom: Please write to *Dept. JC, Penguin Books Ltd, FREEPOST, West Drayton, Middlesex UB7 OBR*

If you have any difficulty in obtaining a title, please send your order with the correct money, plus ten per cent for postage and packaging, to *PO Box No. 11, West Drayton, Middlesex UB7 OBR*

In the United States: Please write to *Penguin USA Inc., 375 Hudson Street, New York, NY 10014*

In Canada: Please write to *Penguin Books Canada Ltd, 10 Alcorn Avenue, Suite 300, Toronto, Ontario M4V 3B2*

In Australia: Please write to *Penguin Books Australia Ltd, 487 Maroondah Highway, Ringwood, Victoria 3134*

In New Zealand: Please write to *Penguin Books (NZ) Ltd,182–190 Wairau Road, Private Bag, Takapuna, Auckland 9*

In India: Please write to *Penguin Books India Pvt Ltd, 706 Eros Apartments, 56 Nehru Place, New Delhi 110 019*

In the Netherlands: Please write to *Penguin Books Netherlands B.V., Keizersgracht 231 NL–1016 DV Amsterdam*

In Germany: Please write to *Penguin Books Deutschland GmbH, Friedrichstrasse 10–12, W–6000 Frankfurt/Main 1*

In Spain: Please write to *Penguin Books S. A., C. San Bernardo 117–6° E–28015 Madrid*

In Italy: Please write to *Penguin Italia s.r.l., Via Felice Casati 20, I–20124 Milano*

In France: Please write to *Penguin France S. A., 17 rue Lejeune, F–31000 Toulouse*

In Japan: Please write to *Penguin Books Japan, Ishikiribashi Building, 2–5–4, Suido, Tokyo 112*

In Greece: Please write to *Penguin Hellas Ltd, Dimocritou 3, GR–106 71 Athens*

In South Africa: Please write to *Longman Penguin Southern Africa (Pty) Ltd, Private Bag X08, Bertsham 2013*

READ MORE IN PENGUIN

A CHOICE OF BESTSELLERS

Paradise News David Lodge

'Lodge could never be solemn and the book crackles with good jokes
... leaves you with a mild and thoughtful glow of happiness' – *Sunday
Telegraph*. 'Amusing, accessible, intelligent ... the story rolls, the sparks
fly' – *Financial Times*

Scoundrel Bernard Cornwell

Five million dollars in gold will buy fifty-three Stinger missiles, which
may be for the IRA but might have more to do with Iraq's invasion of
Kuwait. Or that kind of money will buy retirement for the man hired to
sail it from Morocco to Miami – if, that is, he can outwit the IRA, CIA,
British Intelligence, infamous Palestinian terrorist il Hayaween, and the
ghost of his lost love Roisin.

Devices and Desires P. D. James

'Like the wind-lashed Norfolk headland buffeted by the sea, which is so
tangily evoked, *Devices and Desires* always has an intensely bracing chill
to its atmosphere' – Peter Kemp in the *Sunday Times*

Doctor Criminale Malcolm Bradbury

'The best novel so far about post-modernism. With grace and wit its
author deconstructs fifty years of European thought and history' –
Observer. 'A playful, smart and entertaining work of art with deadly
serious underpinnings' – *The New York Times Book Review*

The Burden of Proof Scott Turow

'Rarely has a plot as political, as sexual, as criminal, as moral, so lip-
smackingly thickened ... A wonderful read from tight start to taut end'
– *Mail on Sunday*. 'Expert and excellent ... a new sort of novel – a
detective story full of people on the make, on the break or settling for
second best: [a] riveting tale' – *Evening Standard*